Prais
This Nigh

"Ronni Davis perfectly captures the terrifying joy of shaking off others' expectations and coloring in your own future—**a sensitive, stirring, deep breath of a book.**"

—Becky Albertalli, #1 *New York Times* bestselling author of *Imogen, Obviously*

"**Swoon. Sigh. Cheer. Cry. Laugh. Repeat.** Brandy Bailey sparkles right off the page, a living, breathing person who yearns to make her dreams come true in spite of the obstacles. P.S. There's also a pulse-racing romance. And it's *everything.*"

—Jennifer Niven, #1 *New York Times* bestselling author of *All the Bright Places*

"**It's official: Ronni Davis is a Drop Everything and Read author!**"

—Jason June, *New York Times* bestselling author of *Out of the Blue*

"**This beautifully written story about a magical, momentous night is the perfect book for any soft, anxious, artistic soul.** Read this on a breezy spring day and hold its words of possibility, honesty, and love close to your heart."

—Claire Legrand, *New York Times* bestselling author of *Furyborn*

"**Charmingly poignant and heart-swooningly funny**, *This Night Is Ours* is a voicy, relatable story of expectation, fear, and love lost and gained. **An instant winner!**"

—Julian Winters, award-winning author of *Right Where I Left You*

"*This Night Is Ours* by Ronni Davis is an enchanting, dazzling YA romance that's **full of humor, swoons, and heart. These characters will immediately pull you into their orbit, making you fall head over heels in love and root for the pair to find their happily ever after.**"

—N. E. Davenport, author of the Blood Gift duology

BY RONNI DAVIS

When the Stars Lead to You
This Night Is Ours

This Night Is Ours

RONNI DAVIS

LITTLE, BROWN AND COMPANY

New York   Boston

Little, Brown and Company
Hachette Book Group
1290 Avenue of the Americas, New York, NY 10104
Visit us at LBYR.com

First Edition: April 2024

Little, Brown and Company is a division of Hachette Book Group, Inc. The Little, Brown name and logo are trademarks of Hachette Book Group, Inc.

The publisher is not responsible for websites (or their content) that are not owned by the publisher.

Little, Brown and Company books may be purchased in bulk for business, educational, or promotional use. For information, please contact your local bookseller or the Hachette Book Group Special Markets Department at special.markets@hbgusa.com.

Library of Congress Cataloging-in-Publication Data
Names: Davis, Ronni, author.
Title: This night is ours / Ronni Davis.
Description: First edition. | New York : Little, Brown and Company, 2024. |
    Audience: Ages 12 & up. | Summary: On the longest day of the year,
    eighteen-year-old Brandy makes life-changing decisions about her future,
    her family, and a budding romance with one of her best friends.
Identifiers: LCCN 2023009287 | ISBN 9780316373616 (trade paperback) |
    ISBN 9780316373715 (ebook)
Subjects: CYAC: Friendship—Fiction. | Interpersonal relations—Fiction. |
    Family life—Fiction. | LCGFT: Novels.
Classification: LCC PZ7.1.D3837 Th 2024 | DDC [Fic]—dc23
LC record available at https://lccn.loc.gov/2023009287

ISBNs: 978-0-316-37361-6 (pbk.), 978-0-316-37371-5 (ebook)

Printed in the United States of America

CW

10 9 8 7 6 5 4 3 2 1

For Aidan, my very own artist kid

1

This Dawn's Early Light

6:45 a.m.

IT'S A BITTERSWEET FEELING, BOTH POWERFUL AND LONELY, being on top of the world (or in this case, the carnival Ferris wheel). Structures, shadowed against the light blues and purples of the summer dawn, rise all around me. The visual is breathtaking, and it's all I can do to hold on to my phone as I steady myself, trying to find the balance between artsy and safety.

"June twentieth. The longest day of the year. Summer. My favorite season. Weather? I've been promised bright sun and blazing heat. I can't wait to feel it on my face. Today is going to be a good day. And tonight? Extraordinary."

I stop recording, then tap the PLAY icon to preview my

first video clip. I wrinkle my nose. The early morning golden hour lighting is perfect, but my dialogue is way too cheesy. Still. I save it in drafts. I might change my mind later. Sometimes, even though I have a few thousand followers, it feels like only eight people ever see my posts. So I don't need to stress. At least not about this.

And I should still give those eight people quality content, right?

Exactly.

Now, the art I just made? I'm anticipating a *lot* more people checking that out. I tap RECORD again, this time focusing on my small drawing of a carnival. The art is stylized in an anime chibi sort of way, with soft blues, pale yellows, seafoam greens, bright pinks, and deep purples standing out starkly against the white background.

The colors are a deviation from the ones in my normal work, which tends to be brighter and bolder. Should I add more shadow? Or would that be too much? I run my fingers along the smooth surface of the Ferris wheel car, avoiding the little cartoon people and bright pink swirls of the mini-carousel and Tilt-A-Whirl I've drawn. A bird's-eye view of the carnival, with inspiration from the real thing, right now.

The drawing's still a bit wet from the markers, and I don't want to smear it. I lean back, tilt my head, and squint. No, it looks good as is, and its story is complete. At least for now.

Maybe I'll eventually add this piece to my portfolio, but

right now, I just hope this post will drive more business to my little online shop, where I sell stickers, iron-on patches, and prints of the art I make. I've only earned about fifty dollars so far, but it's a start, right?

"I call this latest piece *Cotton Candy Carnival*," I say into my phone's mic. "I hope you like it. Link in bio if you want to learn more. This is Brandy Bailey signing off."

I take a deep breath for two reasons: I'm up pretty high, and one slip could mean serious injury. But if I'm being honest, that's part of the thrill of doing this. Climbing into some weird place, luxuriating in the sense of danger, that risk of getting caught. Second reason: I love the morning fresh air, and being this high makes it feel even more pure. There's something special about such newness. It's like a blank canvas, ready for my stories.

I'm up before the town wakes up, so it's just me, the heavy, warming air, and the birds sing-sing-singing away. I snuck out of my apartment early, my mom oblivious thanks to her earplugs and eye mask. Made my way to the carnival grounds, where the rides are still and eerie. Where the lights are dark, the speakers silent. Last night's downpour is a distant memory, except for the steam from the pavement rising into the air and curling my hair.

This is my favorite time of day. Before it's filled with expectations and responsibility. Before everyone's opinions and thoughts and words weigh on me like plates pressing into my chest. Before I have to put on a perfect face so everyone will think I am perfectly fine!

Ever since high school graduation three weeks ago, this is the only time of day I feel actually free. I'm still working out if that's sad or not.

I turn to my drawing again. It's hard to stay sad when I'm so excited about something I've created. The early morning just wakes up my artist fingers. The work flows out of me as easy as breathing. I love that.

The thought that I'll probably have to give this up soon? I don't love that so much. But I'm not thinking about the future. I'm focusing on the here and now.

Because now I need to leave.

I climb down, taking care to keep my balance and to avoid getting another scratch or bruise. My legs are already covered with them from all the other times I climbed to some precarious spot to make my mark. But even though I use the ladder, I still manage to bump against what feels like every single beam.

My phone buzzes with a text and it feels as loud as the thunder that rattled my windows last night. I jump, then go still, holding my breath and willing my heart to stop thumping. I'd be in huge trouble if anyone caught me here. But when no pounding footsteps or flashing police lights materialize, I slowly breathe out and look at the screen.

Shai

OMG

Good lord. It's not even seven. But ever since my best friend Shai (pronounced Shay) had her daughter six months ago, I get texts from her at all hours of the day and night. I guess infants have a way of throwing off your entire schedule.

I wait to answer her until I'm off the carnival grounds and in a good position to run if other people appear.

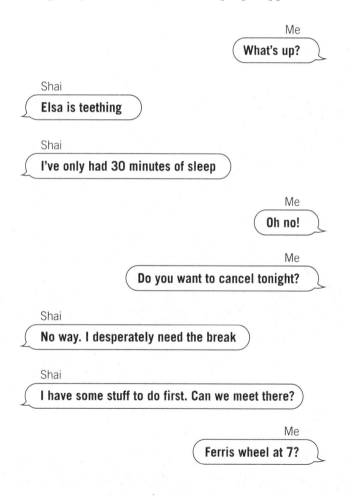

Me
What's up?

Shai
Elsa is teething

Shai
I've only had 30 minutes of sleep

Me
Oh no!

Me
Do you want to cancel tonight?

Shai
No way. I desperately need the break

Shai
I have some stuff to do first. Can we meet there?

Me
Ferris wheel at 7?

My phone buzzes with a new notification.

BenNolanOfficial ✔ has posted a new photo

There's a preview of a picture from an airplane window, the night sky looking like black velvet. I raise my eyebrow. What's he up to, taking what looks like a red-eye? But then I shake my head. Now is not the time to ponder the comings and goings of Ben Nolan, or why the app always randomly picks *his* posts to show me.

I slip my phone into my pocket and start to head down the street, but I pause and take one last look behind me. Carnival rides are so creepy when they're just hanging out, creaking in the wind. But if I'm being honest, I like the creep factor; how the rides seemingly spring up out of nowhere, ready to thrill people and make them happy. It's sort of like art, how we kind of create out of what seems like nothing. Mom does not trust anything that takes only two days to build, no matter how artful it seems, which is why I never got to ride any of the bigger rides until two years ago, when I was finally allowed to come out with Shai. No parental units included.

I can't wait to ride *everything* tonight.

The last night is always the best night, because the food is extra good, the ride operators let us ride as many times as we want, and the fireworks display is always super cool.

It's only fitting that the last night of the carnival coincides with what might be my last night of freedom. I'm expecting an email today that could tip my future in a direction I don't want it to go. I need to at least have one more night of fun before that happens.

My fingers start itching again, wanting to make another drawing, but I'd better not. One is enough for now. Besides, I'm already on the ground. Satisfied, I pat my bag where my markers, pencils, iPad, and sketchpad are safely stashed away, then I start walking briskly down the street. The last thing I need is to get picked up for trespassing. My mom would be super disappointed in me.

And she's the one person I hate disappointing.

2

A Midsummer Dream Deferred

8:00 a.m.

THE EMAIL IS IN MY INBOX.

And yes, there are always emails in my inbox. Messages encouraging me to order more cookies in the middle of the night. Solicitations from random charities because I donated to one once and they apparently shared my email address with everybody. DELETE. Stuff from a site called DailyOM, which Shai signed me up for. ARCHIVE. My horoscope. Stream notifications from Twitch. A couple of emails from my father, but those aren't new. I've already read them a dozen times, and I'll read them a dozen more. He left before I was born, so this is all I have of him.

I'm desperate for some very specific emails, but other than their "confirmation of receipt" canned messages, those senders remain elusive. And there is one website order, which would normally make me feel super happy. Except there's that Email I've been dreading for weeks, blocking everything else.

> **Admissions** 7:50 AM
>
> Congratulations on your admission to the Lucerne School of Nursing!

I close my eyes and shake my head. They have to be playing tricks on me. Because it can't be real, what I'm seeing. I squint at the email, and nope. It's still there, trying to look normal and innocent. But it might as well be flashing in giant, red letters, surrounded by threatening emojis and questionable punctuation.

🔪!!!CONGRATULATIONS ON YOUR
ADMISSION TO THE LUCERNE SCHOOL
OF NURSING!!!🔪

I can't stop staring at it, even though it's making my breath catch. Even though my skin is crawling, and I want to scratch it right off my arms.

No no no no no.

And also:

How how how how how?

Maybe I can delete the email. Maybe it never existed.

Or maybe they made a mistake! Maybe the subject is wrong and the real message—the rejection—is in there.

Then I'll be off the hook.

I guess there's only one way to find out. Rip off that Band-Aid, even though the thought of anyone ever doing that completely grosses me out. My fingers shake as they hover over the touch pad. Then I click the link.

To: ArtisteBrandyB@monroehigh.edu
From: Admissions@LucerneNursing.edu

Hello Brandy,
We are pleased to inform you of your acceptance to the Lucerne School of Nursing!

I don't read further because this is enough to fill my heart with maximum terror.

This is real.

I slam my laptop shut.

3

How to Pretend to Be Happy and Influence People

8:07 a.m.

"BRANDY! OH MY GOSH!" MOM BUSTS THROUGH MY DOOR so hard a couple of my drawings fall off the wall. She's waving her phone around and dancing, and the grin on her face only exacerbates the crawling on my skin. "You got in! Peanut, you got in!"

The room tilts and oh, God, no. Not now. Not the shaking. Not my breath sticking in my throat even more and my heart kicking into high gear. Not me feeling like a prisoner in my own skin. This never used to happen so much, but now, it feels almost nonstop. I don't know what it is. I just know I hate it.

Who even gets like this every time they get stressed out? Most people eat junk food and marathon a show and they're okay. Right? So why can't I be like that? But the more I try to make myself be normal, the harder it is to breathe.

Everything is fine. My breathing is just fine. It's so fine that my head is spinning with how normal my breathing is.

And maybe she's talking about something else anyway. Maybe—just maybe—it can still go away.

Mom thrusts her phone at me, and the room tilts more when I see the screen.

Admissions   **7:50 AM**

Parents: We at the Lucerne School of
Nursing Congratulate You

My skin tightens. I try to focus on the frustration building in my chest. Why would they send *her* an acceptance email? Why? Sure, she paid the application fees, and her name is on the FAFSA, and I was still a minor when I applied, but those are not grounds for them to violate my privacy like this.

Mom throws her arms around me and squeezes me tight. My first instinct is to push her away, not because I don't love a good mom hug, I do, but because I can't stand the way anything feels on my skin right now. But then her scent of jojoba oil and jasmine kind of brings me back to myself. Just a little. Her scrubs are soft against my face. Absorbent, if I were to let the tears in my eyes fall. Which I won't. I can't let her see how upset I am.

"It's what we've been working toward for so long," she says into my hair, her voice thick. "And now it's happening! It's really happening!" She sniffles, and my breath gets shallow again.

"Please don't cry, Mom." Please don't, because that'll just make me feel worse.

"I can't help it." She pulls away and looks into my eyes. The sun rays light her smooth, dark, amber skin, making her glow. My sand-colored skin will never glow like hers, and for years, I hated that. But now I accept it. Just like I should accept that being a nurse is going to be my future.

This morning's freedom already feels like a distant memory. Transient, just like the carnival and its glorious, creepy rides.

"You know what? I'm so happy I'm not going to make you clean your room today."

I take in the sketchbooks and pencils on the floor, the hoodies all over the bed, and the stuffed animals shoved any place they'd squish. *Clean my room.* As if I didn't turn eighteen last month. Still, seeing all my stuff everywhere loosens something in me. I'm here. I can breathe. "My room's fine."

And I'm fine.

I am.

"*And* you deserve a present!" Mom says.

I shake my head. "No. I really don't."

"Nonsense." She bites a nail, thinking. "I know. Why don't I get you a new outfit?"

I glance down at my jean shorts and gray Sonic the Hedgehog hoodie. "I don't need new clothes."

"Brandy. Darling. Humor your mother. We need to celebrate, and I know just how." Her eyes twinkle. "I'm taking you to the President's Club."

"What?" The President's Club kind of intimidates me. It's this fancy, exclusive golf course and city club on the snooty side of town. A couple nights a month, they open to the public and let us "normies" eat in their restaurant. I've never been, but I have to admit I'm a little curious. But am I curious enough to go under these false celebratory pretenses? I don't know.

"You deserve it. And this means you'll definitely need a new outfit." Her eyes light up. "A dress! Ooh, you're going to look so pretty!"

Terror. Pure terror. Mom has this vision of me in her mind that I just don't share. She wants me to wear these cute, really stylized dresses—maxi, mini, or midi. Length doesn't matter. A-line, of course, or skater style. I only know this because she's constantly texting me pics of dresses that she thinks are cute or would be flattering on me.

I'm not a fan of wearing dresses. I feel awkward and like

a kid playing dress up. And some of the materials just don't feel right. I need soft and comfortable things on my skin, like sweatshirts. Plus, I can't climb in a dress. How will I get to my special spots to draw if I'm having to be all proper and ladylike?

I wish I could tell Mom her money would be better spent on pineapple pizza and a gift certificate to an art supplies store. But then I'd be an ungrateful brat, right? Gift giving is totally Mom's love language, and she prides herself on picking out the perfect presents. The only thing she falls down on, in my opinion, is trying to buy me clothes. "I have dresses, Mom."

She gently tugs one of my braids. "When was the last time you wore one?"

"Aunt Rena's wedding." Three years ago.

"Exactly. You've probably outgrown them all."

Honestly, I can't be bothered to care that much. Except for the growing part. "You really think so?"

She grins. "No."

"Oh." I sigh. Being the shortest person in my entire family is a running joke between all of us and I get teased constantly. Cousins, aunts, uncles. I don't usually mind it, but today it grates a little. "But isn't the saying 'good things come in small packages'?"

She hugs me again. "The best things. Like you! Following in my footsteps! And your grandmother's! Just like you dreamed of when you were a little girl! I can't wait to call her and tell her! But first…" She lifts her phone to her mouth. "Hey, Siri, is tonight a public night at the President's Club?"

Please say no, please say no.

"Tonight is a public night at the President's Club," Siri the Traitor answers, loudly and clearly.

"Perfect!" Mom swipes and taps and types. I cross my fingers. Maybe they're all full up tonight. I assume it's a popular place. It's probably been booked for months.

Mom grins. "Yes! Got a reservation."

"Great," I say through a stiff, fake smile. But she doesn't notice. She's too busy smiling for real.

"Since it's so last minute, we didn't get the best time, but we're all set for tonight at four. I'll forward you the confirmation. Ooh, you know what? We should go to that new shopping center! It's super close to—" Her phone vibrates. She looks at the screen and her face falls. "Well, so much for that."

I cross my fingers. "The hospital?"

She nods. "Oh yeah. She's crowning."

On the one hand, I hate that I know what that means. But on the other hand…

Thank.

God.

My breath slowly deepens. The world begins to look less fractured. Maybe if I can sit here and process this, without her expectations pressing on me, I can make peace with it.

"I wasn't supposed to go in until later. And I really wanted to take you shopping." Her mouth turns down at the corners, and the guilt washes over me. She's so happy for me, and I love it when Mom is happy. Especially if I'm the one making her smile like the sun personified. Which is different from how tired she looks when she thinks I can't see her.

I feel crushed inside. I so want her to keep smiling.

But not because of this.

I swallow the huge lump in my throat. "It's fine, Mom. Go usher a new life into the world."

"But I want to celebrate with you! I guess I could ask Maddie to cover for me... except it's my high-risk delivery. I really don't want to pass it off to someone else."

I squeeze her hand. "Your patient needs you. And that new baby needs you."

She rubs at some marker on my thumb. "But what about you? Do you need me?"

I put on my most convincing voice. "I'll be fine."

That's a lie. I will not be fine.

I can come clean. Tell her I do not, under any circumstance, want to go to nursing school. Not anymore. Once upon a time it was all I wanted to do. But now, the thought of it is my worst nightmare.

I dream in street art, and I imagine someday having that street art hanging in fancy galleries. Colors and bold strokes and cute chibi characters. I have the application page for the

Preston Academy of Art bookmarked in my browser. I even signed up for an account because they're too precious to be part of the Common App.

Just thinking about this art school gets my heart racing in the best way. It's one of the best in the country, and I can learn so much, like graphic design and theater tech. I got a small taste of that experimentation during high school, but Monroe High was so busy giving all its money to the varsity football team that the art department had to take what was left over. We had to share most of our supplies, which wasn't ideal because art stuff gets used up so fast. My art teacher, Mr. Conway, did the best he could with what he had, even buying stuff with his own money.

I wouldn't have to share at Preston. They have unlimited supplies. State-of-the-art equipment and facilities. And some of the graduates work on major motion pictures or publish bestselling graphic novels or act on Broadway. Can you imagine being surrounded by all those talented people? Probably intimidating, but also super inspiring, right? Either way, going there would be a dream.

I could tell Mom all about that dream right now, but my throat swells shut. Chakra blocked, as Shai would say. I can hear her bell-sounding voice now. "Here. Write everything down in this blue journal. Blue is the color of the throat chakra, so you'll be able to express your truth here." No, I won't, Shai. Because my truth would break my mother's heart.

When I was six, I told Mom I wanted to be a nurse, just like her. That I wanted to help people, just like she does. The way her face lit up! The way she hugged me and said she'd do whatever she could to help me realize that dream.

And she did. Hiring tutors when I struggled at school, even though we really didn't have extra money like that. Leaving her textbooks lying around for me to peruse before I could even read, let alone understand, most of the words. Letting me have free reign of her copies of *The Anatomy Coloring Book* and *The Physiology Coloring Book* once she was done with all her classes. How could I turn my back on all that support? On all that bonding?

She and I used to dress alike as nurses every Halloween. We would watch *General Hospital* together when I was home sick from school and she could actually take the day off. *Grey's Anatomy* was the one show we made a point to watch every week—until she got so busy with work that she couldn't be around for it as often. And for several years, nursing was all I wanted to do. Until my science and math grades told me another story. Until I almost passed out when we had to dissect that fetal pig during tenth grade biology. Until one of my classmates cut themself with a scalpel in that same class, and seeing them bleed *did* make me pass out. Until I watched my best friend give birth and was up for the next five nights, traumatized by what I had seen.

Mom's heart is so big, and I so desperately want to be

like her. I love the idea of helping others. But as a nurse? Not anymore. Maybe I shouldn't feel so guilty, but I do. It wasn't Mom who changed the rules. It was me. And I don't know how to tell her I want to play a whole new game. So I lie. Again. "I promise."

Mom rubs my head. "If you're sure." It's weird how easy it is to fool her. She got a promotion in February, and ever since, she's been so much busier with work. Before then, she used to be scarily in tune with my moods and feelings. But now it's like she barely even recognizes me. Probably doesn't help that she's been working overtime to keep ahead of all her new work responsibilities, and that I've been working overtime to hide my trepidation over that application. I guess I should be grateful that my efforts are paying off.

Instead, it's guilt, guilt, guilt all the way down.

She frowns slightly. "I'll never understand why you got that thing in your ear."

I touch the helix piercing. It stings only a little bit now, and my cold fingertips (due to Mom keeping the AC set to temperature Arctic Circle) feel good on the cartilage. "I like it."

"*I* would like it if you would refrain from putting more holes in your body," she says. I barely stop myself from rolling my eyes. It's not like it's *her* cartilage that's pierced. "And what's up with those scratches on your legs?"

"Oh, you know me. Tangling it up with the neighborhood strays again."

She sighs. "Seems like every other day a new bruise or something shows up on you. Let me take a look."

"Mom, it's okay. Really. You need to go!"

"You could get sick! Cat scratch fever is a thing."

"I was kidding about the cats. I don't even think our neighborhood has strays anymore."

"Then where *did* you get that scratch?"

"Crowning!" I remind her. I need her to go to work now. I don't know how much longer I can keep up this act. And the last thing I need is for her to start fawning over me even more.

"Wait a second." She rushes out of my room. I take the moment to let out a shaky breath. But then she's right back, so I have to paste on the big grin again.

"Here."

I stare at the wad of cash she's holding out to me. "What?"

"Take this. For the dress."

I shake my head. "No."

"What do you mean, *no*?"

"I can't take this."

"Since when do you turn down money?" She squints at me. "Hello? Is my daughter in there?"

"But, Mom—"

"But nothing. You deserve this. In fact, I'll give you a ride to that new shopping center."

I follow her into the living room. "You don't need to do that. I'm perfectly capable of getting the bus."

"Or maybe you can go with Shai."

"Elsa is teething. I don't want to bother her while she's dealing with that. I can take the bus," I say again.

"With that pile of cash I just gave you?"

I want to sigh for a million years. "I know better than to be flashing it all over the bus."

Her phone buzzes again. She glances at the screen and nods. "All right. But only because I need to get to the hospital ASAP. Text me pictures! I want to feel like I'm there with you."

"Have a good day at work."

Then she looks at me. *Really* looks at me. "You sure aren't acting like someone who's just gotten accepted into her dream school and the most prestigious nursing program in the state."

Tell her, Brandy.

Tell her right now.

I can't do it. She hasn't been so excited about anything in a while. Like, since the day I submitted the application.

I'd pushed it to the last possible minute, even hoping that the deadline would pass. Except... guess what? This school has rolling admissions! Applying after I graduated meant I could potentially attend in the fall. Even the summer if I were so inclined. Lucky me!

I remember Mom and I sitting down, her going over the application a million times. How she'd made sure everything

I'd needed to submit was in my account. And how she'd typed in her credit card number for the application fee. How she'd taken my hand in hers and brought it to her lips, for luck, before selecting submit. Then the look on her face after the submit button was hit. She hugged me so tightly and told me how proud she was that I was following in her footsteps. And Grandma's footsteps.

I should've put a stop to it at the beginning. In fact, Present Brandy is *really* irritated with Past Brandy for not saying something all those weeks ago. And right now Mom looks a million times more excited than that day. I'm not interested in taking that from her. "I'm just in shock."

I'm just a lying liar who lies.

She kisses my forehead. "Understandable. Well, process with some retail therapy. I should be back here by about three thirty so we can ride together to the President's Club, but if not, I'll meet you there. After, we'll accept the admission and I'll pay the deposit."

Never have ten words felt more ominous. "I have the carnival with Shai."

She picks up her purse. "After that, then. I can't wait to see what dress you pick out!"

I give a half-hearted wave. "Bye, Mom."

She dances into the hallway. "See ya later. Eeeee! My baby!"

I'm blinking back tears by the time I hear the elevator

ding down the hall. But I do not cry. It doesn't matter that my face wants to just crumple right now. I'm not going to let it.

I rub my eyes and flick the (non)tears away. And to keep more (non)tears from falling, I focus on counting the bills in the stack of cash Mom handed me. Three hundred dollars. Why on earth would she think I ever needed clothes that cost so much? Did my getting into the nursing academy really call for all this?

I feel sick inside. And I can't sit in this apartment anymore. So I grab my messenger bag. I need to get some air.

4

Overwhelmed in Every Way

10:15 a.m.

THE MALL MIGHT AS WELL BE A MAZE AS FAR AS I'M CON-
cerned. A clothing store at a fancy shopping center might as
well be purgatory. Racks and racks of "upscale" merchandise,
and I can't make heads or tails of any of it. Even the man-
nequins posing in the windows don't help. They're wearing
full-on outfits and doing the work for me. But I'm still hopeless.

The sun beats down on my head, and sweat drips down
my face. The Shoppes at Bishop Haven isn't one of those
vintage malls where all the stores are in a huge building with
fountains and food courts and merry-go-rounds. It's like a
"traditional" mall turned inside out, so the main corridors are

all outside. There are huge movie theaters and fancy restaurants, yoga studios, art galleries, and designer shoe stores. When the Shoppes opened a few months ago, it made a point to call itself a "lifestyle center for the upscale customer." I bite back a snort. Nothing upscale about me, in my cutoffs and Chuck Taylors.

I jump to the side as a mom and daughter come barreling out the door, bringing with them air conditioning and the scent of new clothing. It all rushes at me and makes my breath catch.

Why am I panicking? It's just clothes!

Whoosh. Here comes another satisfied customer, carrying a blue bag and wearing a smile.

It's just clothes.

The thought does not make me push open the door and go inside.

My shoulders slump. It's not just clothes. It's what they represent. If I go in there, then I'm giving in to my mom. Again.

I don't resent my mom. I love her. But look at me now. Standing in this fancy shopping center, rocking on my heels and spinning my wheels. I really don't want to be here. But I don't want to be at home either.

I want to be at the carnival with my best friend. I want to dance on the grounds, ride every single ride, and eat junk food until my stomach hurts. I want to forget every responsibility life's drawn out for me. At least for one night. But instead, I'm here, about to buy a dress I'll probably hate to go to a restaurant I'll probably hate to celebrate getting into a school I know I'll hate.

Whoosh. Another customer. Another blast of artificial air.

"Brandy?"

My brain processes the timbre of the voice coming from behind me. Friendly and light, with just the tiniest bit of grit. Then it registers. Oh my God.

Not the boy who stole at least three of my Tater Tots right off my lunch tray every Thursday. For four years straight. Not the boy whose voice and face and entire presence made my adrenaline spike every day. For four years straight.

I turn around and, yup. There he is. Tall, with wavy dark hair and ivory-colored skin. What some people in my school called "handsome" but I called "annoying." *Why is he here?* Seeing people out of context always throws me off, but seeing *him* out of context has my head spinning.

Ben Nolan had been stealing my Tater Tots since ninth grade, but it wasn't until the summer before junior year that he started following me online. I don't even know how he found my profile. Compared to him, I'm a nobody. He has hundreds of thousands of followers. I have just a fraction of that. But he always likes my videos. Which is actually cool, since that's where I mainly show off my art, and where I get a lot of my commissions.

Once I followed him back, he was suddenly around all the time. Or maybe I just started noticing that he was. We did have almost all of our classes together, his locker was right next to mine, and sometimes he sat with me and Shai and a few other people at lunch.

But I didn't really talk to him after hours unless it was production season, when the drama department and art department came together in a clash of color and cacophony. I painted the sets while he played the parts. (Only once did I smear paint on his nose.)

Okay, fine, it was actually three times, but who's counting, really? He deserved all of it.

"It *is* you! Hey, Freckles!"

And here we go. This is why he did and still does aggravate the hell out of me. Not only was he around all the time, but he teased me nonstop. At our lockers (he made fun of my Kiss & Tell posters). In class (he always sat behind me unless the teacher assigned seats or we were forced to sit alphabetically, so constant braid tugging was afoot). During lunch (when the Tater Tot crimes happened). The last time I saw him was at graduation. I can't work out if I missed having him around or not.

I cross my arms and give him what I hope is a death stare. "My name is Brandy."

"What's that you said?" He cups his hand behind his ear. "Freckles? Got it!"

Ugh. He is so *annoying*. "Why are you even here?"

"I needed a braid to yank. And you have so generously supplied me with two."

I jump back. "Don't you even!"

He gives me an obnoxious grin. How he was voted BEST SMILE in our school superlatives is a mystery to me. "Why are *you* here?"

My mother did not raise me to be rude, but does that apply when your throat tightens so much that words have no chance of escaping? I swallow. Hard. "If you must know—"

He whips off his sunglasses and stares. "Is that my hoodie?"

"Um…" My face is a furnace. And I know for a fact that when I turn red, my freckles pop out even more. Which is the last thing I need him to notice. I don't even have that many freckles, but if you listen to him, you'd think I had a million.

"Didn't I lend that to you four months ago?" he asks.

Five, actually. We had one unseasonably warm day, which triggered our school's new AC system to switch on. Problem is that it decided *stay* on when the temp dropped back to its normal subzero self the next day. Ben saw me shivering and, without hesitation, pulled off his faded gray hoodie and handed it to me.

It was still warm, so it felt like a hug. I'd liked how soft it was. Well-worn and well-loved. It smelled like soap, laundry detergent, and a little bit of Ben. It still sort of smells like Ben.

I shake my head slightly. I *really* don't need this today.

"I've been looking all over for that hoodie!"

I do a mini-flourish. "Ta-da!"

"Why on earth are you wearing it today? It's ninety degrees. Aren't you all sweaty?"

I huff. "Excuse me. I do not sweat."

"Okay." He makes a goofy face. "Next you're going to tell me you don't go number two either."

"You're gross."

He laughs. "Sorry. It's just that I'm roasting, so I thought you'd be, too. But apparently you are a superhuman weirdo who can withstand extreme weather."

"Why I gotta be a weirdo, though?"

"Because you are. Weirdo."

"Call me that one more time and you'll never get this hoodie back."

He shrugs. "Whatever. It looks better on you than it does on me anyway."

What the hell is *that* supposed to mean? Then I shake my head. He said it in such a throwaway manner. There's no way he meant anything by it.

He slips his sunglasses back on. "How long have you been standing here?"

I turn toward the store, where more customers are coming in and out. *Whoosh. Whoosh. Whoosh.* "I'm supposed to be getting a new dress."

He raises his eyebrows at me. "You?"

I punch his arm. "Oh my God!"

"It's just that dressing up isn't exactly your style."

He knows my style?

Okay, fine. It's not that hard to figure out. Jeans. Hoodies. Hair in two braids. Nothing special. Easy to blend into the background.

But still. He noticed.

Why do I care that he noticed?

"What do you need a dress for?" he asks.

Ugh. I screw my face up. Tight. What do people even wear to the freaking President's Club?

"What's going on, Freckles? You're standing here like a zombie and you look like you're consti—"

"If you want to live, you will not finish that sentence."

"You look sad," he says instead. Which punches me right in the gut. I thought I was hiding it pretty well. But then again, Ben says that in his acting classes, they do a lot of exercises that dig into how people are feeling. So that's probably why he can see it.

"I got into nursing school today."

His mouth drops. "That's amazing, Brandy."

"Yeah. Everyone seems to think so."

He stares at me. At least I think he is. Hard to tell through the dark lenses. "What do *you* think?"

"I think I would rather shit in my hands and clap than go to nursing school," I say, then I slap my hand over my mouth.

He throws his hands up. "Um, okay. Was not expecting you to say that. Who'd've thought? Little ole Freckles, using language like that!"

"I am not that little! And my name is *Brandy*."

"Why in the world did you apply to nursing school if you hate it that much?"

"Do you even care?"

"I'm asking, aren't I?"

I tilt my head toward the door. "I'm here because my mom wants me to pick out a nice dress."

"You said that."

"Because she really wants to celebrate. My getting into nursing school."

He gives me another strange look. Then understanding dawns. "Ohhh."

"At the President's Club."

"Your nursing school is at the President's Club?"

Now it's my turn to give him a strange look. "That's where Mom wants to celebrate."

"Oh." He wrinkles his nose. "Wait, really? That place is—"

"Fancy, I know. And as you just *so helpfully* pointed out, not exactly my thing."

"Always happy to be of assistance." He wrinkles his nose again. "Sounds like you're in quite the pickle. What are you going to do?"

Quite the pickle. This boy's obviously been reading too many old plays.

"What do you *want* to do?" he asks.

Time slows down again. I can't think of the last time anyone's asked me that. I guess it never occurred to me to mind, because everyone else had more important things to worry about. Like my best friend *having a baby.*

When Shai told me she was pregnant, I immediately dropped everything to be there for her in any way I could. Then her parents kicked her out. I can't even imagine how scary it was, and probably still is, for her. No way was I going to make her go through that alone. And no way am I going to bother her with my crap now.

"I don't know if what I want even matters," I mutter.

"Of course it matters."

"Will you go away if I tell you I want you to go away?"

He laughs again. "No one ever wants me to go away. So not even a chance. Talk."

"Ugh, you're so arrogant."

"*Confident* is the word I'd use." His joking expression

clears. "But seriously, Brandy. Why don't you think what you want matters?"

My guard drops ever so slightly as I let out a deep breath and twirl my braid around my finger. I stare at my feet while the words pour out of me. "Because it doesn't *feel* like it. It's like I'm at the top of a roller coaster, only it's not a fun roller coaster. It's a coaster of destruction—that destruction being my entire future—and gravity is about to take over any second. And gravity is everybody's expectations and things. I guess I'm freaking out. Just a little bit? I mean, I'm telling this to you of all people, so I must be out of my mind."

"Hey." He waits until I look up at him. "It's going to be okay."

"Is it?"

"I mean, only you know in your heart of hearts, so only you can answer that."

"I guess."

"Feels like you've been holding that in for a while."

I nod. "Yeah, maybe I have. I'm really sorry. I didn't mean to dump like that."

"Hey. I said it's okay."

I nibble my bottom lip. "Thanks."

We are quiet for a bit, so the only sounds are random conversations around us mixing with the classical music being piped in. Ben gestures toward the door again. "I guess it couldn't hurt to give the store a shot. Since we're here and all. Maybe you'll get lucky and find that fancy dress. And maybe I'll find a new black shirt."

"Is that why you're here? To get a new shirt?"

He runs his hands through his dark waves, making them even more messy. "And I need to do something to get out of my head. I've been spiraling since this morning."

I blink up at him. Ben spiraling? He's the most cheerful person I know, always looking on the bright side and trying to get everyone else to do it, too. Like when our senior skip day got rained out. I'm talking torrential flooding, end-of-the-world, where-the-hell-is-the-Ark raining. Not only did he acknowledge our collective disappointment, but he somehow got us all into the auditorium and arranged an impromptu board game day/talent show. We still got to skip class. People got to show off their skills, and everybody stayed dry. Ms. Fanning, our English teacher and drama coach, even ordered pizza for us.

So my curiosity? Super piqued. "Do you want to talk about it?"

I'm not sure how I expect him to answer. We never really got into super deep stuff at school. There just wasn't time when there was torment to be had. But he's not himself right now, and I need to focus on something else, *anything* else, to get out of *my* head.

His expression is thoughtful. Then he tilts his head in a "follow me" motion. We find a seat on a stone bench that's directly in the sun. Which explains why it is available.

He takes off his sunglasses and leans close to me, bringing with him the scent of coconut sunscreen, something that reminds me of spring, and that familiar Tide detergent. The spring scent is new. It should be cloying, but on him it's nice. And this close, I can see the pores on his nose, the very faint freckles sprinkled across the bridge. (And he has the nerve to tease me about mine!) Just for a moment, he seems human, rather than a thing to torture, and that throws me off. I try to discreetly let out a deep breath. Something to calm my sudden racing heart. *Why is my heart racing?* This is Ben. The bane of my existence. Yes, he's cute, but everyone knows that. Plus, there's a lot of cute people, and they don't make my heart race. So what the heck? And sure, he's funny. But so are clowns. And fine, yes, my heart's been doing this weird skipping thing around him ever since he stuck giant googly eyes on my locker the second week of ninth grade. But that doesn't explain why I'm feeling a little weird right now.

Maybe the nursing school thing is messing with my head even more than I thought.

"Promise not to tell anyone?" he asks.

His voice is low and all mysterious. So I lower mine, too. "Who would I tell?"

He raises one perfectly manicured eyebrow at me. I teased him for five days straight when I found out, during junior year, that he got his brows waxed. I mean, who does that?

"I promise I won't tell, Eyebrows. Not even Shai."

"Did you just call me *Eyebrows*?"

"If I have to be Freckles, you have to be Eyebrows."

He takes his own (not discreet) deep breath. "Can't believe I'm telling you this. But. I had an audition yesterday. A big one. The biggest of my life. And today I'm supposed to find out if I got the part."

Then he doesn't say anything. And he keeps not saying anything.

"Ben."

"Why are you looking at me like that?"

"Obviously I need details! *What was the audition for?*"

He buries his head in his hands. "Ugh, stop making that face."

I want to wring his neck. "Benjamin David Nolan."

He cuts his eyes over to me. "How…how do you know my middle name?"

Oops. No one knows about my late-night IMDB stalking (Benjamin David Nolan, actor, born January 31, 2006), and I plan to keep it that way. Look, knowledge is power, and I was just doing reconnaissance. "Never mind that. Please spill the tea. I'm begging you."

He shakes his head, but then gives me a little smile. And hold on. Since when is his smile adorable? I mean, wait. No. It's not. It's just a smile. A regular, plain old smile with straight white teeth and tiny dimples in his cheeks. Boring.

"Okay. I'll spill. It was for a lead role. In a major motion picture. And Freckles, I have to land this role." His eyes flicker with passion.

"Like a *movie*? In actual theaters that serve popcorn and nachos? Or a straight to streaming movie? Or both?"

He nods. "In theaters first, with a big premiere on a red carpet. Then eventually streaming. All of that."

"So...Hollywood?"

He nods again. "Yeah. Hollywood."

I stare at him. Because holy cow, that's huge. That's *real*. "Wow. That's...wow."

This boy's been in my face for some reason or another just about every day in school for the last four years. But today, for the first time, I really *see* him. Not just his faint freckles, but *him*. It's written all over him how much he wants this, and it's sinking in just how hard he works for it.

Everyone at school knew that Ben had big dreams and big aspirations. He was a fixture in the drama club, snagging lead roles even during freshman year, when those roles always go to seniors. While the rest of us goofed off during rehearsals, Ben took every part he played seriously. Instead of partying, he was taking acting classes or working to earn money to pay for those classes. And he auditioned during a lot of our lunch periods. (Unfortunately, he never had an audition on a Thursday, so my Tater Tots were never safe.)

"He's got something special," Ms. Fanning always said. I guess some super important people are starting to believe it as well. Hollywood people. Maybe producers and directors and stuff like that. Holy cow.

Ben is already sort of locally famous. He's had recurring roles on national TV shows and a regular role on a cable variety show, so our local media goes nuts over him. He gets to do things like throw pitches at baseball games and interview farmers at the state fair. And like I mentioned earlier, his social media is gangbusters huge. He's getting thousands of new followers all the time because I guess people love his anecdotes about being an aspiring actor from a small(ish) town. He posts about his auditions and does acting challenges and funny random skits. But even with all that, and although he's been to Los Angeles for those sitcoms and for some auditions, he's not what I'd call Hollywood Famous. At least not yet.

Or maybe I just have no clue what I'm talking about.

"I'm both excited and freaking the freak out," he says. "But I'm probably getting all worked up over nothing. It's such a long shot and I don't even know if I came close in that audition."

"I'm sure you nailed it," I say. "Aren't you an expert at that stuff?"

He shrugs. "I don't know. Maybe? I like going on auditions. But…ugh. I've never been as nervous as I was yesterday. I fumbled my slate twice, and then I knocked over a prop. The only thing that maybe saved me is that this character is supposed to be awkward, so I hope they think that was all part of it."

I have no clue what a slate is. And I've never seen Ben look so terrified.

I don't know what goes on in auditions, but I do know this: I cannot imagine standing in front of a bunch of important people, being like "pick me." And even though he's as white as chalk right now, I know that Ben is a special kind of brave. He's been gunning for his dream, a big dream, for as long as I've known him. I've been hiding mine behind bridges and buildings. Literally. I don't know whether to admire him or to be irritated that I'm so much the opposite.

Curiosity takes over and eclipses both choices. "Have you ever not gotten a part?"

"Sure. You just have to not take it personally," Ben says. "At the end of the day, it's a business, and I'm just one brand in that business. When you look at it like that, it takes the sting out."

I tilt my head. "Does it?"

He laughs. "Nope. But I keep telling myself that and hope I'll believe it one of these days."

I manage a small chuckle. "That makes sense." Even though Mr. Conway gave me feedback on my work, most of it was encouraging. And the people who buy my commissions always leave glowing reviews, and then they tell their friends, who order more. I've never had my art really critiqued outside of that, so I don't know that sting.

I think about the emails I'm waiting for. Mr. Conway

had to push me hard to enter a bunch of art contests, but ever since I sent off the emails, I've been both eager and anxious to hear back. Some of them have a critique component, and I'm super nervous. Ben treats his acting like a business. Will I ever be able to think of my art as a business? It's so personal, and if people hate *it*, I'll feel like they hate *me*. But I'm going to need to learn to not hold it so closely, and soon. Else I'll never be able to stay grounded ~~if~~ when I do make that leap from hobby to career.

"How *do* you learn not to take it personally?" I ask him.

His expression is thoughtful again. "It's like picking out clothes or something. Maybe nothing is actually wrong with that hoodie or whatever, but it's the wrong size or color, so it's not right for me. So I try to think about auditioning like this: There's nothing wrong with me as a person or an actor, I'm just wrong for that particular project."

I nod slowly. That's such a good way to look at things. "Huh. That's actually helpful."

"Yeah?" He gives me another smile and okay, *fine.* I fully admit that it's an adorable smile. Objectively. And how had I never noticed how kind his eyes were? I guess it's something you don't really pay attention to when you're busy thinking of ways to torment the tormentor.

"I've never gotten this far for something this big," he adds. "And none of my other auditions ever mattered as much as this one."

"What does that mean? Are there stages to auditions?"

He nods. "Most of the time, yes. Especially for movies. I had my first audition last month, and a callback last week. Then a chemistry test yesterday. I literally got off a plane from LA a couple of hours ago."

"Chemistry test? Do you need to know about molecules and stuff for the role?"

He laughs. "Not that kind of chemistry! It's when the director makes you audition with the other actors to see how you get along."

"Oh. *That* kind of chemistry." Not that I'm great at either kind, to be honest. "That sounds like a lot."

"It can make or break a movie," he says.

"Are the other people in the cast really famous?"

"Yeah."

"Whoa. Can you tell me who? Not that I'm, like, a climber or anything. I'm just curious." I try to imagine Ben on-screen with someone like Chloe Winters or Julian Coleman. Ben kind of shines in that way, so it comes easier than I thought it would.

"I wish I could," he says, "but NDAs and all that. I could get in big trouble."

"Oh. Well, I don't want you to get in trouble. Even if you do call me Freckles. See how generous I am?" It would've been a nice distraction from my own situation, but I'm not that selfish. I hope. "Are these tests a normal thing?"

"At this stage, yeah."

"And do you think you had good chemistry?"

He nods. "That, I'm confident about. I did some awkward stuff, but getting along with the other actors wasn't an issue at all."

"Well, duh. I can't imagine anyone not getting along with you."

He gives me a side-eye.

"You started every single thing that went down between us," I say.

"Hey, I didn't start the eyebrow teasing."

"You're right, that was me. Sorry not sorry. You know, no matter what happens, you'll be okay, right?"

"Will I? Every superstition I've ever heard is bouncing around in my brain and I can't shake it," he says.

"Don't you have a black cat?"

"Lucky is the very best cat."

I start singing. "She's so lucky, she's a star!" Then in my regular voice, I say, "Just like you're going to be."

He closes his eyes. "Please don't make fun of me. Not today."

"Dude."

"You always make fun of my acting."

"I do not! I make fun of *you!*"

But I get it. Because I feel that same thing. That desperation to prove I can do the things people don't believe I can do. Most of the people I knew from school did believe Ben would make it big. But there were definitely some haters. Just like there are for me—even if they mostly live in my head. I still understand the need to make people see that I'm serious, that this is not fleeting or a fantasy.

What I can't relate to is actually doing something about it. And that makes me ~~slightly~~ very envious. There's my little online shop, and I do the commissions, and I have a portfolio. But what is that in the grand scheme of things? A bunch of small things that I'm not sure will add up to the career I dream of.

Ben's been working his way up to this for a while. I would watch him on local TV shows and commercials (then tease the hell out of him the next day at school). Then a few national commercials about hot dogs or whatever (and tease him even more). There was the cable show where he disappeared for two entire summers so he could sing and dance and act in front of live studio audiences. Shai and I would watch the shows after school every day—her fresh from dance class and trying to learn their choreography. Me doodling about the show's Theme of the Day and how they incorporated everything they did in the episode into the theme. It was actually a really neat show and I hate that it got cancelled. Because although the boy got on my every last nerve, it was still fun to see Ben in his element. He *shined* on that show.

And then there were the national TV shows. Granted, most of those parts were on the small side—a fast food worker here, an obnoxious moviegoer there—but it sounds like this one is *huge*.

The point is: Unlike me, Ben is out there with his dreams. I hold mine tight and have been ever since the day I hinted to Mom that I wanted to pursue art and she shut that right down. Despite my best efforts to forget it ever happened, the memory pops into my mind.

"This is really good." Mom looks over my drawing. Original characters sitting on a graffiti-covered wall, both looking at one phone. The colors are a surreal pastel, like being inside a dream. "They look like best friends who share everything and love each other like sisters."

"That's exactly what they are," I tell her. I'm so excited that she sees what I was trying to do.

She puts her arm around my shoulders and squeezes me. "I'm not well versed in art, but you're really talented, Peanut. Your drawings tell stories."

"Thanks." I bite my lip. It's time to start planting the seeds, so I do. "I'd be happy doing this the rest of my life."

She looks at me, her forehead wrinkled. "Like a career?"

I nod.

"What happened to nursing? I thought you wanted to be like me and your grandmother."

"I—"

"Nursing is what we've been working for. Don't tell me you're changing your mind now."

I don't say anything, but I guess my expression speaks for me.

She purses her lips. "You know art isn't going to put food on the table, right?"

This pisses me off. "But why couldn't it? If I work really hard?" Which duh, of course I plan to do. Even though making art is the only thing that doesn't *feel like work.*

She sighs. "As much as I'd love to tell you that hard work will pay off, that's not always the case in this field. And it makes people reckless. Your father left us because he was so busy chasing his art dream."

"And he made it."

She purses her lips. "Well. That's not typical."

I bite my thumbnail. "So?"

She brushes a spirally strand from my forehead. It takes everything in me not to flinch away. "Your father is an outlier, a shot in the dark. My job is to keep you alive and make sure you have a secure future. Prepare you for the real world. Art's not the way to guarantee that, Peanut. You've talked about being a nurse since you were three, and I'm going to help you to get there every step of the way. As long as you have those credentials, you'll never have to worry about eating."

"Hey, you look worried. Are you okay?" Ben asks me.

My stomach churns with nausea. "You're making me think about my future. And I don't know how I feel about that."

I know exactly how I feel about it. There are few things more nerve-wracking than thinking about *the future*, let alone having a discussion about it.

"I mean, it is yours, so you should have a lot of thoughts about it. And feelings, too. Especially if it's coming like it is."

I sigh. Again. "Yeah."

Even though I kept my dreams of being an artist pretty quiet, almost everyone at school knew I liked art. They paid me for doodles all during my senior year, which helped me stash away a few hundred dollars that no one knows about. And there is my website, which is growing. Slowly, but it's there. Shai has an illustration that I made of her and Elsa as a "new mommy" gift, and it's hanging above Elsa's crib. And there's my modest social media following. But I haven't been able to tell anyone else that I want to make this my life. Even though Mr. Conway figured it out ages ago.

The world needs to see your art he'd signed in my yearbook. *Don't be afraid to put it all out there.*

Except I *am* scared. I'd be devastated if the world shot me down, too.

Still. Study halls spent hanging out in Mr. Conway's classroom were my favorite times of the day. He'd let me have run of the studio, and he was always there to answer questions whenever I needed help. He taught me the subtleties of using pastels, the boldness of broad paint strokes, and the intricacies of penciled lines. He encouraged me to play with all the mediums he had and find the one that speaks to me most, the one that makes my fingers tingle with the longing to create. It was in his classroom that I found my home in colorful, cute cartoon letters, whimsical landscapes, and tiny chibi characters. It was in his classroom that my thirst for more knowledge was awakened.

He pushed me to take risks, and even though they scared me, I did it. He even encouraged me to apply for a scholarship at the Preston Academy of Art. I still have the PDFs saved on my iPad.

I just need to work up the guts to actually apply to the damn school.

"When does nursing school start?" Ben asks.

"This fall."

"So you still have time to change her mind."

"Except she wants to pay the deposit this evening."

"Okay, less time."

It seems so big, picking art school over nursing school.

But Ben's doing big things. Why can't I? Why on earth do I have to be such a chicken?

"Everything feels so *real* all of a sudden," I say.

"That's because it is. It's *been* real, Brandy. All of it. Me. You. Our careers. And it could be the biggest thing to ever happen to me. I *have* to get this role." Ben looks me right in the eyes and my breath catches. The determination in his gaze feels too familiar. A thought pops into my head, but it's just as quickly swept away, because Ben is super intense right now. And it's kind of...hot? Wait, no! Ew! Except...I swear he is getting cuter and cuter by the minute. How is that even possible? I mean, okay. We can start with his eyes. I guess they're pretty, with their layers of greens, browns, and golds. And his hair. Shampoo-commercial shiny dark brown waves getting all tangled up in the breeze, and what am I even doing?

I shake my head slightly. Obviously, I'm not thinking straight. But also, he needs to stop looking at me all cute like that! It's not like everyone doesn't know he's objectively good looking. It was one of the Universal Truths of Monroe High.

People talked about him all the time. Once, Raquel Delgado, who was super popular, made a list of the best-looking guys in school. She passed it around in the locker room after gym class. Some of the names were expected, like Jason Brooks, who was on the football team, and Marcus Cho, who was just hot in general. Seeing Ben on that list made my insides all squirmy, but not as squirmy as knowing how many people wanted him to ask them to prom. Except he didn't even attend. He was in Los Angeles that weekend.

Not that I was keeping tabs or anything.

"Sorry." He swallows and looks at his lap. And something flips inside of me. I've been going to school with this boy for years, stealing his fruit and hitting him upside the head, but also accepting his help when math kept getting the best of me and letting his shenanigans distract me when I was frustrated over another chemistry equation, but I've never felt closer to him than I do right now. It's weird and I don't know how okay I am with this. I almost want him to call me Freckles again, just to set the world back to its rightful self.

But it doesn't sit well with me that he thinks I don't take his work seriously. I'd hate it if he made fun of my art. I don't want his opinion, or anyone's, to matter. But it does.

"Ben."

He turns to me. "Hmm?"

"I never meant to make fun of your acting. I actually think it's cool, what you do."

He gives me another small smile. "Thanks, Freckles."

Three times today he's given me that sweet smile. For years, all I ever saw was a wide, shit-eating (and infuriating) grin plastered across his face. This feels more personal. More special. Even if he does insist on calling me that heinous nickname.

I'm sweating.

"And I know you weren't being mean or anything," he adds. "I'm just stressed. It sucks."

Maybe now it's my turn to distract him. But I'm not ready to spill my guts to him just yet, not anymore. So I tilt my head toward the store. "Should we go in now?"

He nods and hops up. I don't even have to push open the door to go in. He does it for me.

5

Insert Shopping
Montage Here

10:35 a.m.

Shai

You're awfully quiet down there

Shai

Are you even home?

Shai

I just put my ear to the floor

Shai

No I'm not being creepy why do you ask

Shai
You're def not home

Shai
Brandy

Shai
Brandy

Shai
Brandy

It's almost always a blessing and every once in a while a curse to have your BFF living in the apartment above yours, but that's the least of my worries right now. I'm too busy using every ounce of willpower to hold it together. Everything in this store is too much. Too much bright light. Too many fragrances wafting through the air. Too many racks of bland, preppy basics. It's kind of hard to breathe, but I try to take a deep breath to keep from panicking. Big mistake. I can actually *taste* all the cologne floating through the air. Blech.

At least the music is lit. "Heartbreak Fever" bumps from the speakers, knocking my panic back a few notches. Normally if the feelings are too much, a song with this much rhythm only ratchets up my anxiety. But today, the beats are helping. And I'm grateful.

Ben wrinkles his nose. "Is this Kiss & Tell?"

"Yes, and if you say one word against them, I will eviscerate you."

"Which one do you love the best? Hunter?"

"Hunter is out of my league in more ways than one, and—ew, why am I talking about this with you?"

"Fangirls are so passionate."

"I am not a *fan*girl," I growl. "I just like their songs."

He gives me one of his grins. "And you just happened to have a poster in your locker."

Ben's entire being lights up every time he smiles like that. Honestly, it's usually hard to stay in a funk around him because he radiates such good vibes. Just like Shai does. I never realized how much I surround myself with bright people. But right now, I don't care how bright his smile is. The boy is walking on thin ice. "If you make fun of them or me for liking them, I'll never speak to you again."

"God, you're defensive AF. Why would I make fun of you?"

"You always make fun of me."

"Well, if it means anything to you, I like them, too. And Kayla *is* a fangirl, and that exact same poster from your locker is up in her room." He pulls out his phone and starts tapping. "We should look up the dress code at the President's Club."

I'm not sure how I feel about liking the same music as Ben's five-year-old sister, but then I figure, who cares? Good music is good music.

54

He scrolls, then frowns. "What the hell does 'country club casual' mean? Ugh, the Wi-Fi here sucks."

"That's because you have a Samsung." I pull out my phone, swipe away those million texts from Shai, and google "country club casual."

"What's wrong with my Samsung?" Ben asks.

"I'm not about that green text bubble life," I say. I tap on the first page I see. It loads super slowly, but it eventually gets there. I frown. Big. "Golf shirts? Skirts? Ugh!"

He huffs. "Whatever. At least I don't have to buy a new phone every two years because it gets bricked."

"At least mine doesn't blow up!"

"That was the battery, and it was years ago!"

A bunch of new (blue, the superior color) texts appear, and they're from a number I never expected to hear from. A number I never even assigned a proper contact.

I stare and stare and stare at my phone. But the messages don't go away. They're real.

I'd been stalking this man since I was old enough to have my own tablet and figure out Google. I'd perused his website. Read about his gallery openings and installations all over the country. But I never reached out to him until the beginning of my senior year, when Mom started really pressuring me about nursing school. I didn't realize how desperate I was starting to feel about everything, but something made me fill out the contact form on his website. I didn't expect an answer, or if I did get one, I figured it would be from an assistant. Surely, someone like him wouldn't be checking his own messages, right?

But then he wrote back. And he told me he'd been keeping tabs on me all along.

There's a big question there, but I've been too scared to ask it. I'm still too scared to ask it. The answer might devastate me.

> MF
>
> **Hey. I'm not sure if you got my email. I'm in town at NEO Gallery this week.**

> MF
>
> **It would be cool if you stopped by. I'd like to see you.**

"Who is MF?" Ben asks.

I'm still too busy staring at the texts to answer him.

"Hey, Freckles." He waves his hand in front of my face. "Hello?"

"Yeah, fine!" I shove my phone into my pocket. "Shall we?"

He gives me a look like he is not convinced. (And he shouldn't be. I wasn't that convincing.)

"Tell me who MF is."

"No."

"Fine."

"Fine."

My phone buzzes again.

Mom
> **Where are you?**

Mom
> **You should try this store! It's supposed to have good contemporary teen fashion.**

Mom
> **The Shoppes at Bishop Haven**
> Directory
> bishophavenshoppes.com

I don't even get a chance to tap on the link before a new text from her pops up with five images of dresses I wouldn't be caught dead in.

Mom
> **I'm going to get a few sent to the apartment. Try them on if you get a chance! We can return them if you don't like them.**

Mom
> **It'll be like I'm there with you in a way!**

More texts start pouring in, and my hands start shaking so much I almost drop the phone.

MF
> **I'd like to see you.**

> **But only if you want to. No pressure.**

Ben snatches my phone. "I'm picking your dress for tonight."

This snaps me back to the present. "Do you have a death wish? Give me my phone!"

"They want golf-chic? You should *give* them golf-chic!"

What is he even talking about? "Ben."

He darts over to a rack and starts flipping through. How he even decides on a rack is a mystery. There are *so many*. And they're all full of so many colors and shapes and styles. How do people do this? How do people *enjoy* this?

Ben holds up what looks like a hot pink tennis dress. "Golf chic!"

"Phone."

"No. Whatever is happening on there is freaking you out and you need a distraction."

"I'm not freaking out!"

"Your face is like cinnamon-speckled milk and you've been rubbing your arms for the past thirty seconds. You're not fine."

I force my hands to my side. "I. Am. Fine! And also, describing people of color as food? Kind of racist, dude."

"My bad. Seriously." He tilts his head. "You look like paint-speckled porcelain. How about that?"

I sigh. "I guess."

He holds up the dress again.

I shake my head. "That ain't it."

"Okay." He hangs it back on the rack. "But if you snooze you lose. No take-backsies."

"Whatever. This is silly."

"It's fun. You remember how to have fun, don't you?"

"You are infuriating!"

"How about this?" This time, it's a soft green button-up ruffled hem shirt dress. I consider it. It's not too dressy, but it might still be conservative enough to fit in at a fancy dinner. And the color is nice.

"Possibility. I don't think it's my size, though."

"You should try it on anyway," Ben says. "My older sister constantly complains about how sizes for women's clothes aren't consistent."

I'm not convinced, but I follow his advice. The thing hangs on me like drapery, and I hate that because it really is such a cute dress. I come out and show it to Ben. "Told you so."

"It was worth a shot," Ben says. "The color looks amazing on you, though. Hey, don't get offended. But I meant to ask you." He gestures toward my legs. "What is up with that?"

I'm so used to the scrapes and bruises that I hardly ever notice them anymore unless I'm trying to avoid getting a new one. "I'm remarkably clumsy," I say.

"Huh. I never noticed you being clumsy before," he says.

What else has he (never) noticed about me? I ponder that when I'm back in the dressing room and wiggling into my own clothes. It makes me blush.

I come out and plop onto a bench. "All right. Your turn."

"Yes. Black shirt." Ben hands me my phone. The screen keeps lighting up with notifications, which I keep ignoring. "Kayla spilled salad dressing on my old one."

"Oh man." Kayla is highly spirited. He'd come to school with evidence of her chaos at least once a week, and his stories are always gold. The child is a firecracker, that's for sure. "You can't just wash it?"

"Oil-based salad dressing."

"Ew." I wrinkle my nose.

"Exactly. What five-year-old even eats salads? Mom said I can use vinegar to clean it up, but I can't stand the smell of it. So that's a hell no right there." He raises his eyebrows at me. "Since I helped you with the dress, will you help me pick out which shirt to get?"

"Deal."

He disappears into the dressing room with his nine hundred shirts, and I catch up on my notifications. Some DMs asking about stickers. A couple of emails from Lucerne that I swipe away. A weather advisory. And some new texts from Shai.

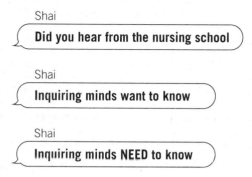

Shai

Did you hear from the nursing school

Shai

Inquiring minds want to know

Shai

Inquiring minds NEED to know

Ben comes out of the dressing room in a white button-down shirt and raises his eyebrows at me. But the expression on my face must show that I'm not a fan, because he disappears again.

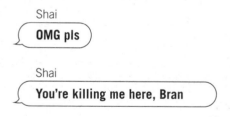

Shai

OMG pls

Shai

You're killing me here, Bran

Now Ben's wearing a dark gray shirt. He checks the mirror and scrunches up his forehead. "This is going on the 'maybe' pile. I don't hate it, but I don't love it."

I nod. "It looks nice on you, but it doesn't really stand out. Or capture who you are."

He meets my gaze in the mirror. "Who exactly is that to you, Brandy?"

"Uh..."

Who *is* he to me? My memories of him are a blur of good-natured torment. But now? *But now?*

He's definitely different from how he usually is around me. He's not teasing me quite as much as normal, and that feels decidedly *ab*normal. I'm not the kind of person who gets married to routines, but seeing him like this—not his usual infuriating, overconfident self—is throwing me off. Because I think I don't mind him like this. I feel like it's even kind of sweet.

Hold on. *Sweet?* Him?!

Yeah, I've officially lost my mind.

For the first time in forever, I am speechless around Benjamin David Nolan. I'm still speechless when he goes back into the dressing room. I'm still speechless when my phone buzzes again.

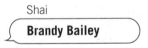

Shai

Brandy Bailey

I can't answer her. I can barely breathe. What even is *happening*?

"How about this one?" Now Ben's modeling a dark blue shirt. But he shakes his head almost immediately and goes back into the dressing room.

Shai

If I don't hear from you in five minutes, I'm calling a search party

I shake myself back to reality.

Me
I'm out

Me
Shopping

I don't know why I don't tell her I'm with Ben.

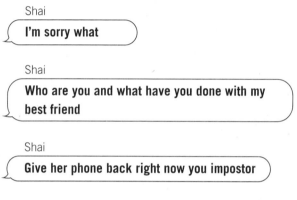

Shai
I'm sorry what

Shai
Who are you and what have you done with my best friend

Shai
Give her phone back right now you impostor

"Okay, this is the last one," Ben calls.

Me
It's me

Me
I promise

Me
Long story

Me
Will catch you up later

My phone buzzes like crazy, but I barely notice it. Because Ben has just come out of the dressing room again.

And he looks like an actual Prince Charming.

My heart forgets to beat. Then it beats too much.

It's just a shirt. A regular old shirt that hangs on him just right. Like it was made for him. But we're in a chain store, and I didn't even know chain stores made clothes that could fit on people like this.

Lines appear between his brows. "What? Why are you looking at me like that?"

The green in the shirt accentuates the green flecks in his hazel eyes, and his jawline has never been so square and perfect. Ben Nolan looks like the leading man he dreams of being and I don't know what to even think.

Or if I can think at all.

"You have to get that one." My voice is strained. And that's because I'm having a hard time breathing. Again.

I should probably get that checked out.

Ben looks down at the shirt. "Yeah? But it's not black."

"Black is overrated. Right now, you look…" Amazing. Unreal. Good enough to eat.

Good enough to eat?

"Good." The word flies out of me before I can stop it. "Really, really good."

Ugh. What the heck. He is attractive, but that attractiveness never affected me much. Not like this. I don't like it. It's probably just a fluke anyway. When he puts on his regular clothes, he'll just go back to being annoying, obnoxious Ben Nolan.

Just like how I like him.

He grins. "Okay then. Let's go pay. Then we'll go somewhere else to shop for you."

"You don't have to go dress shopping with me."

He shrugs. "But why wouldn't I? I take Kayla all the time."

"Kayla is your little sister."

"So?"

"So. It's different."

"How?"

"I mean, we just happened to both be here. But now we're actually *going shopping* for me. It'll be weird. Won't it? I mean, what do you know about"—I think about the text my mom sent me—"contemporary teen fashion?"

And for that matter, what do *I* know about "contemporary teen fashion"?

He tugs one of my braids. "You're my friend."

"Am I?"

He ignores my question. "And face it." He glances at my hoodie again. "You need the help."

I cannot stand him.

6

Chasing the Sun

11:45 a.m.

TIME'S A-TICKIN'. MOM'S EXPECTING PHOTOS, AND AT SOME point I'll need to go home and take a shower and change and all that stuff before meeting her at the President's Club. So I suck up whatever I need to suck up and decide to let Ben do his thing. I hate to admit it, but he's right. I *do* need all the help I can get. (And this definitely also applies to other aspects of my life, but I'm not thinking about that right now.)

"Let's start walking. Maybe something will jump out at us."

And off we go. No plan. Just wandering. I look around at the stores, having no idea where to begin. For a supposed "lifestyle center for the upscale customer," this place sure is an interesting mishmash of cultural and bourgeois. A shop selling designer handbags sitting next to a place that sells charm jewelry. A café whose aromas are making my mouth water blasting techno music, which spills out through its open door. An art supplies shop that has a discreet NOW HIRING sign in the window. I tilt my head, thinking.

But then we're walking again. A lot of the shops are outright rejects. Stores that are too much or too little. Places that only sell jewelry or shoes or leather jackets. But we don't pass up the handmade cosmetics store because Ben needs to get some kind of special soap. The scents here are strong, but they're less cloying than the ones in the clothing store, so they don't bother me at all. There are a lot of signs talking about ethical this and cruelty-free that, so maybe that's why.

Ben picks up a bottle of shower gel. "I discovered this scent a few weeks ago. It's all I use now." He holds it out to me, and I take a small sniff. It matches the new spring scent I noticed earlier.

"That's really nice," I say.

"Nice? That's it?"

"What do you want me to say?"

"Try 'yes, Ben, you're a walking fresh spring' or something like that."

"It's different from how you used to smell."

His cheeks darken. "Are you telling me I smelled bad?"

"No. Just different. You used to smell like a bar of soap. That Coast one." I take another breath of the shower gel. "Now you smell like this. It's nice. I guess."

It's more than nice. It's comforting and reassuring. I kind of want to bury my face in his shirt.

Nope!

"Did you just sniff me?"

Busted. So totally busted. "No!"

Lying. So totally lying.

He grins. "You totally sniffed me."

"Shut up."

"And you knew which soap I used." He waggles his eyebrows.

I am mortified. *Mortified.* "Benjamin Nolan."

He heads toward the counter to pay. "Yes?"

"It just so happens that your soap had a very distinctive scent. Stop smiling like that!"

He does no such thing. If anything, the grin gets even bigger. "For what it's worth, I know what scent you wear, too. It's that soft rain stuff."

I stare at him. "Looks like someone else has been sniffing."

"Ah, so you admit that you sniffed me." He slides his card into the chip reader. "I knew it."

I blink at him. Then I blink some more. "Knew what?"

"That you're a weirdo. Who goes around sniffing people."

"Excuse me, Mr. Rain Scent. I had your hoodie for months. Of course I know how you smell."

"That...doesn't make it any better."

The clerk is watching us, his eyebrows raised. My face warms up despite the blasting AC. "We should get going."

Ben just keeps grinning.

"Enjoy," the clerk says with a knowing smirk. Then he mouths to me, "He's cute!"

Now my face is really hot.

Outside the store, I turn to Ben. "I can't believe you did that!"

He puts on his innocent expression. Disney eyes, hand to heart. "Did what?"

"I...you...argh!" I try to stalk away. Except it's less dramatic when the storefront across the pathway registers, and I stop short. NEO Gallery.

NEO Gallery! How on earth did I not know it was *right here*? This feels too easy. Like a setup. Because honestly, what are the chances?

Maybe it's a sign! Yes, that has to be it. A ray of hope shoots through me. Maybe this is my ticket out of all of this. Lucerne, nursing, whatever the hell is going on with Ben, everything. "There."

Ben looks me. Then he looks at the storefront. Then back at me. "NEO Gallery?"

I nod.

He gives me a knowing look but doesn't mention the texts. "No offense, but I think the clothes in there are out of both of our price ranges."

I couldn't give two cowlicks about the clothes in there. If NEO is like any other gallery I've visited (I'm ashamed to admit there aren't many—not yet anyway), the clothes are eccentric and super expensive and truly not my style at all. But maybe they could be. Maybe this is where I begin. A new, flamboyant me!

"Okay, but hear me out," I say.

"No. I'm not letting you walk around dressed like a peacock." He pauses and grimaces. "Yeah, I just heard that."

"Dude. What makes you think you'd have any sort of say?"

"Sorry, won't happen again." He tilts his head. "Now that I think about it, you could probably pull it off anyway. So are we going dress shopping in there or what?"

I shake my head. "No. There's someone in there I need to see."

Ben studies my face, then nods. "Okay."

NEO Gallery has an urban loft feel, with ruddy brick walls and small walls of various artworks scattered all over. Natural light streaks through large plate-glass windows, throwing prisms into the air. A shelf stands, holding a variety of art books for sale, and a rack of art supplies tempts me with its shiny markers and high-quality canvases. And there is clothing so far out of my comfort zone I don't even kid about trying any of them on. Ben checks out a price tag on a bright orange dress with large leaves patterned all over it and his eyes pop out of his head. I giggle when he gently pats the dress and steps away. Far away.

I pull out one of the art books. I'd had my eye on it for a long time but could never find it in person. I like to hold the books before I buy them, and the weight of this one is perfect. There's also another one, considerably thinner and paperback, featuring NEO Gallery's current exhibiting artists. I grab that one, too. After I pay for the books, Ben gives me a questioning look. I take a deep breath and nod, then we head toward the actual artworks.

But then I freeze in place.

I'd seen pictures. Of course, I'd seen pictures. But pictures and in person are two completely different things. Here I can feel his energy, the beaming charisma permeating the entire space. The gallery is small, but he still feels a world away. Still, I study him, looking for any and all traces of myself in his face. The way he stands. His hair.

"He looks familiar. Who is he?" Ben asks.

It's hard to get the words out. Because it doesn't even feel real that he's standing right there. That I'm breathing the same air he is. That he's here. In the flesh. Real. Alive.

"My father."

Understanding dawns on Ben's face. "MF."

I nod. Then I stand there.

"Is the double meaning intentional?"

I nod again. And I keep standing there.

"Brandy?" Ben sounds like he's a million miles away.

It's hard to move. It's hard to breathe.

The emails my father and I exchange are never emotion-filled missives. Basically, they're just a way to make sure the other is still alive. I never go deeper because it feels like a betrayal in a way. So we just send each other shallow little updates here and there. He knew I was graduating. I knew he was touring. I knew he was going to be in town. But until he sent those texts, I didn't know he was going to be *right here*.

It kind of feels like a betrayal now, standing here and staring at him. I'm 99.9 percent sure Mom will be hurt if she finds out that he and I have secretly been in contact.

But don't I have a right to know my father? The man who helped create me? I do, right?

My father. This is my first time ever seeing him in person. I've never even heard the sound of his voice. Never knew what it was like to have a dad hug me or tell me he was proud. And as I stand here now, a million feelings are rushing around my brain, crashing through my veins. Anger. Frustration. Resentment. And a deep, deep sadness.

He shines, almost blindingly, like I'm staring at the sun. Contrasting his exhibit: dark, swirling, stormy paintings that remind me of black galaxies spinning out of control. They look exactly how I feel when my skin gets too tight and the room tilts and breathing gets hard. It's like my brain is on blast, right in front of me, and I swallow, trying to push that feeling away right now.

I pull my eyes away from the paintings and look at him again. He murmurs something to a couple—an astonishingly beautiful boy with chestnut colored hair and perfect teeth, and a gorgeous girl with big copper curls and golden skin—and they chuckle in response. All three of them hold glasses of dark, red liquid. *Wine in the afternoon?*

I tilt my head, regarding this couple. The girl asks questions about black holes and space, while the boy looks at her like she's his whole world. They don't seem that much older than Ben and me, but how would I know? People mistake my mom for my sister all the time. And everyone thinks I'm younger than I actually am. (Which sucks, especially when all I want to do is buy one single scratch-off lottery ticket and the people behind the counter give me a hard time, and yes, I'm talking to you, Mr. Armstrong, owner of the ice-cream shop in the center of Preston Township!)

If I drew strangers, I would definitely draw them. I love looking at pretty people.

And I know I'm staring at them to keep from staring at my father. To keep from thinking about him and to squash those feelings that are still rushing me.

A gentle poke to my shoulder makes me jump. But it's Ben, watching me. His eyebrows are raised, and the look in his eyes asks, "All good?"

But I can't answer because I don't know.

My father looks over and I try to imagine what he sees. A short girl with Pippi Longstocking braids, gawking at him like the world's biggest loser. The recognition is instant. So is the shock that washes over his face. Then the smile comes. He waves us over.

I turn and run out of the gallery.

7

That Feeling When

12:05 p.m.

"ARE YOU OKAY?"

I sigh for a million years. "For the last time, I'm fine. Just like the other five times you asked me." I head toward the popcorn stand. "I want caramel corn."

He doesn't follow. "I don't think you're really okay."

I stop and turn to him. "Then why do you keep asking me?"

"Because." He catches up to me. "There's power in speaking things out loud."

"Who told you that? Your therapist?"

"Actually," he flicks my braid, "it was Shai. And I only overheard her talking about it."

I let myself relax. Because of course it was. Shai = Happy Sunshine. Earth child personified. Always going on about breathwork and crystals and other assorted mystical things.

"And I want you to trust me," he says. Then his forehead wrinkles. "How do you know I go to therapy?"

"Technically I didn't know. But," I point finger guns at him, "I do now!"

"You…you did not just *point finger guns at me*."

"I believe I did," I say in a snooty voice.

"Do *you* go to therapy?"

"Nope."

"Pity."

"What do you mean, *pity*?"

"I'm saying that you told me you'd rather shit in your hands, which is really disgusting by the way, than go to nursing school, and excuse me but you just saw your father for the *first time ever* and you're acting like it's no big deal. So yeah, I'm thinking you could use some therapy."

I just stare at him, mouth wide open. "Did you just *diagnose* me?"

He smirks. "I believe I did."

This boy is infuriating. If only because he might be right, and I don't know if I have the grit to process all of that right now. "What kind of popcorn do you want?" I growl.

"The same as you and I got this."

"I'm paying!"

"Nope!"

"Oh my God, please. It's the least I can do."

His forehead scrunches up. "What the hell are you talking about, Freckles?"

"I mean, you didn't have to hang out with me today."

He holds up his hands. "Stop it right now. This?" He points between us. "This is not a transactional relationship, okay? We both want caramel corn and I want to buy you caramel corn, so let me do that. Please."

Properly chastised, I nod. "Okay. Thank you."

He gently tugs one of my braids. "I'll get us a big one to share."

"And I'll call Shai while you're doing that. She's been blowing up my phone all day."

He grins. "You two are so codependent."

"We are not! We're besties! That's what besties do!" I pull out my phone and tap the FaceTime icon.

✧ ✧ ✧

"Where in the Lemony Snicket are you?" Shai squints into the camera, as if that's going to give her answers. She is a bona fide cutie, with her peachy freckled skin, heart-shaped face, and long, wheat-colored hair. I bet her front camera never scares her like mine does when it comes on unexpectedly.

"I told you. I'm shopping."

"Bitch, I know that. Where?"

I affect a snooty accent. "The Shoppes at Bishop Haven."

She giggles. "Seriously?"

"I know, right?"

"What on earth are you doing there?"

"Ugh. Where do I start?" I outline the whole thing about Mom being so excited about Lucerne and the big dinner later. The need for a new dress. Hence. Shopping.

Shai's face falls. "Fuck."

"Yup. Also. I saw my father today."

It's not often that Shai is taken by surprise, but the expression on her face (eyebrows shot to the hairline, eyes super wide, mouth open) shows me that today's revelation is a whopper. "You might've led with that, Brandy Bailey! What the fuck? Are you okay?"

"I'm fine."

"How the fuck are you fine?" she squints again. "Are you dissociating again?"

"What does that even mean?"

"Is that Shai? Tell her I say 'hey,'" Ben says from behind me.

I close my eyes, sigh, and then open them. "Ben says 'hey.'"

She blinks. Hard. "You're with Ben? Ben Nolan?"

He bends down (way down) so his chin is resting on my shoulder. "The one and only!"

"Ow!" I squirm. "Why is your chin so sharp?"

"The word is *chiseled*, thank you very much."

"I promise we didn't come together," I say to Shai. "He just appeared. And then he never left."

"You never asked me to leave," Ben points out.

I wiggle so that sharp chin leaves my shoulder. "Are you trying to cause me permanent nerve damage?"

"Do people even have shoulder nerves?" Shai asks.

"That's a good question." Ben frowns thoughtfully. "You're the one who got accepted to nursing school, Freckles. Do you know?"

Honestly, how any of us made it out of high school is a mystery and a miracle. "If you weren't so tall, I'd poke *your* shoulder with *my* chin so we can see."

"Ahem." I snatch my head back around. Shai's eyes are lit up in a way that makes my stomach drop. Because Shai is the Queen of Scheming, and her inner schemestress has just switched on.

She looks from me to him, then smirks in her knowing way. "You should meet us at the carnival later," she says to Ben.

Absolutely no hesitation on his end. Just a big grin and a loud "Okay!"

She gives him the details while I stand there. Frozen. I'm holding the phone, but it doesn't occur to me to just... end the call. She's thrown a big wrench into something I was looking forward to using to forget every damn thing. Lucerne. The dress. My father. The list keeps growing.

Everything feels *off* today and I don't like it.

"I have to run," Shai says. "Bran, sorry you got into that school. I know that's not what you wanted. But we'll figure something out. Okay? Love you!"

The call ends. Ben holds the caramel corn out to me. I take a few kernels, then I close my eyes and try to focus on the salty-sweet crunchy goodness. And that's when my stomach reminds me that I haven't eaten a thing all day.

I smile, relieved. Of course! I'm not thinking straight because I'm hungry! I've had no fuel. Between sneaking out this morning and the emails and the shopping, plus seeing my father, my stomach's been too tied up in knots for me to even think of having a decent meal. Everything makes sense now!

Whew. Everything is fine.

It is.

8

Playing to Win

12:15 p.m.

Mom
Have you found anything yet?

Mom
I want to seeeeee!

Ben asks, "Shai again?"

"It's my mom." I show him the screen, and he properly responds by crinkling his nose.

I plop down on a bench and grab another handful of popcorn.

He sits by me and hands me the box. "So. I don't want to pry—"

"But you're about to, aren't you?"

He purses his lips in this way that I can tell he's thinking. Really hard. "Why can't you just tell your mother you don't want to be a nurse?"

I sort out my thoughts before answering. "Your family supports your dreams, no matter how huge they are, right?"

He leans forward and purses his lips again. "Yes and no. I pay for my own acting lessons, and I drive myself to auditions. But they don't stop me, if that's what you mean. Half the time they don't even notice what I'm doing."

"How can they not notice you? You're Benjamin David Nolan."

He turns to look at me. "You never did tell me how you know my middle name."

And I never will. "You've been on TV. Like, real TV."

"Yeah but. Okay. My older brother and sister have done the most. Like, *the most*. One's a lawyer, one's a surgeon. And there is Kayla, who my parents definitely did not plan on having. She takes up a lot of attention because she's you know, five. And the cutest thing ever."

"Ever." Well, maybe except for Elsa. But I don't say that out loud.

"So I'm kind of lost in the shuffle. But when I'm on stage or in front of a camera? Everyone's looking at me. I'm the one people are paying attention to. It's like...I finally matter. I can't even describe how it feels."

I stare at him. His entire being lights up when he talks about acting, and his energy is so contagious it crackles. It's hard to imagine Ben not mattering because his presence right now is so solid, so consuming that I'm having a hard time noticing anything *but* him. "You don't think you matter? To your *family*?"

He sighs. "I mean, I know my family loves me. But lately I've been completely at sixes and sevens, and I just spiral all the time. I feel like a background character in my own life."

"Wow." Ben is so bombastic and charming, and people definitely notice him. The whole time we've been sitting on this bench, people have been giving him double takes as they walk past. I don't know if it's because they recognize him or if he just stands out like that, but he's definitely not being ignored.

And at school, he was one of those people who got along with anyone, sliding between cliques like liquid. Teachers loved his upbeat attitude and positivity. He's the kind of person who makes people happy just by being around them. Even me sometimes. Even when he's getting on my every last nerve.

But everyone's home life is different. And I wonder what people think they know about me. Or if they even think of me at all.

I rub my arms. I don't like wondering this. I prefer flying under the radar, hiding behind my art. Drawing random things and sticking them in people's lockers? Let's go! Losing myself in any number of projects in Mr. Conway's studio? Yes, please. Someday maybe standing in a gallery, talking to strangers and trying to get them to buy my creations? Maybe step on the brakes a little bit.

But something about Ben makes me want to share, especially in these quieter moments—when his bombasticness is down a few notches. There's something soft about him, but not in an "I will run screaming from a spider" way. More in a quietly strong way. A safe way.

A background character in his own life. While I feel like the unwilling lead in mine.

"I'm going to say something and I'm not teasing, okay?"

He chuckles. "I love that you have to have a disclaimer."

I scrunch my nose at him. "See, I was trying to have a nice moment and you had to go and ruin it."

He quickly smooths his expression into a serious one. "Okay. I'm being serious now."

"Maybe I won't say it now."

"Please?"

It's the *please* that gets me. So earnest and sincere and really unlike the way I mainly see Ben. Except for today. "I was going to say that I hate that you feel like you don't matter. I can't imagine how they can't see what I see."

He keeps looking at me. "And what *do* you see?"

My throat closes. I swallow, then force myself to speak.

Throat chakra open. "I think...I see someone anyone would be lucky to know," I say. My voice is husky, so I try to clear my throat without him noticing.

"Th-thank you," he says. His cheeks color. "I really appreciate you saying that."

"I mean." I shrug. "You might get on every last one of my nerves, but I wouldn't put up with it if I didn't think you were a decent person."

He bursts out laughing, his eyes crinkling at the corners. A real smile, not a Hollywood smile. "It's my pleasure to torment you," he says. And the teasing Ben is back. I let out a sigh of relief. This feels right.

✧ ✧ ✧

12:45 p.m.

We're in another clothing store. This one is tiny and chaotic and stuffy, with dubious patterned clothing shoved into every free space. How this store managed to find its way into the "upscale lifestyle center" is a mystery to me.

"We should find the ugliest dress possible," I say.

Ben's face lights up. "Yes!"

"And whoever picks out the ugliest has to buy funnel cakes at the carnival tonight," I say.

He shakes his head. "We should make this more spicy. If you find the ugliest, I buy the funnel cakes for everyone. If I find it, you have to wear it to dinner with your mom."

That would stress Mom out so much and serve her right for stressing *me* out so much. Do I feel guilty at the thought? Of course. But I'm running on caramel corn, I'm a little dehydrated, and I just saw my freaking father. I deserve something. The train to this-is-a-bad-idea-land is chugging along, and I've already settled into one of the nice, plushy seats.

Plus, this is kind of a win-win. Because if I win, I get free funnel cake. Except... "Buying funnel cake is getting off too easy," I say. "I think if I pick out the ugliest dress, you should post a picture of you wearing it on your profile. And I mean the grid, not the stories."

"Okay."

"Really?"

"You doubt me?"

"I mean..."

"I can't believe you're doubting me! You're so on."

"Okay then. On the count of three. One... two..."

"Go!" Ben makes a beeline for a rack, snatches something off, and shoves it behind his back. I just shake my head. Some people just have it so easy in these places.

I make my way to the sale racks at the back of the store. Literally everything in my size is... not bad. Basic, yes. Boring, of course. But boring isn't really awful, now that I think about it. It'll make me less likely to be perceived, and that's always a good thing.

But then I realize my mistake. I'm looking at stuff that would fit me when I should be looking at things that fit Ben.

And there it is. It's a skater dress, but the dancing banana pattern on a hot pink background looks like those hideous leggings Aunt Colleen tried to get Mom to sell with her a few years ago. Just imagining Ben in this makes a giggle well up in the back of my throat.

It is perfect.

I dance up to him, triumphant. But I hold it behind my back. "I got it."

"So do I. But," he taps his chin thoughtfully, "I have a proposition for you."

That familiar shit-eating grin of his sets off all my warning bells. "No."

"You haven't even heard it!"

"The look on your face speaks volumes. Absolutely not."

He plows on like I haven't even spoken. "You wear what you have picked out"—he gestures toward my hands, which are still behind my back—"or you take the risk of what's behind my back. But you *have* to wear what I'm holding, no matter what."

"Oh hell no. That was not part of the deal, Eyebrows."

"I have altered the deal. Pray I do not alter it any further."

"That is not fair."

The shit-eating grin turns into an infuriating smirk. "Are you too chicken to even try it on?"

"I am not chicken," I say through clenched teeth. "You are a cheater!"

"Prove to me that you're not a chicken."

"I don't have to prove anything."

"Ba-kok! Ba-KOK!"

A middle-aged white lady with silver streaks in her hair glares at us from the next aisle.

"Shh! People are staring at us!"

"That's because you're a chicken." He turns to the old lady and throws her one of his movie star smiles, which softens her expression. "She's a chicken," Ben says to her.

"Give me the dress," I growl.

"Are you *sure*?"

"Now!"

The smirk is now *way* too satisfied. (One day I'm going to smack it right off his face, I swear.) He thrusts a purply-pink pile of fabric into my arms.

I stare at the monstrosity in disbelief. "You have *got* to be kidding me."

"Cluck, cluck."

If my eyes could convey the amount of sheer frustration I'm feeling right now, Ben would be dead meat. "You are infuriating!"

He waggles his eyebrows and gestures toward the dressing rooms. "Tick-tock."

So here's the thing. I pull on the dress and...I actually

don't hate it. The top has strappy shoulders and a heart-shaped bodice, and although I don't have a lot going on in the boob department, the dress makes it look like there's a little something-something there. The bottom flares out, like a skater dress, and the skirt hits just above my knees. But the best part is that the material is stretchy and soft, and it doesn't feel awful on my skin. I turn this way and that, admiring how it doesn't look like it's trying too hard. I'm not sure the color is right for the season, but then again, how would I even know? I have no idea what's in style or not.

I don't know how to pose like those girls on social media, all flattering and dramatic and stuff, so I come out of the dressing room and just stand there, arms dangling by my sides. "Hi."

Ben's leaning against a pillar and looking at his phone. He glances up and his mouth drops. "Wow."

"*Wow* as in I'm the winner? And don't tease."

"I'm not teasing." And he isn't. He just keeps looking at me and looking at me. He's looking at me like he never wants to stop.

It unnerves me.

"You should get it," the lady from the next aisle says.

"Ben," I say in a shaky voice. Then I can't talk anymore.

He is still staring. Then the corner of his mouth twitches. "I know."

I point to him. "You *tricked* me!"

He shrugs. "Maybe."

"That's not fair at all!"

He shrugs. "The end justifies the means, Freckles. But I'll hold up my end of the deal. I always imagined wearing a dress feels really breezy on the—"

Gross! "Benjamin Nolan, do not finish that sentence!"

"You double won," he adds, which I'm not sure is better. "How does it feel?"

"Suspicious." I squint at him. "Why are you being so nice to me? What are you up to?"

He stuffs his hands in his pockets. "What? Can't a guy just be nice, but not in a creepy *I'm a nice guy way*? Like, just regular nice?"

"Are you a nice guy, though?"

"Remember a certain hoodie?"

"Okay, fair."

"So? Your dress?"

I turn and look in the three-way mirror. "I should send pictures to my mom."

"I mean, you can, but you're the one who has to wear it."

He's right. Plus, the more I look at it, the more I like it. And finding clothes that feel okay on my skin is a miracle half the time, so I'm going to take this win. My first real one of the day. "All right. Let's go pay!"

9

Pressing, Pressing Pressure

1:30 p.m.

Mom

Exciting news!

Mom

I talked to my director, and I've been given approval to have you do your practicals here.

Mom

Everyone is so excited that you'll be on our team. You know how everyone loves you. And once you graduate, you'll have a spot here. We're always looking for good nurses.

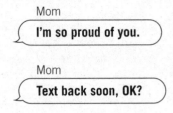

Mom

I'm so proud of you.

Mom

Text back soon, OK?

"Brandy?"

Ben's voice is distorted, like it's swirling through a tornado. Or one of my father's galaxy paintings. The sun is beating down on the top of my head, but I feel like I'm in a cold, dark tunnel.

"Brandy."

The world flips and flips. I stumble onto a bench. All I can think about is how much I want out of my skin. How I want the dizziness to go away. How much I just *want her to stop.* I close my eyes to stop the whirling. The world keeps spinning. My stomach churns.

"Freckles!"

The nickname snaps me back so hard it feels like an explosion.

He's staring at me. "What the hell?"

I thrust my phone at him. He ignores it. "Brandy, what happened?"

"Mom's plowing on with planning my life, full speed ahead, and I'm feeling more stuck than ever, and that roller coaster is happening and I'm just going to crash at the bottom and—"

"No. What happened to you? Just now?"

I wrap my arms around myself. "I don't know. It keeps happening and it's awful every single time."

"Is there anything I can do?"

This slows my spiral. The fog starts to drift from my brain. "Did you happen to drive today?"

"Yeah. Do you need me to take you to the doctor?"

"What? No. Somewhere else. Are you in?"

"Brandy, that was pretty scary. Are you sure you don't want to go to the emergency room or urgent care?"

I shake my head and look up at him. "No. I need this other place. Now. Please?"

He nods slowly. "Okay."

10

Decorating My Canvas

2:00 p.m.

THE COLD METAL TUBE SHOVED UP MY NOSE WOULD PROBA-
bly be nerve-wracking enough for most people, but it's the
bright fluorescent lights and my eyes watering from the sharp
sting of alcohol that's making me question every life choice
that has brought me to this point. All the strings pulling me
in a million directions and making my head spin.

One string wants to say screw it to everyone and just...
follow my dreams. Chase the path that's calling out to me
even though I have no idea where it'll take me. Be like my
father and throw everything away. Even though I know Mom
won't like it. Even though it might even devastate her.

Art never makes me feel like I need to jump out of my

skin and run screaming down the street, but the thought of being stuck in a sterile hospital for twelve hours every day surrounded by white walls and being assaulted with constant beeping does. The thought of seeing all the blood all day, every day makes me want to bury myself.

Art's always busting to get out of me. Nursing makes me want to hide.

Another string holds me in place, next to this boy who I never really thought could be so sensitive. This boy drove me here even though he kept saying he'd prefer to take me to the nearest hospital.

But there's that last string, the most powerful one, wanting to yank me away so I can hide from everyone and everything. No more responsibilities. No more shame because I keep running away. No more nursing. No more whatever the heck is going on when I look at Ben.

Maybe this is how I hide.

"On the count of three."

"You sure you want to do this?" Ben asks.

"Absolutely." My voice sounds a lot steadier than I feel. I ball up my fists to keep my fingers from shaking and to distract me from the clenching in my stomach. I nearly jump when I feel Ben's warm hand covering one of mine.

He's holding me. And I'm letting him.

Before I can think too much about it though, I hear the other voice, soft and calming.

"One…"

I squeeze my eyes shut.

"Two…"

I'm a brave girl, I'm a brave girl, I'm a brave—

Forty wasps attack my right nostril all at once. Despite how tightly they're closed, my eyes start watering like *whoa*, the tears running down the sides of my cheeks and into my braids. I blink my eyes open slowly, and the light rushes in. I lie still for a few seconds and stare at the ceiling, willing the stars to leave my vision and my breath to re-regulate.

"Take your time," the piercing tech says.

It's only after a few deep breaths that the endorphins start flooding in. When I got my helix pierced, it took much longer. I sit up slowly.

"Oh wow, Brandy." Ben smiles. His eyes shine with what I think is approval.

"How does it look?"

The piercer hands me a mirror. "See for yourself."

All year I've been feeling this push and pull. Pleasing everyone I know. Pushing my own shit aside, except for those precious mornings when I sneak out of the apartment and make my own mark. And I am tired. Ready for all the yanking to stop so I can be still. Just for a moment.

This moment.

I grin through the tears at the tiny, sparkling stud in my nose. "My mother is going to kill me."

11

Pretty Promises

2:30 p.m.

DEATH ISN'T COMING FOR ME YET, BECAUSE MOM'S STILL AT work. The apartment is cool and quiet, and I sip from a bottle of Evian as I flip my laptop open. The acceptance email from Lucerne glares at me from the screen. So does the latest email from my father. I starred it and kept it as new so I could read it over and over.

> To: ArtisteBrandyB@monroehigh.edu
> From: GalaxyAaronArt@galaxyaaronart.com
> Subject: Re: Re: Hi

Hey Brandy,

Sorry it took me forever to get back to you.

Life on the road is busy as usual.

How was graduation? Did you go to prom? I'd love for you to send me pictures if you did.

I hope everything is okay with you and your mother.

Graduation gift sent through Venmo. Don't spend it all in one place!

A

To: ArtisteBrandyB@monroehigh.edu

From: venmo@venmo.com

Subject: Galaxy Aaron Art paid you $250.00

Graduation Gift

Transfer Date and Amount:

June 20, 2024 PDT • + $250.00

Like   Comment

Is it sad that the little bit of attention I get from him means so much to me? When Mom's been here all this time? Why do I feel fine accepting money from him, but I'm always tempted to refuse it from Mom? My stomach clenches with guilt again, and I hate how familiar it feels. I stare at the screen until my eyes cross, trying to make sense of it all. But I can't.

This is what I type:

This is how I feel: 😣

I decide to edit and post my video from earlier. This is a meticulous operation. I have to perfect the cuts so that the timing is just right. Then I need to pick the best song to fit the mood of the video, the length of the video, and to fit what's sort of trending at the moment. It takes me about fifteen minutes to come up with something I like, and once it's posted, a notification immediately pops up.

Huh. Now that I think about it, Ben's always the first person who likes my posts. Every single time. He even beats Shai, but her notification usually pops up right after his.

💙 MaybeShaiBe liked your post

Social media makes me feel both invisible and seen. At least I can count on those two.

I drop my phone onto my bed and pick up one of the packages that had been waiting in the hall. Sometimes our next-door neighbor will grab them out of the mailroom and set them in front of our door. Super sweet of her. But when I open the first bag, *sweet* is the last thing on my mind. A dress tumbles out—the kind of super pastel pink, flowing, feminine thing my mother dreams of seeing me in. The kind of thing I would never, ever pick out for myself, not the very least because the material feels terrible on my skin. The dress is beautiful and I hate it. Absolutely hate it. But I especially hate the expectations that come with it. I drop the dress onto my bed and hop into the shower.

I need to wash those expectations away.

I'm in the shower forever, but the stress doesn't leave and it doesn't leave. Even though my skin is turning pink. Even after I close my eyes and let the water run over my face, taking care with my new piercing. Ha, brave? Not even close. I saw my father and *ran away*. Who does that? I squeeze my eyes shut, but the shame still lingers. And Lucerne pounds in the back of my mind, like a low drum.

Plus, there's dinner with Mom. Which is quickly approaching.

My headache increases.

It's just a dinner, so why am I so apprehensive? Is it because

I have no appetite at all? Is it because it's at a fancy place and I'll be completely out of my element? Or is it because it feels like just one more thing forcing me over that roller coaster hill?

Maybe it's because I wish I could skip everything until the carnival, where I'll be with my best friend, riding all the things, eating all the things (if my appetite is back), and trying to win all the things.

I don't have time to fuss with my braids, which leaves me with a bit of trepidation. I hardly ever wear my hair down because it tangles like mad. Flyaways plague me no matter how much product I use and especially if I air-dry, which I have to do right now. I actually do like my hair, though. It hangs down below my bra strap. It's fine and wavy, a dark brown accented with copper highlights. Or is it lowlights? Whatever it is, it's kind of cool, especially in the sunlight. Or moonlight. I guess tonight, I'm showing it off in all its glory.

Still wrapped in a fluffy, yellow towel, I look from the skater dress to the flowy dress. I could wear the flowy dress and make Mom happy. Or I could open the other packages, which must be dresses—the return address is the same—and try those on. See if I like them better. No doubt that whatever she picked for me would help me fit in with all the other people having a fancy dinner at a fancy place, and I'd look like the princess of Mom's dreams.

Or I could wear the skater dress and make me happy. As

well as keep up my end of the deal with Ben. Not that he'd know or anything. But I'd know, and it would be nice not to renege on one thing today.

I look back and forth, from one dress to the other. Then I make my choice. I just hope it's the right one.

12

A Helping of Get Me Out of Here

4:00 p.m.

THE MAÎTRE D' GIVES ME A DOUBLE TAKE WHEN I WALK INTO the opulent lobby, and his eyes zero right in on my nose. He wrinkles his own nose and stares at me. His expression isn't welcoming at all, and that makes my throat clog.

"Hi," I say, my voice a little shaky. "I'm meeting my—"

"Brandy." Mom's voice comes from behind me. And well. It's time. I whirl around to face her. She looks beautiful, in a light blue sundress that falls just below her knees, her hair a luscious pile of curls on top of her head. She must have changed at the hospital, or else we'd have run into each other at home.

Thank goodness for small favors.

"Hi, Mom."

"I barely managed to escape in time," she says breathlessly. "That baby was not in any hurry."

"But all is good?"

"All good. Mom and baby are healthy and doing well." She looks me up and down. "Your hair looks good. You should wear it like that more often." Then she focuses her gaze on my nose. Laser focus. She raises her finger, leans forward, and—

"How can I help you, madam?" asks the maître d' in a French accent. Saved! For now, at least.

Mom whirls around and puts on her professional voice. "I have a four o'clock reservation. For Bailey?"

"Ah yes," he says. He turns to a blond man with shocking blue eyes who is wearing a black vest over a white button-down shirt and black pants. "Please take care of our guests."

The host nods. "Right this way."

We follow him into the dining room, which is like entering another world. There is marble everywhere. Crystal chandeliers throw rainbow-colored lights over all of the white-clothed tables. A giant fireplace stands at one end of the room, and even though the biggest heat wave of the year is happening outside, a roaring fire warms the entire space and softens the air conditioning rushing over my arms. The host pulls out a chair covered in rich, maroon velvet, and I gingerly sit. I'm stiff as he gently pushes the chair in, and I watch as he does the same for Mom. "Enjoy your meal," he says, then gracefully bows out.

Mom picks up the menu.

"It's all in French," I say. Unfortunately for me, I took Spanish. I decide to order one of the two dishes I recognize: coq au vin. The other is escargot, and I am never trying to eat any kind of snail.

"A bottle of Château Latour, 2012," Mom orders when the waiter arrives. "And a Sprite for my daughter."

The waiter nods and then leaves, taking our menus with him.

"So. You picked out a dress after all. You never showed me any pictures."

"I got busy."

"Did you get the ones I sent to the house?"

"I opened the pink one. Didn't like it."

"But it's gorgeous!"

"And I hated it. Why did you tell *me* to pick out something nice if you were just going to buy me something anyway?"

"I wouldn't exactly call that nice. And why aren't you wearing sandals? Sneakers are not what I would've paired with any dress, personally."

I squirm. "I like the dress. Okay? And the shoes are comfortable."

She closes her eyes and sighs. "I guess I'll take the win, since you never wear dresses anymore."

"Some of the materials feel terrible on my skin," I admit.

Her eyes pop open. "But you've never told me that."

"Because it's a new thing. It never bothered me until a few months ago." I shrug and pick at my napkin. "It's silly."

"Brandy, it's not silly to want to wear comfortable clothes. Why do you think I'm in scrubs ninety percent of the time? But it *is* silly to wear sneakers to the President's Club. And to get *that*."

She doesn't need to point. I know exactly what she's talking about. I touch the stud, which isn't the smartest idea. The sting makes me flinch. "I like it."

"It's crass."

"It's *cute!*"

"Shh!"

The anger rises up in me, like bubbles boiling to the surface. "I'm eighteen," I whisper. "I'm allowed to get a nose piercing."

The waiter discreetly sets down our drinks and some bread, then slips into the shadows.

"Where on earth are you even getting the money for all these piercings?" Mom screws up her nose. "Did you use the money I gave you today for that?"

"No. I have my own money."

"From where?"

"My art."

She crosses her arms. "Your art."

I nod. "I do commissions and I have a shop."

"A shop."

It would be really nice if she'd stop repeating me. "Online."

"I don't remember giving you permission to start a website."

"I opened it after I turned eighteen." I pull out my phone and navigate to my webpage. "See?"

Mom doesn't even check the screen. "Is that what you've been doing at school instead of studying?"

"What? No! I did it so I could have time to study. People kept asking me to draw for them and it was too much. So I started charging them."

"I still don't understand how you flunked English and got an A in Spanish. My guy, you speak English!"

"But I fixed it the next quarter, remember?" I hold up my phone. "This is proof that I can make money with my art!"

"And spend it on silly things like piercings."

"It's not silly. It's adorable."

"It's undignified."

"It's staying."

"Not if I have any say so."

"It's a good thing it's my body then."

She sits back like I slapped her.

I clap my hand over my mouth. I've never talked to her like this before. I'm shaking because I don't know how I feel. On the one hand, this new, powerful sensation is kind of nice, even if it is scary. On the other hand...this is Mom. And her storm cloud expression is making me sad.

"Brandy, what has gotten into you? We're supposed to be celebrating, so why are you acting like this?"

"You didn't even let me order my own drink."

"But you always get Sprite!"

"Maybe I wanted to change it up. Get a Coke or a Mountain Dew!" My voice is rising, and while I hate it, I can't stop it.

"Brandy, please. People are staring."

Those were the right words to subdue me. I fold into myself until the spectators grow bored and turn back to their own meals. Then I grab a piece of bread, just to have something to do.

"Don't tell me you're this upset over some Sprite."

I'm deflated now. "I'm not upset over Sprite." I look at my phone again.

"It's nice that you're making pocket change from your art, but that's not sustainable. Nursing school is what's going to make you secure. That's what I want you focusing on."

"But—"

"Are you nervous about starting school? Is that why you're acting out?"

"I'm not acting out."

She doesn't seem to hear me. "That's completely understandable. This is a milestone and a big deal. But this is what we've worked for, and I'll be by your side the whole time. You're already set up for success. Didn't you get my texts earlier?"

The waiter slides our salads in front of us and disappears

again. I drop the bread, pick up a cherry tomato, and roll it between my fingers.

"Why aren't you more excited?" she asks. "Do you know how much I would've loved to have the chances I'm giving you? You'll never have to worry about security. Or money."

"I do appreciate everything you do for me."

"You sure have a funny way of showing it. Wearing sneakers when you should be dressed up. Putting holes in your body. Sulking at this expensive restaurant."

The guilt builds and builds. "I never asked for any of this. The one thing I want—"

"—is right here, Brandy, so please. Show me something."

"I'm trying!"

"I thought your dream was nursing school. It's all you talked about when you were little."

I can't do this. "I know."

"We used to dress up as nurses every Halloween and watch *Grey's Anatomy* together every week."

"I *know*."

"Remember how you used to pretend to give medicine to your dolls? And how you'd check my heart with your little stethoscope?"

"Of course I remember. I also remember the way you looked at me when I'd do that stuff. I'd give anything for you to look at me like that all the time. But I can't do it anymore. I can't pretend anymore."

"What are you talking about?"

Be brave.

I have to do this. "I want to go to art school."

She crosses herself. Three times. Then she takes a deep, *deep* drag of wine. "Art school."

"I mean, I don't know if you noticed, but I do art and I'm kind of good at it."

"We talked about it one time, Brandy. Once."

"That's because you pretty much told me to give up on it."

"I didn't mean for you to give it up *as a hobby*. I'm just saying it's not a viable career. Art isn't going to put food on the table."

My turn to sigh. "So you keep telling me."

She shakes her head. "But now, I'm thinking you need to be done with art for good."

Terror strikes my heart and my stomach drops to the floor. "Done?"

She doesn't seem to hear me. "It's interfering with your judgement and messing up your priorities. You barely graduated on time because you couldn't stop drawing."

"But I did graduate!"

"And your head is always in the clouds, and I know it's because you're dreaming of something that *cannot* happen."

"My father made it. Why couldn't I?"

The way her expression falls shatters me into a billion pieces, and I hate that I'm the one who did that to her. Bringing up my father was probably a low blow, but I'm getting desperate. I can't be done with art. I *am* art, and if that goes away, I'll disappear, too.

"I keep telling you. Your father was . . . *is* an anomaly. His story is not typical, and need I remind you that he left us to pursue that art?"

"My story is not his story. I can create my own. I *am* creating my own."

We stare at each other. I don't know what she sees in my expression, but her sadness suddenly transforms to stone. "You're done with art, and that's final."

"No."

"I'm done talking about this."

I squeeze the tomato. Juice runs down my arm and drips on to the fancy white tablecloth. "You have to listen to me!"

"This conversation is finished. And wipe that up." She fumbles with her napkin. Drops it. "Where is that waiter? How long does it take to get service around here?"

The waiter materializes with our meals, and the scent, which would be divine under any other circumstance, makes my stomach flip over and over and over. I stand up and drop my napkin into my chair. "I can't do this."

Mom jumps up. "Brandy Bailey, you sit down this instant."

"I'm sorry."

She reaches out to grab me, but I jerk myself out of her reach. And with tears clouding my vision, I run out of the restaurant.

13

Chasing the Sun

4:35 p.m.

THE BUS DRIVER GIVES ME A STRANGE LOOK, AND I CAN'T blame him. I probably look like a hot mess. I'm out of breath from running. My face feels like it's on fire. I never cry, but sometimes tears leak out, and they've been rolling down my cheeks nonstop ever since I left the President's Club. I haven't bothered to wipe them away.

I take a seat in the back and pull out my phone. Stare at the screen, which is lighting up with a million missed calls from Mom. Then a bunch of texts start rolling in. Boom boom boom.

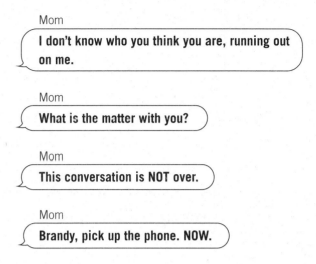

Mom

I don't know who you think you are, running out on me.

Mom

What is the matter with you?

Mom

This conversation is NOT over.

Mom

Brandy, pick up the phone. NOW.

The screen lights up with her picture again. I decline the call. It lights right back up. But I can't deal with her right now. I just can't.

I'm about to shove my phone into my bag when a social notification pops up.

BenNolanOfficial ✔ has tagged you in a video

I've never opened someone's profile so fast. And it does not disappoint. There Ben is, dancing away in that banana-patterned hot pink monstrosity. I recognize the steps from one of his musical numbers from the variety show—a lot of flourishes and turns and even some tap dancing. He looks like a total and utter fool, and I am here for it!

the breeze is quite nice @artistebrandyb

#actor #dancer #triplethreatmixparty #uglydresscontest

#ezbreezy

The tears are freely flowing now, but now it's because I'm laughing too hard to breathe. I might be slightly hysterical. I sense people are staring at me, especially since my AirPods are in and they can't hear what I'm hearing, but for once, I can't be bothered to care about how I'm being perceived.

I pop open the comments.

JordanReedOfficial ✔ WTF

LittlePlumLady14 Mommy? Sorry, mommy? Sorry, mommy?

TT4512 are u ok

NolansGurlLOL Omg marry me already 😍

I raise an eyebrow at that NolansGurl because how dare she? Is Ben dating someone? I frown. I don't like how that thought's making me feel.

Wait. Why do I even care? It's not like he and I are close like that, even though we did spend a lot of time together today.

Nope. Not going there. It was only one afternoon. *One.*

So why did I start replaying the video again? Why am I looking at how he tagged me on his verified profile of hundreds of thousands of followers and feeling like it's something special? It's silly. People tag people all the time. It's really no big deal.

So why does it kind of feel like it is?

I must really be messed up from fighting with Mom. When I think about the look on her face, before I ran out, my heart breaks. I can only imagine what her expression is like now. The murderous glare that's surely in her eyes. We've never argued like that before, and the whole world feels upside down and inside out. Everything is all wrong. Because Ben is the last thing I should be feeling possessive over, and yet, the emotions are flip-flopping in my head. Sad over Mom. Confused about Ben. Ashamed that I ran out of that gallery. Drawn back to thinking about Ben.

That one hurts less than the other thoughts.

The video repeats again and again, so I give it a double tap so it can both register a like and pause. He freezes mid-turn, his grin wide and twinkly. But the charisma permeating from it—from *Ben*—is still flowing. It's almost palpable.

I've been following him on social for ages. My locker's been stuck next to his for years. I've definitely seen how charming he can be, but something changed today. I watch the clip again, thinking. And then it hits me: Just like how I've never really given a second thought to how cute he is, his charms have never affected me like this. *He's* never affected me like this.

Could he be affecting me now?

The video plays again. I notice more things. How carefree and confident he seems. How he looks like he's having the time of his life. How all of those things are suddenly super attractive.

I let out a shaky breath. He's *definitely* affecting me now.

Well, that's scary as hell. I shake my head so I can come to my senses. My hair falls in a curtain around my face, startling me and comforting me at the same time. At least these tangles are a constant in a sea of topsy-turvy *everything*.

I send the video to Shai. Her response is immediate.

Shai
Bruh

Shai
Do I even wanna know

Me
It's a long, LONG story

Shai
You have a LOT to tell me tonight, young lady

Mom's photo flashes. She's calling me again, but I can't deal with her right now. Guilt follows the anger, and just like that, my joviality is squashed. The bus feels too stuffy, too hot, too heavy. I yank the cord and jump off, not even checking the stop. I take huge gulps of air to slow my racing heart. But the guilt keeps rising, like bile in my throat.

I open my messages. Navigate to the conversation with Mom.

Three dots immediately appear, but I throw the phone into my bag. Then I look up. I'm at the Shoppes at Bishop Haven.

Maybe this was meant to be. Being brave backfired big time at the restaurant, but I do have another parent. And he's waiting for me.

14

Papa Don't Preach

4:45 p.m.

NEO GALLERY CLOSES IN FIFTEEN MINUTES, AND THE CLERK right inside the door has a cordless phone in her hand and is staring at me like she's already dialed the nine and the one.

Move, I tell myself. *Move now.*

The gallery is super quiet now. My father's back is to me, and he is adjusting one of the paintings. I stand at the doorway separating the gift shop from the installations, just watching him. Despite the blasting air conditioner, sweat is pouring down my back.

I can't believe he's right here.

Almost as if he senses me there, he whirls around. We

make eye contact, and this time he doesn't beckon. He comes to me.

I stare at him, hungry. And he stares at me just as deeply. The resemblance is uncanny, almost like looking in a mirror. Our eyes are shaped exactly alike, and they're the same shade of honey brown. Freckles sprinkle across his nose in a pattern identical to the way mine fall. I can see where I got the fine texture in my hair. We even have the same ridiculous cowlick in the widow's peak. Automatically, I reach up and smooth mine down.

Two things the pictures don't show: My skin color is closer to his fair tones than my mom's deeper tones, and the pink in his cheeks reminds me of the pink that I get whenever I blush. Which I am surely doing right now if the heat in my face is any indication.

"You came," he says.

I swallow the lump in my throat. Unblocking that chakra. "I did."

His grin widens and our smiles are the same, down to the dimples in our right cheeks.

"Hi," he says.

"Hi."

And now it's a bit awkward, with my father and me still staring at each other like we're strangers. Which we are, I guess.

"It's good to see you, Brandy," he finally says.

Is it good to see him? I'm not sure. More like shocking,

if I'm being honest. And what the hell do I do now? Should I hug him or keep standing here, shuffling from foot to foot? Should we shake hands? And how do I even address him? Absolutely not "Dad." Maybe Aaron, his first name? The sheer panic on my face must be comical. It'd be really funny if I weren't the one experiencing it.

"Would you like to see my art?" he asks.

I let out a breath. "Yeah. Okay."

"Right this way."

My feet carry me to the exhibit, where canvases of all sizes grace the walls. Up close, his art is even darker, literally and figuratively. Blacks, navy blues, dark grays. The heavy, swirling galaxies draw you in and won't let go. This is the artwork that sells for big bucks to dignitaries and celebrities and wealthy collectors. And now it's right in front of me.

My father—Aaron—turns back to his work in progress. "I'm not sure how I'm feeling about this one," he says. My eyebrows jump up. This man is one of the best artists of our time. If *he's* doubting his work, what does that say about mine? So different from his, more on the whimsical side. Silly cartoons of me and Shai. Funky lettering. Comics and more comics. If art is meant to evoke emotion, his brings storms. I want mine to bring joy . . . especially the joy I feel when I make it.

"I think it's beautiful," I say. Because I can appreciate good art even when it's nothing like the art I make. Maybe especially so.

He studies the canvas, frowning. "I don't know. Something feels kind of off about it. How does it make you feel, Brandy?"

I stare at the work so hard my head starts to spin. Scrubs. Needles. Blood. I try to squash the thoughts of Lucerne back down. Except they won't stay. They're rushing my brain and putting stars in my eyes. They're making my breath come in short spurts. I sway a bit on my feet.

"Brandy?" My father grabs my shoulder, and I shudder.

"Are you okay?" he asks.

Absolutely not. "I don't know."

"You look like you need to sit. Let's go sit."

I need to scratch my skin off. "Yeah, okay."

My father grabs his bag and walks me over to a café of sorts. There isn't an official barista, just a few coffee machines, a box of assorted teas, and a napkin-lined basket of random pastries. My father—Aaron—fills a paper cup with decaf and stirs in a bit of cream before we settle into a couple of squashy chairs. Except I *can't* get settled. I'm sitting ramrod straight.

He studies me. "You are really pale right now. What's going on?"

I clear my throat, then I clear it again. "I mean, I'm meeting my father in person for the first time in my life, so..."

He nods, then sighs. "This is strange, huh?"

"Can I sketch you?" I blurt.

He nods again. "Of course, you can."

The medium I choose often depends on my mood. Right now, my heart is beating like hummingbird wings and my head is spinning. So I pull out my sketchpad and a pencil. I need the roughness of the newsprint, the scratch of the granite to help me feel like I'm here. That I'm real.

My father leans forward, resting his elbows on his knees and holding his cup with both hands. There are furrow lines between his eyebrows. He stares at the steam swirling from his coffee, and I stare at him.

And then I draw.

"This is strange for me, too," he says quietly. "Your mother managed to track me down right after you were born. Just so I'd know you existed. But other than occasional updates and school pictures, I didn't know much."

I erase an errant line. "You can't blame her for that."

"I know. And I don't blame her for wanting to protect you."

"Protect me?"

He looks up from his cup. "I hurt her. I guess she was scared I'd hurt you, too."

"Oh." I lower my eyes and use the side of my hand to blend.

"I didn't know if she'd told you anything about me, so I was surprised when I got your email. No one knows I have a daughter, so I knew it wasn't some sort of prank. Then I checked out your profile, and I knew it was definitely real."

He's seen *my profile*? My face warms again at the thought. From embarrassment or pride, I'm not sure yet. But this means...he's seen my art. "How did you even find me?"

"I put your social media handle in the search bar. I'm not that old."

A horrifying thought pops into my brain. "You don't think I'm here to get a leg up or something, do you? Because I want to do this on my own merit. I'm not a nepo baby."

"Noted. But just so you know, it's not a bad thing to get that leg up. Especially in this industry. If someone offers you a gift like that, I'd advise for you to take it."

He speaks so formally. I wonder if this is how he talked to Mom when they were young, or if it came from years of traveling the world and meeting famous people.

The sketch is finished. It's super rough, and the guidelines are still there. I'm not sure what to do with it yet. "What should I call you?" I ask.

"You can call me 'Aaron.' "

I nod. "Aaron." I let it roll around on my tongue. It feels okay. I show him the sketch. "What do you think?"

He reaches out to take my sketchbook, but I hold on to it. I don't gift my work to just anyone, and he and I are not there yet.

"It's good," he says. "Really good."

"Really? You're not joking?"

"Why would I joke about that? I've seen your posts. I even have this." He lifts his messenger bag, and there's one of my patches, right on the flap.

"Oh my God. You bought—"

"Of course I bought from your shop. And not just because you're my kid. And not because I feel guilty, although I do."

I'm stunned. He bought from my shop?

He gestures toward my sketchbook. "You're talented. And I promise those aren't words I throw around lightly."

"I don't know what to say."

"Your art is also very safe," he continues. "I'd love to see you take more risks. I think you have it in you. I hope you're going to art school to cultivate that talent and try new things."

And we've arrived at last. Interesting that he assumed I was going, though. "About that."

His eyes narrow. "What do you mean, *about that*?"

"I haven't applied."

The furrow in his forehead deepens. "Why not? What are you waiting for? Do you know how many schools would want someone with your skills?"

I slide my sketchpad back into my bag. "Mom is desperate for me to be a nurse."

"Hold on. She's not letting you apply to art school?"

I shake my head.

"But why are you letting that stop you?"

"You don't get it. You left us. And she had to do it all on her own. Nursing gave her stability. And she thinks that's the way I should go. It'll give me security and a marketable skill, and I'll be contributing to society in a meaningful way."

His eyebrows jump up. "Art is not meaningful?"

I pick at a loose thread on my bag. "Not like delivering babies, I guess."

"Huh. I mean, art is very important in babies' development, so..." He trails off, frowning. "Do *you* want to be a nurse?"

The million-dollar question. Again. "Not even a little bit."

He sits back. "Then don't be a nurse."

It sounds so simple, right? But it's not. It absolutely is not. "That's easy for you to say."

"You're right. It is. I shouldn't be so flippant."

"She's got everything planned out for me. She's even talking to her boss about me, and I just want it to stop! My life is spinning out of control and there's nothing I can do to rein it in. Coming here—seeing you today—was one thing I could control, I guess." I pause. "She told me I had to give up art. Today. Right now."

Anger flashes across his face like a ghost. Then his expression is neutral again. "I'm sorry, she did what?"

"Yeah."

He blinks rapidly and buries his head in his hands. "This is definitely on me."

"She does blame you," I blurt out.

"God, Brandy. I'm so sorry."

"I can't give it up."

His head pops up, and he looks tortured. "Believe me, I know. Hell, I've lived it. I'm still living it."

"I *need* to be an artist. A good one who can get a job, support herself, and...I don't know. Be like an adult."

"Or you know, you can be young, make all your mistakes now. Get them out of your system. Take your big risks now, while you have the space in your life to do it."

The air thickens. "Is that what you did?"

The corners of his mouth turn down. "I was young and reckless. Definitely not in a position to be a good father."

"Mom was also young."

"And I was selfish, Brandy. Nothing—and I mean *nothing*—was going to keep me from my art. I had to chase my dreams. I would've withered away if I'd stayed."

What he's saying resonates. Big time. If I don't chase my art, if I don't take that leap, I will shrivel up in a swirl of darkness, just like the paintings on those exhibit walls. Still. Another question tugs at me. "You didn't love her? Or us?"

He shakes his head. "It's because I loved you both that I had to go."

That makes no sense. Until it does. He simply loves art more than he loves me. That stings, it really stings, but at the same time, I get it, at least on a small scale. I know what it's like to get so wrapped up in a project that nothing and no one else matters in that moment. I know what it's like to be so deep in a drawing that I forget to eat or sleep. That I disappear while Shai blows up my phone with thirty thousand texts. I know what it's like to feel such a wall of resentment at being interrupted that I want to throw something. And I know that feeling of pure contentment when I'm in my flow state, lo-fi music in the background as the art pours out of me. I can understand why someone would give up everything to feel that all the time. Because too often I imagine walking away from everything so I can revel in that sort of high.

But can I turn my back on everyone in my life? Could I *really* walk away from Mom, after everything she's done for me? Would I be able to leave Shai and little Elsa behind?

I don't think I can.

My father's expression is thoughtful. "In a way, I can see where your mother is coming from. Starting out in this business is rough. I spent a lot of nights sleeping on couches and floors and eating ramen noodles if I was lucky. Sleeping in my car with a rumbling stomach if I wasn't. Sometimes I wish I'd had something decent to fall back on while I was working for my break. And a break is not guaranteed, Brandy, even if you're super talented. A lot of it is luck. Being in the right place at the right time and getting in touch with the right people."

"But don't you think that if you were doing the thing you

didn't care about that you'd have missed out on that break? Like, if you were stuck on a twelve-hour nursing shift and missing that one soiree or whatever that could've put you in the path of your destiny or whatever?"

"That's the flipside of the artist coin. Both sides are pretty tarnished, if you ask me. And I'm one of the lucky ones. Even the most talented people don't always get to do what they're passionate about, even if they have a degree. You're the one who has to decide your limit. How far are you willing to suffer for your dream?"

"But nursing will be suffering, too! I *hate* it. And science and math and blood and fluids and—" I shudder. "Ugh. It seems like no matter what I pick, something's going to suck. Why?"

"Because we live in the real world. There's always going to be sacrifice. You just have to figure out *what* you're willing to sacrifice."

I bury my head in my hands. "I hate this."

He sighs. "Believe me, I get it. I lived it. I'm living it. But let me give you some real talk. This profession will break your heart a million times. It will force you to give up everything, then if you do make it, it'll shove you into a corner, and you'll be doing what they want instead of what you want because that's where the money is. That's what you'll you need to do to survive. And you'll spend your life trying to paint yourself out of that corner. Because what's the point of *surviving* if you're not living?"

"If I'm not making art, I might as well be dead."

The intensity in his eyes scares me. In fact, this whole conversation is scaring me. Not sure what I came here for. Validation? A nudge to tell me that turning my back on my mother's wishes is okay? Permission to leave everything and everyone behind?

"You won't die, Brandy. But if doing this is the most important thing, if you feel like it's your life's destiny, then you *need* to do it." His stare is unwavering. "Do you feel like it's your destiny?"

I think about how I felt, so early this morning, in the quiet dawn. Squinting to get the outline right until the sun came all the way up, brightening my canvas and showing me the perfect colors. The sensation of *rightness* that took over my entire being. The true feeling of yes, this is where I'm supposed to be. This is what I'm meant to do.

I could live forever chasing that serenity.

Mom's face flashes in my mind. I blink to clear it away. "So. Everything else be damned?" I ask quietly.

He nods. "Yeah."

"Do you ever regret?"

And now he looks sad. "For years I didn't. Then I got an email."

15

That I Would Be Good

7:00 p.m.

THE BUS DROPS ME OFF RIGHT IN FRONT OF THE CARNIVAL. I run onto the grounds, my messenger bag banging against my knees. I lost track of time at the gallery, missed the bus, and had to wait twenty minutes for another. And Shai is waiting.

But then my phone buzzes. I'm this close to shoving it back into my bag when I see it's actually not yet another message or call from Mom. It's my email.

International Illustrators Union	**7:00 PM**
Your Contest Entry	

I almost drop the phone.

Okay, breathe. It's easy. In...out. In...out. Oh my God. It's happening. This is it. The moment of truth. The time to see if people in charge of art funds and contests and who may or may not have connections in certain industries agree with Mr. Conway's assessment of my talent...or if he was just being nice. Time to see if all my worrying was for nothing, and that the universe has decided my future for me.

My finger shakes as I go to tap the message. But before I can open that email, another one pops in. Then another.

Colors United Pop Art Contest	7:01 PM
Your Contest Entry	
NEO Gallery Artist's Choice Art Contest	7:01 PM
Your Contest Entry	
Breaking Free Art Competition	7:01 PM
Your Entry	

I have an important choice to make now. There's my date with Shai, which means I should absolutely not be standing in the middle of the sidewalk trying to decide what to do. But I really want to open these emails.

This is not good. Why would they all send results on

the same day? What if they all think my art stinks and that I have no business even holding a crayon, let alone trying to be a real illustrator?

Be reasonable, Brandy. All those likes and comments on social count for something, right? And Mr. Conway never took as much time with other students as he did with me. Plus, my father told me I was talented, and he's one of the most famous artists in the world. Then there's my shop. I can't forget my shop, where people *give me money* to make art for them. So I can't be terrible. Right? Besides, whatever's in those emails can't be worse than going to nursing school.

But they could be what sends me there.

My head is spinning. I have to do it. There's no way I can wait.

I close my eyes and breathe.

Then I tap the first message.

16

Cotton Candy Dreams

7:08 p.m.

WHEN GEORGE W. G. FERRIS WHIPPED OUT A NAPKIN DURING a banquet and sketched out his concept for something bigger and better than even the Eiffel Tower, he certainly didn't have little ole me in mind. He was going for the big dreams. World's Fair dreams.

I've never seen the Eiffel Tower (in person), and that original wheel was torn down a long time ago. And now I'm here, staring up at our dinky little carnival wheel and loving it just as much as I'm sure I'd have loved that original masterpiece. The Ferris wheel is one of the most popular carnival rides ever. It's romantic. You can take a breather while still having fun. It's a thrill to hover above an entire carnival from a little car perched at the very top of a giant, slowly turning apparatus. Getting to watch all the twisting rides, the twinkling lights, the families scooting around below. Getting to hear the laughter and squeals and thrills. All of it right there, to take in, to marinate.

I like those things, too. But I *love* the Ferris wheel because it's art.

So intricately put together, this giant wheel with spokes placed just so. Seats that swing enough to give you a thrill but are snug enough that you feel safe when you're at the top. A classic, the Ferris wheel.

My favorite, the Ferris wheel.

One day, I'll make my mark like George W.G. Ferris did. I have to. But this night, I'm going to do everything I can to escape the bullshit blocking my way.

✧ ✧ ✧

The contest results were as follows:

- International Illustrators Union: 3rd place, with a $50 prize
- Colors United Pop Art Contest: Honorable mention, no prize

- NEO Gallery Artist's Choice Art Contest: 2nd place, $100 prize
- Breaking Free Art Competition: 1st place, with a $500 prize

First place!

I'm still shaking. Breaking Free was my pie-in-the-sky entry. A longshot that Mr. Conway convinced me to apply for. I never thought I'd win. To be honest, I didn't think I'd win any of them. But now the results are shining at me from my screen, and I can't help but feel so proud. And grateful.

All of the emails had feedback. Breaking Free's is my favorite:

> The colors in your piece really popped, and your characters were whimsical and fun. We really enjoyed all the tiny details about your town, and we felt a real connection with your work. However, your piece feels very safe. There is nothing wrong with safe, but we would love to see you take more risks.

Take more risks. I feel like this applies to my life, too. Not just my art.

I touch my nose ring. Standing up to Mom was kind of

a risk. Seeing my dad was another one. I wonder what other risks I can take?

Breaking Free also offered me a spot in their three-day mini-workshop. My heart beats faster when I really think about what that means: A chance to study directly from Breaking Free artists. That's up there with getting accepted to the Preston Academy of Art. In fact, some of their artists actually graduated from Preston. My father mentioned knowing the right people. This could be a way into that world. For real.

After I freaked the freak out, I forwarded all of the emails to Mr. Conway. I didn't even know if teachers checked their email over the summer, but I thought he'd want to know how I did.

✧ ✧ ✧

"Brandy Angelica Marie Bailey!" Shai's hair blows around her face. "Only ten minutes late this time. That must be a record!"

I hug her gently, careful not to squash my cotton candy, but also because strapped to her chest with a complicated-looking blanket carrier thing is Shai's little baby. "I didn't know you were bringing Elsa. Hi, princess!" I bend down to boop the baby's nose, and she shrieks in delight. Then she reaches a drool-covered hand toward me.

Shai gently guides Elsa's hand away. "The last thing you need is cotton candy," she says to Elsa in a singsong voice. Then she looks back at me. "Em backed out of babysitting."

"Again?"

Shai pulls out a cloth and wipes Elsa's chin. The child is a drool machine. A by-product of growing new teeth, I guess. "I mean, I get it. She's doing me a favor every time she watches Elsa. And if my parents found out, they'd probably disown her, too."

"Ugh. If they keep this up, they won't have any daughters left."

"Tell me about it. Plus, Julia had to work, so she couldn't help either. So I'm on my own tonight. It was rough, scrambling to get everything done, but I finished my homework, fed Elsa, and even got a shower!"

"And the carnival goers thank you profusely." I wrinkle my nose. "Homework in summer is just cruel."

And if I'm being honest, so are Shai's parents. Die-hard super fundamentalists who rally against premarital sex, anything LGBT, and interracial relationships. Hence the reason she lives above me in an apartment with her older sister, Julia—who was disowned when she brought home her awesome Latine partner, Sofia—instead of with her parents and Em, who is fourteen and still figuring things out.

You'd think the birth of the most adorable baby in the

world (who happens to be their freaking grandchild) would soften Shai's parents, but they're too busy clinging to their rosaries to even look. Let alone see.

Which is a damn shame. *I* see, and Elsa's the cutest thing ever.

Shai stops that cute little thing from reaching for my cotton candy again. "It really is, but I'd rather get ahead before this one," she kisses the top of Elsa's head, "starts walking."

"You could've cancelled tonight. Or I could've come over. It's a super long and difficult trip, getting all the way to your place, but I would've been willing to make the sacrifice."

She snorts. "And miss our gorgeous carnival? No way!"

Real talk: Our carnival is janky as hell, but I completely understand how Shai's feeling. Because our carnival is also magical, especially now that all the lights are blinking on, the yummy scents of popcorn, corn dogs, funnel cakes, and deep-fried Twinkies are wafting through the air, and the sounds of laughter and cheers and pop music are filling my ears. Kiss & Tell again. I bop my head to the tunes of "Come Say Hello." Such a damn good song. "I don't know how you do it all."

She shrugs. "I do it because I have to keep a human alive. But it still kind of stinks that Em bailed, because I was looking forward to hanging out and just being me, ya know? Being a mom 24/7 is not easy." She looks at Elsa and her face softens. "But it's fine." She catches me staring at her. "I'm *fine*."

I twirl a lock of her hair. "Are you though?"

She raises her eyebrow at me and points to my nose. "Like you can talk. What's up with your new accessory? Is that why you were late?"

I touch my nose piercing and hiss at the sting. I really need to stop doing that until the thing heals. In about six months or so. "That's not why I was late. I was reading my email."

She blinks at me. "Why would you be reading your email instead of hanging out with me?"

I tell her about the contest emails, and she squeals and throws an arm around me. Then she pulls away, her eyebrows at the top of her forehead. "Okay, first of all, amazing! Well done! Second of all, I didn't know you were entering contests?"

"Yeah, a few months ago. Mr. Conway's idea."

"Why didn't you say anything? I could've put some good vibes into the universe for you!"

I shuffle from one foot to another. This girl would give me the world if I asked for it, but I never will. She's the one who deserves the entire universe. "You do enough, Shai. I'm good."

She looks me up and down. "So what are you going to do with your contest money?"

"Put it in savings for now."

She opens her mouth and then closes it.

"What?"

She strokes Elsa's nose. "Nothing."

"Shai?"

She shrugs. "Seems like this is the perfect opportunity to take control. Maybe apply to that school. Show your mom that you're really serious."

My shoulders slump. "She won't listen."

"So? It's not her money, and you aren't beholden to her. Or anyone. I still think you should try."

"Maybe." I say it to appease her, but she wasn't at the President's Club earlier. When Mom's mind gets made up, it stays made up.

She shakes her head. "Anyway. I still can't believe you got your nose pierced. That's bananapants!"

"Do you like it? Is it too much?"

She giggles. "First the helix, then this. Next, you're going to get a rose or some questionable kanji tattooed on your bicep."

"I still haven't ruled it out." I pause. "Mom hates it."

She scrunches her nose. She's got a good one—perky and freckled. Easy to draw. She got hers pierced right before she had Elsa, and the gold stud only accents the cuteness. "I mean, you're eighteen, and it's really not *that* big of a deal—"

"Except it is. Because Mom hates it so much. But you're right. I'm an *adult*!" Maybe if I keep repeating it, the conviction will stick. Unfortunately, I've never felt less like an adult than I do right now. Shai just seems so grown up, and I feel like a kid trying to play catch up. With everyone. Most of the time it doesn't really bug me, but shit's been real all day and it's messing with my head big time.

"I do like it," Shai says. "It suits you."

I flush with pleasure. That validation thing again, I guess. "Thanks."

But the scrutiny doesn't stop. Shai has this way of studying me that makes me feel like I'm under a microscope. She's doing it right now, and I can't help wishing she'd turn those moss-colored eyes elsewhere. "You seem off. Are you okay?"

"What do you mean? I'm fine." Never mind that I'm bouncing on my heels and want to do something. Anything to get out of my head.

But Shai has her "I can fix you" face on. "How are you feeling? After seeing your dad and all?"

"He's not my dad. He's a sperm donor."

"Do you really believe that?"

My shoulders slump. "It's complicated."

She nods. "I know. It has to be confusing."

"Super confusing," I say. "I feel like I should hate him, but I don't? And he's kind of cool, even. But I'm still pissed because of—" My eyes sting. I wave my hand around, as if that's going to stop the tears from threatening to spill. "You know. So."

Shai's mouth turns down at the corners. "I always

wonder..." She trails off and looks at Elsa. "It's weird, isn't it? How Elsa's life kind of matches yours?"

"Maybe that's why I love her so much."

She gives me a wry smile. "Sure, that's it. Wait, hold on. We FaceTimed. Oh shit. Bran? Did you get your nose pierced to avoid thinking about today?"

"No!"

"Liar."

"I'm not lying."

"Bullshit. You are the queen of dissociating," she says.

"Again, what does that even mean?"

"Well, the kind that you're doing? Distracting yourself by doing a bunch of weird stuff so you won't have to think about the hard things. Like, who even are you right now?" She looks me up and down. "You're wearing a dress? And your hair!"

"I didn't have time to braid it." I stroke the fine waves. "Do you like it?"

She gives me a sideways glance. "Yeah, it's gorgeous. You're gorgeous. But...what's really going on with you? You're acting super sus."

"Et tu, Shai?"

"Always me, Bran. Here to pull you back when you try to avoid hard things. No, Elsa, babies don't eat cotton candy."

"I dressed up for dinner with Mom. And...dinner did not go well."

"Oh no. Was it because of the piercing?"

"Because of everything."

She kisses the top of Elsa's head. "Parents suck."

"You don't."

"That remains to be seen." She yawns. "I'm exhausted."

She really does look exhausted; she never used to have those dark circles under her eyes, but I'm surprised they took this long to show up. She's studying to be a midwife, and she started working ahead right after graduation so she can begin her official training early. Mom loves that Shai is going into medicine, and I know she wants Shai to be more of an influence on me in that way. But Shai's path is so much like my mother's. Teen mom, giving up everything for security first and foremost—so she and her baby can have a good life.

But that's not my life. I don't even know if I want kids. It's not that I hate them. I adore Elsa with everything in me, but the thought of being pregnant? Giving birth? That's a great big ball of Hell No. The thought of sex freaks me out, and while I know there are other ways to get babies, all of it seems so big and out of reach.

Is it normal to feel like this?

"Where are you, Bran?" Shai's bell-sounding voice pulls me out of my thoughts.

I blink to clear my head of the blurry lights and distant carnival noises. "Sorry."

"Welcome back," she says. "You know you need to process seeing your father, right?"

"I know. But it doesn't even feel like it really happened, so how can I even start?"

"You just start."

I sigh. "I just want to forget all of it and hang out with you and Elsa on the official first day of summer. So can we talk about something else?"

Frustration flashes across her features before they morph into her normal expression. "I just want you to be okay."

"I will be. I promise."

I don't know if I believe that, but I have to pretend. At least for now.

Shai studies me for a bit. Then her mouth curves into a minx-like grin. "Soooooo...why were you hanging out with Ben today?"

Dammit. Maybe we should've stayed on the other subject. "I told you. He just appeared. And never left."

"Okay." She raises an eyebrow. "Did you *want* him to leave?"

I open my mouth, then close it. "I mean, I guess it was nice of him to be there and keep me from spiraling about all the things."

She nods. "Yeah, but you didn't answer my question."

"Oh my God, please. I can't."

"Do you think—and don't get mad—but do you think

there is the slightest possibility that you no longer think of him as a rival? And dare I say, you might be getting a little crush on him?"

I choke on my cotton candy. "Okay, what's with all the fancy talking?"

"What's with you avoiding the subject?"

Ugh. "We spent one afternoon together, and he still gets on my first, twelfth, and two-hundredth nerve."

She tilts her head in that knowing way that drives me crazy. "Does he?"

"I can't even believe you're asking me this with your whole chest. You know the boy is a pain in the butt!"

Shai just keeps looking at me with that maddening expression. The thing is, when it comes to matters of the heart, Shai is annoyingly clairvoyant, and she gets overexcited when she thinks she's right about things. Not sure I can handle that right now.

And besides, Ben *does* get on my nerves! I mean, yes, I fully admit that he's cute, and his video was hilarious and the perfect distraction from the fight I had with Mom. He made it a point to tell me that he really liked my new piercing while he was dropping me off today. And waited until I was safely inside before driving off. We're not going to talk about the slight emptiness I felt as soon as his Toyota disappeared from in front of my apartment building.

It's almost too much. I've never been a girl who gets

crushes. I can appreciate when someone is attractive on an aesthetic level, and I love looking at pretty people of all genders. And while drawing them is a challenge I'm not sure I'll completely overcome anytime soon, the thought of doing… *things* with any of them makes my stomach feel funny. I've never daydreamed about prom dates or homecoming dances. And normally, the thought of just kissing anyone freaks me all the way out. And I wonder, all the time, am I normal?

"Brandy, it's okay for you to like him," Shai says quietly. "You know that, don't you?"

"That would be reassuring. If I actually—"

"Speaking of," Shai interrupts loudly. Then a hand reaches over my shoulder and snags some of my cotton candy.

I whip around and, sure enough, Ben's standing there, strings of pink candy floss hanging out of his mouth. "Mm, delicious. Even more so because it's yours."

I ignore the swoop in my stomach. "Why do you always have to steal my food?"

He grins. "Because it's funny when you're aggravated. And you totally like it."

"Not even a little bit."

The grin grows. "You totally like me."

"Hate you."

The grin is now covering the entire bottom half of his face. "You wish."

Ugh! He's changed into the green shirt he bought today. The green shirt that accentuates the flecks in his eyes and makes him look like royalty and nope, I'm not doing this right now. Not in front of Shai.

"You're not wearing my hoodie anymore!" he says to me.

"You were wearing Ben's hoodie?" Shai asks. "Interesting."

"Not that interesting," I say. "It was the only thing I had clean this morning."

Liar, liar...

"Were you talking about me?" he asks.

"No!" I say at the same time Shai says, "Yep!"

"Ah." He waggles his eyebrows. "All good things, I hope."

"In your dreams," I mutter.

"Something's different about you," Ben says to me.

"Indeed," Shai pops in.

"Let me figure it out." He rubs his chin like he's thinking very, very deeply. Shai quietly hums the Jeopardy theme while Ben looks me up and down. He's looking and looking and looking, and his brain must be burning up from concentrating so hard. And let me tell you, I'm feeling some type of way about this boy studying me like I'm a math problem. My brain flashes to earlier today, at the little dress shop, and how he looked at me like I was a marvel. Back to right now, and how he's looking at me like he'd rather look at nothing else. My breath catches.

I've got to stop him. It's making me *feel all the things.* Too many things. I bounce on my heels. "I don't know about you, but I'm ready for some rides!"

Ben doesn't move. He just keeps looking, and so I look back. Really look back.

And oh.

Oh.

17

And Just Like That

7:20 p.m.

ONCE UPON A TIME, MOM READ ROMANCE BOOKS LIKE THEY were going out of style. "They're like popcorn," she used to say. "Easy to get through, simple, and satisfying."

When she'd work late, I would sneak and read those books. The characters were always different, and the settings were all over the world. The way they met was different, and the way they'd fight for their love always changed. But one constant thing from every book stuck with me: how feelings could explode after a moment of profound and sustained eye contact.

How did I never notice how *deep* hazel eyes could be? It's not just the color, although the golden green is absolutely gorgeous, especially from an artistic standpoint. But now there's something beyond the obviously pretty colors reflecting the carnival lights, the flashes of mischief when he torments me, and the way they shine when he laughs. Something he's never shown to me before. Or maybe it was always there and I never noticed. I don't know.

What I do know is that I suddenly can't move. I can't think. I can't do anything but stand there and get lost in those waves of gold.

"Maybe it's just the lack of hoodie," Ben finally says. "I can't remember the last time I saw you without a big shirt on. Except the day I lent you mine."

"Sure, that's it, Ben," I manage to choke out.

Ben and his hazel eyes with golden flecks and obnoxious grin and perfectly manicured eyebrows. Ben, who is tall and confident and whose floppy dark hair is curling in the humidity.

The roller coaster feeling comes back, and my stomach swoops. If I'm being honest, I'm kind of offended that the feelings I so politely asked to leave earlier today have decided to unpack their suitcases and tuck themselves right in. Clearly, they're planning to stay awhile.

But if I'm being *really* honest, the thought of him being close to me actually doesn't feel so weird. I'd say it was an intrusive thought, except I'm not exactly kicking it out, am I?

And now Shai's looking from me to Ben, her schemestress expression full and clear. "Look closer," she says to Ben.

"Rides?" I try again. My voice is weak. My knees are shaking. "I'm ready when you are."

I'd even ride the Tornado at this point, and I hate that one. It makes me sick every time I ride it, no matter how slowly I turn the wheel. But I'm willing to endure that just to get the focus off of me. I don't know if I can handle him looking at me like that again.

Elsa squeals, pulling me out of...whatever that was. Ben turns to her, and the pressure on my lungs eases. My heart starts to slow down. The world starts to clear.

"Hang on, is this your baby?" Ben asks Shai. "She's so cute!"

"Meet Elsa!"

He bends down and grins at the baby. "You are the most adorable thing ever. Yes, you are!"

Elsa grabs some stray strands of Ben's hair and squeals again. Ben giggles (he *giggles*!) and why do I think *that's* the most adorable thing ever?

My heart speeds up again.

"She's a sweetie," Ben says to Shai.

"I agree. I kind of like her, ya know?"

"I get that. When my mom told us she was pregnant, I was really weirded out because gross," Ben says, then holds up his hand. "Not that I'm saying you're gross. Because you're totally not. Wait. That didn't come out right either."

Shai nods. "I get it."

"When Kayla was born, I swore I would protect her with everything I had. And the first time she smiled at me I knew I would do anything for her. I know it's not quite the same as being a parent, but there's something about their little faces, you know?"

Shai smiles down at Elsa. "I do know."

Talking about Elsa is probably the only thing that's keeping me rooted right here. I ruffle Elsa's soft curls. Because I get it, too. The first time I saw her, I melted into a big ole puddle of goo. And when Shai asked if I wanted to be Elsa's godmother, I immediately accepted. Didn't even have to think about it. Just a resounding, "Hell yes."

I'll do anything for that little baby.

Ben disengages Elsa's fingers. "I just remembered I owe you funnel cakes, Freckles. Stay here." And off he goes.

I'd never really seen Ben walking before. Wait, that makes no sense. It's more that I've never *watched* Ben as he walked. But I'm looking now. He moves confidently, with the slightest bit of swagger. It's the kind of walk that calls attention, the kind of walk that says, "I Am Somebody." And with the dreams he has, it's fitting.

"Why does he owe you funnel cakes?"

I jump. "What?"

"Explain about the funnel cakes, please," Shai says.

"Oh!" I turn away from Ben and focus completely on Shai. "It ties in with the video earlier." I explain to her about the ugly dress contest. The way he picked out the sundress I'm wearing now. And why he was dancing on social earlier today. The whole time I'm talking, the more soppy Shai's expression gets.

"That is the cutest thing I have ever heard!" she says when I'm done. "Bran, he is so into you I can't even stand it."

"No way. He's just nice. He said so earlier today."

"How many guys do you know will shop with a girl who they're not related to and who they're not dating?"

"I mean, I only know the one guy, so..."

"And how many would wear that hideous thing and *tag you in the post?*"

"He was proving he held up his end of the bargain." My argument is weak. What Shai's saying is weaseling into my brain and mixing with the stuff that's been kind of blooming ever since I saw the video. Or maybe ever since he held my hand at the piercing parlor.

"He has a nickname for you."

"The nickname is annoying."

"You make the cutest couple," Shai says. "He's attractive, you're attractive."

"He's out of my league. I don't even know how to play the game."

"I wouldn't say he's out of your league. But I can totally see him on a movie screen."

Movie screen!

I wonder if he's heard back about the part yet?

"He breezes in like fresh air," Shai says.

I cross my arms and stamp my feet. Because no. Just no. This can't happen. I'm such a mess, and Ben's such a pain in the ass, dating him would be exhausting. Can you imagine how tiring it would be to think up ways to best him all hours of the day and night?

But it would also be fun, a little voice in the back of my head says. *And you do it anyway, so nothing would change.*

Too many feelings. I want to run all over the carnival, screaming at the top of my lungs and purging all the shit that happened today. I want Shai to stop trying to get me to talk about all these things, and I don't want to psychoanalyze why I couldn't tear my eyes away from Ben's, or why I want to think about him, or why I kind of want to keep talking about him with Shai.

The need to *go* intensifies.

"It's just that I've never seen you look at someone the way you just looked at him."

"Shai, it would be incredibly ridiculous for me to ever like Ben." The denial rolls off my tongue like water.

"Why?" She screws up her face. "What aren't you telling me?"

"Nothing. It just wouldn't work."

She studies me a bit more, then shrugs. "Okay, suit yourself."

I was honestly expecting more of an argument, so I watch her face carefully. "What do you mean by that?"

"You'll get there."

"Funnel cakes have arrived," Ben says. "Let's find somewhere to sit."

"Already on it," Shai says, and leads us toward an empty picnic table.

"I could only carry one plate, along with the drinks, but I got the biggest one I could manage." Ben sets the plate of crispy fried dough dripping with syrupy sweet cherries and fluffy powdered sugar in the center of the table. And now I can see the bottles of water shoved under his biceps.

His nice, toned biceps.

Hmm. Does Ben lift?

No!

I turn to the doughy goodness in the middle of the table and my stomach roars. All I've had to eat today was caramel corn and cotton candy, and I just want to shove my face in the cherry syrup and suck it all up like a vacuum.

"It's important to stay hydrated," Ben says.

"You're so thoughtful," Shai says. "Thank you."

My appetite disappears again, because that's when I have to admit defeat. Ben is cute, and he is kind. He's been a steady presence during a shaky day. And he has gorgeous eyes and an amazing walk. His name is suddenly a sweet soft sigh floating through my thoughts. But it's the out loud, to *his* face, BFF endorsement that does it. Not that Shai would ever lead me astray, but it hits different when it's spoken into the universe by a person who is very intentional about the things she wants to manifest.

I peek at him out of the corner of my eye, and my heart rate speeds up. This is not good.

I think I'm falling for Ben Nolan.

Oh shit.

I think I'm falling for Ben Nolan.

Now I don't know how to act. Ben and Shai are shoving forkfuls of dough into their face holes, and I'm sitting there in a trance because what if I do something that makes him figure it out? He'll never let me live it down!

I glance at him again. God, he is really, really freaking attractive.

He turns and gives me a strange look. "What are you waiting for, Freckles? Dig in!"

He gets on my damn nerves.

18

Please Keep Your Emotions Inside the Ride at All Times

7:30 p.m.

I DANCE IN MY SEAT. THE RIDES ARE CALLING MY NAME AND it sounds like the sweet, sweet melodies of screams and cheers. "You are a clown and a half, do you know that?"

He puts his hand over his heart. "I'm hurt. I should at least be two whole clowns. Half is just cruel."

Cruel would be not telling him that he has a powdered handprint on his green shirt. And a crumb on the corner of his mouth. I point toward his chest. "There's something…"

"Nope. Not falling for that."

"What are you talking about?"

"You just want to make me look down so you can flick my chin."

"Ugh! Projection much?"

"You know you'd do it to me," he mumbles. Then he looks down. "Huh. You were actually right." He brushes the powder off his chest. "Anything else?"

I point again. "There."

He leans closer. "Where?"

"Your mouth."

He swipes, no luck. The crumb is a silly, stubborn baby.

"Maybe you should get it for him," Shai says.

I squirm on the hard bench. "I think he'll find it."

"No, you can help me. I don't mind," Ben says.

"Okay, fine." This is decidedly *not* fine but I can't back out now.

My breath catches and my hand is shaking. And when I brush the crumb away, a bolt shoots through me so violently that I jump up. "I think it's time for the main attraction."

"Yes!"

"Pass," Shai says.

"Oh." Ben glances at Elsa. "Right. Sorry."

"It's not because I have Elsa. I just can't do them."

"It's true," I say. I'm so happy for this distraction. "Girlfriend gets seriously motion sick."

"I'm her designated bag holder since the summer before eighth grade, when our parents let us come on our own and she"—Shai gestures toward me—"could finally ride everything she wanted."

"That doesn't seem fair," Ben says.

"I don't mind. Every single thrill ride kicked my ass that summer. Hence, Designated Bag Holder and also Game Player. I win all the things."

"And I appreciate you so much for it," I say. "Truly."

"I miss when I could turn with the best of 'em," Shai says. "Remember all those fouettés?"

"What's a fouetté?" Ben asks.

"A literal act of god," I say.

"Yeah," Shai sighs. "I used to whip around and around with no fear back in the day. Not now, though. Everything makes me dizzy."

"She used to do ballet," I explain to Ben. "And she's played Odile in *Swan Lake* too many times to count."

"I don't understand what any of that means, but cool." He nods, then turns to Shai. "I don't want you to be left out."

"It's fine, I promise. I'm not going to hold you kids back. But I will get on the Ferris wheel with you two when you're ready to settle down."

You two. Not sure how I feel about the way she says that. But I do know this: Ben and I have to be a package deal now. At least until we meet back up with Shai for our last ride of the night.

"Hand over your bag," she says. Then she gives me a knowing smile. "Have fun."

I obviously didn't think this through. Because my escape *from* Ben is going to be *with* Ben. And I need a wild ride more than ever.

I point to the Zipper. "I want that."

"That?" Ben's voice cracks. "Maybe we should work up to that one."

"What, you scared?"

"I'm never scared. But we did just eat, so..."

Sure, I believe that. I grin, then point to the Tilt-A-Whirl.

He instantly brightens. "Absolutely yes."

The line is short, and we're settled into a red, dome-shaped car in no time.

"Ooh, you should let me control it!" Ben stretches out so his arms cover the entire lap bar. "That way we'll get the ultimate whirling experience."

"You are so freaking cocky. What makes you think I can't provide the"—I deepen my voice—"ultimate whirling experience?"

"That is not how my voice sounds."

"Says you."

"I've sent in eleventy-billion audition tapes. Believe me, I know how I sound."

I shove his hands off the bar and put mine in his place. "That's not even a real number!"

His hands cover mine. "It's the perfect number. The best number to ever exist because I made it up."

"You know what—"

"Here we gooooo!" The ride starts and I can't shake his hand off no matter how hard I try. But while I'm gripping the bar like it'll explode if I let it go, what he does is much worse. He keeps throwing his body to make us spin so furiously that I can't help sliding across the car. "Ben, stop making me crash into you!"

"I'm not doing anything! That's the ride!"

"You are such a liar!"

He lets out the most spectacular evil laugh, and now I am fully convinced he's throwing his body this way on purpose. We spin and spin and spin so much, *but only in one direction*, that I'm permanently stuck to his side. I can smell his deodorant and that spring scent and his shampoo. His laugh is so big and loud that it's all I can hear, over the music, the mechanics of the ride, the screams of the other passengers.

When we climb off, my stomach is spinning, but for a whole different reason.

"That was most excellent," Ben says.

"I didn't know you could scream like that," I say.

"Like what?"

"You literally sound like a banshee."

"Do you even know what *banshee* means?"

I shove him. "What about 'hate'? As in *I hate you*. Do you think I know what that word means?"

He just grins his cute little grin, and I just want to wring his neck.

"What next?" I growl.

He points to the Power Surge. "That."

My mouth drops. "Are you serious? What happened to 'we just ate'?"

"I'm cured now." He raises an eyebrow at me. "You scared?"

"How dare you?"

"I mean, you're the one hesitating."

I really, *really* cannot stand him. "Not even. Need I remind you that you're the one who skipped out on the Zipper?"

He snorts. "That was a precaution. But the truth is that no carnival ride can defeat me."

Even *looking* at the Power Surge is enough to get my adrenaline rushing. Three different kinds of rotations up in the air, loud music, flashing lights, the works. It's the perfect attraction to shut my mind up and make everything go away.

"I've never done this one," I admit. "But *not because I'm scared.*"

He bursts out laughing. "You sure about that?"

"It the kind of ride one should experience with someone else." I look up at the flipping, twisting, screaming riders, and my heart races with excitement.

"Well, I'm here. Unless..." He starts clucking under his breath.

"Oh hell no. Let's go."

The line isn't super long, which I guess makes sense. Not a lot of people willing to risk their lives on a ride like this. But I'm bouncing on my feet by the time we show our wristbands because this is exactly what I need. Right now. We race to our seats and climb in. Already the thing is swaying, and my stomach is flipping with anticipation. "Have you ever ridden this one before?" I ask him.

He looks around the entire mechanical wonder. "Nope. It'll be our first time."

Now it's my turn to raise an eyebrow. There's no way this boy doesn't realize exactly how that sounded. But I can't dwell on it for too long, because the music starts. And the ride cars start rising.

"Um, Freckles?"

"What, Eyebrows?"

"Maybe I wasn't ready."

I lean past the harness so I can see him. He's definitely paler. "Are you joking?"

"No."

Shit. There's no going back now. Without even thinking, I grab his hand. And now my heart is racing with a different type of excitement.

The next two and a half minutes are some of the most flippy, twisty, turny minutes I've ever experienced. I'm screaming and kicking my legs and living my best life as the lights of the carnival blur around me. As my stomach swoops and my hair blows wildly. My cheeks hurt because I can't stop laughing. My heart is full because this is exactly what I needed.

But in the back of my mind, I keep wondering if Ben is okay.

When the shoulder harnesses release, Ben stumbles out of the ride. I watch him closely. He has more color in his cheeks, and the shit-eating grin is front and center. He stands up straight. "That. Was. Awesome."

"You were totally scared."

"Was not."

"You screamed like you were on fire!"

"I know! Wasn't it great?" I wonder if my eyes are shining even half as brightly as his are. "Best ride ever."

"Let's get on the Scrambler next," I say.

"No." He points. "That."

When I realize what he's pointing at, my stomach sinks clear to the ground. "Oh no."

"Oh yes. Whoever can ride the Tornado without puking wins."

The Tornado is the one ride that defeats me every single time. The tilting and swinging mess me up in a way that the Power Surge and Tilt-A-Whirl don't. "Wins what?"

"The night."

I throw my hands up. "What does that even mean?"

"That's for me to know and you to find out."

164

I stare at the ride as it swings and whirls and swirls. Kids are screaming and laughing, parents look like they'd rather be stung with hot needles. Repeatedly. "You have no idea, do you?"

"Not even a clue. You in?"

"Only if you ride the Zipper."

He stops. Swallows. "Okay. How about we scratch this last ride and go play some games?"

"And we breathe not a word of this to anyone."

"Deal."

But as we make our way toward what I call Game City, something strange happens. A small crowd of middle schoolers starts following us, and it keeps growing bigger and more spectacular as Ben and I wander down the modest midway. Well, as spectacular as a carnival crowd consisting of twelve-year-olds can get. So far, they're keeping their distance, but there is a lot of whispering and staring. The attention's not on me, but it's close enough that it's bothering me. And I don't know how much longer they will stay away.

"Ben," I whisper.

But he's busy taking in the sights and sounds of the carnival. "We should play that one."

I step in front of him to make him stop moving. "Ben!"

"What?" He leans down to hear me better, and his springtime scent floods my nose, but not in a bad way. It really is a nice scent.

"I think you have a fan club."

165

His face turns bright red. I mean, like a freaking straw-berry. "I'm sorry, what?"

I try to gesture discreetly. "They sure aren't following *me*."

Ben peeks out of the corner of his eye and his blush deep-ens. "What should I do?" He whispers furiously.

"I don't know!" I whisper back.

"Well, *I* don't know what to do!"

"This hasn't ever happened to you before?"

His eyes are so wide right now. "No!"

"You haven't considered this happening? Ever? Mr. I Tried Out for a Motion Picture Lead?"

He yanks me close. "Keep your voice down!"

"My voice *is* down." Tingles travel down my arms from his touch. "I'm just saying. You get that role, you get mega famous, and this will happen all the time."

He pales. "I'm not even thinking that far ahead right now."

"You're not?"

"Okay, I might've been practicing my autograph and how to pose for selfies with people," he relents.

I suck in my lips to keep from snorting.

"But it's different when it's real. Are you laughing at me?"

"No."

"You are laughing at me. At this time of great distress. I'm so sad." And his mouth actually turns down as he widens his eyes even more. Puppy dog eyes. I swear, this boy. "See how sad I am?" He blinks, and now I understand what Shai means when she laments about how unfair it is for guys to naturally have the best eyelashes.

"Do you think we should carry on like normal?"

"Maybe that's for the best," he says. He glances over my head and his face brightens. "Ooh, Whac-A-Mole!"

"Benjamin!"

He's gone. I shake my head and follow him. By the time I've caught up to him, the small group is a bit closer. They're still a respectful distance away, but there's no way of knowing how long that's going to last. I turn my head quickly when I see the phones come out.

"They're taking pictures," I mutter.

"Like, on the one hand, I want to turn around and pose, but on the other hand, I want to run behind this game and hide."

"I don't like getting my picture taken by strangers."

"Then don't turn around," he says. "Or you can leave. I can deal with it."

He looks like the last thing he wants to do is deal with that on his own. "I'm not leaving you, Ben."

He looks at me, his expression soft. "You mean that?"

I shove him so hard he stumbles. "Duh."

"I am touched. Truly."

"You're welcome."

"All right. As long as they stay over there, we should be safe. So..." He grins that lighting up grin. "Watch me take these carnies for everything they've got."

19

Game On

8:00 p.m.

"IF YOU COULD HAVE ANY PRIZE FROM HERE, WHAT WOULD you get?" he asks at the basketball game.

"Like you can win." I'm only saying it to antagonize him. The boy has shown me that he's a master at Whac-A-Mole and pop-the-balloon and other assorted games. I've never seen anyone hit so many targets so perfectly. Now I'm the Designated Person, only instead of someone's bag, I'm carrying a fluffy, stuffed blue bear, a bright yellow banana plush, and a random assortment of keychains and stickers. So maybe he could win. Except I have never seen a person win anything at this one. Not even Shai. "But I'd pick the strawberry."

"Yo." The guy behind the counter gestures at the cash in Ben's hand. "You can give me your money if you want, but this game is hella rigged."

"You should heed his warning," I say. "I've seen gamemasters go down with this one."

"I'm better than a gamemaster," Ben says. He eyes the baskets, and the calculations in his head are almost visible. Then he turns to me. "I got this."

"Prove it."

Without taking his eyes off of me, Ben slaps a ten-dollar bill onto the counter. "You'll get your strawberry."

I'm aware of the fan club coming closer. I refuse to look at them, but I can feel them. The energy is frenetic and eager, one I haven't felt from myself in years.

But I can't take my eyes off of Ben. The way he braces his legs. Mimes a few practice shots. And shoots.

BONK.

"He shoots. He misses!" I say in a sportscaster voice. "A great first attempt though!"

Ben ignores me and shoots again. And misses again.

"Yo, you really should just give me all your money now," the game attendant says.

"No way," Ben says. He's intense again, like he was earlier today, and yeah, it's definitely hot.

"This is it," I say in a sportscaster voice. "Can he prove that one can win even if the odds are stacked against him?"

"You got this!" Someone squeaks from behind me.

Ben straightens his stance. Eyes the basket. And shoots.

Swish!

The eruption of squeals is ear-breaking. I whip around and sure enough, the crowd is a lot closer than even just a few minutes ago. The game attendant tosses Ben his prize. I grab Ben's arm and we take off, ducking behind a trash can until that heavy energy dissipates.

"Do you think it's safe?" he asks.

"It's now or never."

By dodging and skipping, we eventually make our way back to Shai, who is dancing with Elsa in the middle of a walkway.

"What'd you do, rob a Chuck E. Cheese?" she asks once she eyes the bounty.

"No, he's just freakishly good at carnival games." I hand the rest of the prizes to Ben. "You should've seen him. He's almost as good as you."

"Almost?"

"I see that Elsa has been released," I say to Shai.

"She has. She was getting super squirmy. Weren't you, baby?" Then she looks up at me. "Hey, I got some pictures of you two on the rides. I've already texted them to you."

"What do you mean, *almost as good as* Shai?"

"Just what I said! Thanks for the pics, Shai." I resist the

urge to whip out my phone right now and scrutinize every single photo.

It's hard, though.

"I can't believe you rode that one thing!" Shai points to the Power Surge. "That's bananapants!"

"I loved every second of it," Ben says.

"Oh please. He was totally screaming for his mother."

"Excuse me, I was screaming for my grandmother, thank you very much. Hey, I got this for Elsa." He hands the bear to Shai.

"Oh my God!" She beams at him. "You continue to be the nicest person I know."

I cross my arms. "Hey!"

"Besides my beautiful best friend, of course," she says. Elsa grabs the bear and immediately chomps on its ear.

"That's right." Not really. I'm nowhere near as nice as Ben is proving himself to be. I look over at him, and something in me softens. It's been happening all day, but in this moment, it's feeling extra real.

"And this, my dear Brandy, is for you." He gives me the stuffed strawberry from the basketball game.

I gasp. "Wait, what?"

"You asked for it, and I saw how your face lit up when I made that last basket," he says. "So it's all yours."

"But, Ben—"

"Ugh. Don't make it weird."

That's fair. I was about to make it weird. I stroke the strawberry's little leaves and smile at the little face. "Thank you."

All remaining slivers of animosity I might have felt toward him are gone. Completely wiped out. I feel a little bit dizzy, a little bit light-headed. Because I know I don't *think* I'm falling for this boy. It's happening.

Oh.

Crap.

"Um, I don't want to alarm anyone, but are we aware that there is a posse of middle schoolers all with their phones pointed at us?" Shai asks in a low voice.

The blood drains from Ben's face. "They're still here?"

"Do you need bodyguards?" Shai asks. "A publicist?"

His cheeks darken. "No."

"Not yet," I say under my breath.

"What?"

I give him the sweetest smile ever. "Nothing."

He stares at me, and I can tell he doesn't believe me at all, but I keep smiling anyway. Because even though I'm somehow falling for him (oh God), tormenting Ben still sparks joy.

"Do you think it's safe to close out the night with the Ferris wheel?" Shai asks.

We both turn to Ben.

"We can't pass up the Ferris wheel," he says.

I grin. This is all I wanted. And they can't get us while we're in the air. "Let's do it."

In line, Ben pokes my shoulder. "Did you know the Ferris wheel was invented for the 1893 Chicago World's Fair?"

"Of course, I did," I say. "The H. H. Holmes fair."

"Exactly. Wait, what?"

"What?"

"How do you know about H. H. Holmes?"

I gesture toward Shai. "True-crime goddess here."

"Oh yeah. He was nuts." Shai dances back and forth, her way of rocking Elsa while standing upright. "But there was never a murder castle. I bet you didn't know that."

"You're lying," Ben says.

"Would I lie about something like that?" She shakes her head. "I need to get you clued in to the podcasts I listen to."

"*Anyway*," I say. Because once Shai gets started, she'll run down that rabbit hole for hours and we'll be standing here all night. Plus, stories about notorious killers like that freaks me the freak out. On the one hand, I want to get into their head to see what makes them like that. But on the other hand? I believe, one hundred percent, that I am better off never, ever knowing.

"How many?" the ride operator asks.

"Four," Shai answers. "One car for me and the baby. And those two"—she points to me and Ben—"get their own car."

She is such a *traitor*! Normally it's me and Shai sitting at the top with our mouths open so wide that gnats probably fly right in, and these cars are big enough for all four of us. It's going to be weird not riding with her. I glance at Ben. He's making funny faces at Elsa, and she's giving him a gummy grin back. So I turn back to Shai.

"We're going to have words after this," I mutter. She just smiles and whips out her phone.

"After you," Ben says to me. I squash the irritation I feel at Shai and climb in. And there's really no reason for me to be cranky. I've been hanging with this boy on and off all day. Why not in my favorite ride ever? I should be feeling neutral, if not happy.

Feelings are so confusing.

Once we're settled, he lowers the lap bar, so I get a good look at his long, slim fingers. Piano player fingers. Beautiful fingers. Wait, no! Regular fingers that probably do play the piano well. He's already a triple threat. Why not add another one?

"Do you play the piano?"

He gives me a strange look. "Where did that come from?"

I shake my head. "Just a random thought. So do you?"

He nods. "Not very well, though. I gave it up a few years ago. I prefer the guitar. It's more portable. But it hurts my fingers, so I don't play that all that well either."

"That's two more instruments than I know how to play," I say. "What other things about the Ferris wheel do you know?"

"Too much. It wasn't cheap. Cost $380,000 in 1893, which is more than eight million in today's money. Can you imagine having eight million dollars to design whatever you want?"

The wheel slowly starts moving. "I think it would be awesome. I'd make the most amazing art installations all over the world, with representation of everything I love but that's also universal in a way? Because when you think about it, most people want the same things, right? So I'm desperate to stand for those things in a way that's relatable but also deeply personal." I think about all the secret art I've "installed" around town. "I would make it so people who can't afford it get to see it for free, but rich people still have to pay. What about you? What would you do if you had eight million dollars?"

"I'd build an acting school and consulting firm for kids who don't have connections in the industry. I'd hire people who would help them build their skill and help them find agents and learn how to audition and stuff. It's something I could've used a few years ago."

"How did you break in?"

The wheel stops and Ben leans over to see who's getting on and who's getting off. "Oh boy. My, quote, 'fan club,' unquote, is down there."

"Did you just—?"

"You have to admit it's better than using the finger quotes."

"If you say so."

Ben smiles at me, and I sigh. *I sigh.* Oh my God.

We kind of just sit there looking at each other, then the wheel jolts and starts moving again. Ben shakes his head like he's coming out of a mini-trance. "What was your question? The one before the finger quotes one."

"How did you start? Acting, I mean?"

"Oh. I always liked pretending to be someone bigger than I actually was, but I really got into it during eighth grade. We did *Little Shop of Horrors*, and I played Seymour. Except I wasn't just playing him, I *became* him. I can't describe how it felt, other than just *right*, you know? I went to acting camp that summer, and then started acting school right after. That's where I 'got discovered.'"

He hardly ever talks about this part, and I suddenly want to know all the things. "Tell me about getting discovered."

He bites his lip, then nods. "Okay. So my last workshop? It was like a graduation, and agents came to observe us doing monologues and scenes and stuff. I was really nervous at first, but once I got on stage, I forgot they were even there because I was having such an awesome time. The next day, I got an email from my acting coach telling me that some of the agents were interested in me. So I went on this audition binge and ended up liking Megan the best. And now I'm here."

"Yeah, you are. It's really neat to see you talk about your acting and how much you love it."

He smiles again as the wheel comes to a gentle stop at the top. Usually at this point I'm looking around, taking in the wonder of our little carnival from the very best view. But I keep looking at Ben and his smile. "Thanks, Brandy. When did you—"

The rest of his question is drowned in an explosion of noise and color. I jump, then glance up at the sky just as the first fireworks bloom across the night sky.

"Awesome," Ben says. I turn to him, and I can't tear my eyes away from the flashing reds, blues, and greens reflecting off his face.

I can't tear my eyes away and I kind of hate myself for it.

Ben leans close. "This is nice."

Yeah. He is.

I mean *it* is. The fireworks. The ride! The carnival!

No, it's definitely him that's nice. Especially this close. I bet he's nicer even closer.

He's looking at my lips. And I'm wondering which his will taste like: the colors in the sky or the funnel cakes or the pink cotton candy he stole from me.

He reaches up and brushes a trembling thumb against my cheek. I close my eyes and let it crackle through me.

The charge, the spark.

And then. And *then*.

Then the ride jolts into motion. And so do we.

Bonk!

"Ow," Ben says, rubbing a red spot on his head. "That's gonna leave a mark."

I can hear Shai laughing behind us. Because of course she is.

This is why we can't have nice things.

"Are you okay?" I ask him.

"Yeah, I'm fine. How about you? Are you okay?"

I nod. "I'm seeing stars but it's fine."

He gently touches my forehead. "You have a red spot."

"So do you."

He smiles again. "Then we match."

Finally, the ride finishes loading and unloading and we're in our three-round rotation. But the moment from earlier is gone. Now Ben is leaning forward, inspecting the car in front of us. "Hold on. Who the hell climbed this thing and tagged it?"

I shrug. Innocently and sweetly. "I wonder."

He glances at me sideways, then nods. "Indeed."

"Dude. Why do you sometimes talk like you're some lord from the Regency era?"

"What's a Regency era?"

I blink at him for approximately fifty minutes. "*Pride and Prejudice?*"

"You think I'm into *Pride and Prejudice?*"

"I mean, if you want to be a leading man, you should be."

Now it's his turn to blink at me. "I have to read *Pride and Prejudice?*"

"Yes, and watch at least one adaptation. I recommend the Colin Firth one."

"Should I know what that means?"

"Benjamin. What the hell?"

He laughs. "Don't get it twisted. I know who Colin Firth is. And I actually think I would make a great Mr. Darcy."

After seeing his more subdued side earlier today, I have to agree. He really, really would. "Literally never say 'don't get it twisted' again."

He puts his hand to his heart. "I'm so hurt right now."

I smile sweetly. "You always hurt the ones you love."

He waggles his eyebrows. "Are you saying you love me?"

I cannot wait to get off this damn ride.

20

Dress Rehearsal

8:30 p.m.

TROUBLE STARTS WHEN WE HIT THE GROUND. I *FEEL* THEM before I hear them. Seriously, it's amazing that a gaggle of middle schoolers can move so much air mass. And then... we are surrounded. No, not *we*. Ben. *Ben* is surrounded by squealing bubblegum-and-fruity-body-wash-scented people who are begging for selfies and autographs. Shai jumps out of the way quickly, shielding poor Elsa from the madness.

How could I have forgotten so quickly that they were waiting for Ben? And Ben, gracious Ben, tries to deliver, but he's quickly overwhelmed. People are trying to get closer to him so they can touch his hair or his shirt, and I'm getting roughly shoved aside. "Hey, hey, no pushing," Ben says. "I'll try to get to all of you, but you have to stop pushing!"

It's no use. There can't be more than fifteen of them, but they're pressing in and it's getting scary. I stumble and Ben reaches out for me. But no dice. He can't reach so he holds up his hands. "Seriously. You have to chill or I'm going."

Like he could extricate himself from the middle of that crowd crush. My heart is pounding and I have no idea what to do. But I have to think of something, because Ben's starting to look panicked, and it's an expression I've never seen on his face and never want to see again (unless he's doing it in a movie or on TV).

I look around frantically and thank *God* I spot a security guard. He's turned around, completely oblivious.

I cup my hands and yell. *"Hey!"*

Nothing. I yell again. *"Hey!"*

The guard turns around and sees the crowd. Then he mutters something into his walkie and runs over. Somehow he manages to part the crowd and subtly maneuver himself in front of Ben, separating him from everyone without them noticing. "Please, ladies. Give him some space."

"Okay, boomer!" someone yells.

"Hey, I am not a boomer!"

"And I'm not a lady," a gorgeous curly-haired, brown-skinned person says.

The guard sighs for a thousand hours. "All right, *people*. Please give him some space," he amends.

Another guard jogs up to help manage the crowd. One by one, the fans get their selfies and their autographs. They don't ask for much after that and they leave with no issues. I guess that moment was all they needed.

But for Ben, it was a lot of moments, and he looks overwhelmed. Once things are calm again, he grabs on to my hand and holds on for dear life. "What the hell. Was that."

Boy is seriously shook. His tan has completely disappeared into the whiteness of fear. "Ben, are you okay?"

"I don't know? Is that...is that what it's always going to be like?"

"I kind of hope so," I say. "It would mean you're doing well. But you'll have bodyguards to keep it from getting scary, won't you?"

"Speaking of guards, thanks for grabbing them. I'm really sorry you were getting shoved and that I couldn't stop it sooner."

He was the one getting felt up and asked to sign people's shirts. Why on earth is he concerned about me? "I'm fine, Ben. But I don't think you are."

"I'm a little freaked out." He shuffles, his cheeks flushing. "I don't think that's something I'll ever get used to. That was intense."

I'm pretty sure super famous people have had *way* bigger crowd crushes, but I'm not about to say that to him. Because someday that might actually *be* his crowd, and he does have to know how to deal with it.

Shai appears beside me and yawns. Elsa half sleeps against Shai's chest. Shai's exhaustion is radiating from her, and Elsa's eyes are droopy.

"All good?" Shai asks. "Sorry I had to run but—"

"Don't even mention it," Ben says.

"At any rate, it's time for me to call it a night," she says.

I give her a gentle hug and kiss Elsa's forehead. "I feel like I hardly got to spend any time with you and that's the whole reason I came."

"Liar. You came for the funnel cake."

"Also true."

She squeezes me back. "I can give you a ride home if you're ready?"

"I got it," Ben says.

"Are you sure?"

We all know when someone asks "Are you sure?" they mean "Thank God you suggested it so I don't have to."

"Positive," Ben says.

"Maybe I *want* to go with Shai, did you ever think about that?" I cross my arms. But I'm grinning so I hope he knows I'm joking.

"Ugh. Why are you so difficult?"

"See you later!" Shai calls and she's gone in a blink. Just like the magical fairy she is.

21

And Then There Were Two

9:00 p.m.

THE CARNIVAL IS WINDING DOWN, WHICH ALWAYS HAPPENS after the fireworks. The food stands packing up, the rides thrilling their last passengers, people making their way to the exits. Souvenir stands are open, but I have no desire to buy anything.

Actually, I'm still feeling really antsy, like I need to do something more extreme than riding a super thrill ride or warding off a bunch of screaming preteens. But there's nothing. Not at this hour. Too many people are around, too many eyes to catch and report. Plus I'm with Ben.

We start making our way toward the street and my apartment complex.

"That was fun," he says. "Except for being mobbed by all those kids. *That* was freaking weird."

"You were so sweet to all of them. They'll always remember that. You know that, right?"

"Maybe."

"They will. You made their nights. That means a lot to people who look up to you. I'm glad you're not like that actor from the con."

"Con?"

"Oh my God. Yes. This bitch. So last year, Shai and I went to BananaCon. And she wanted to get a photo op with that one actor from *Creekvale*—the one who plays Rocky."

Ben screws up his face. "Him?"

I nod. "Exactly. I don't get it, but Shai was so excited. When we were lined up, he got escorted past us to get to the photo room. People were freaking out, but his nose was so far in the air he didn't see any of us. And he was strolling along like 'I'm an important man. Everyone look at me!' I didn't care for me, but for Shai's sake, I wanted to shove a stick up his nostrils. And also? Who the hell wears sunglasses inside a damn hotel corridor?"

"Wow. Who hurt you?"

"He did!"

Ben bursts out laughing. "Yeah. Never want to be that guy. I don't know how my career is going to go, but I always want to stay grateful. You know? Not everyone gets to do this. I don't want to ever take it for granted or become a jerk."

I bump against his arm. "You could never be a jerk."

He smiles uneasily. "Thanks."

"Because if you turn into one, I will personally kick your ass all the way to Jupiter."

His laugh is like sunshine personified. "I'll keep that in mind."

"Believe me, I'm up for the job and more than capable."

"You're scaring me, Freckles."

"Good."

We walk silently for a while. The night feels really good now. The breeze has picked up and the faint scent of carnival foods follows us down the streets and through neighborhoods. "You don't need to walk with me," I say to Ben after about seven blocks.

"Remember what I said about the transactional thing?" he asks.

"Right. Sorry."

"You don't need to be sorry. I just want you to never think that I'm doing stuff with you just to get something in return."

"So...why have you been spending so much time with me today?"

"I could ask you the same question."

"I asked first."

"Ugh, no fair. I'm having fun, okay? Is that a crime?"

I shake my head. "Nah. I'm having fun, too. A lot."

"I always have fun with you." He gives me a side-eye. "Even when you're teasing me."

I laugh. "Teasing you helped get me through so many crappy school days. Just imagining the look on your face after I unleashed my latest chaos was enough to make things better, but actually *seeing* it? Easily the best."

"Wow. Well, I'm glad I could help!" He scrunches his forehead. "I think."

"Do you know how many times my mom took away my iPad because my grades weren't great? She kept telling me I needed to be more serious. She couldn't tell that I *was* being serious. It was just about art instead of all those other classes."

"When did you know you were an artist?"

It takes me a few seconds to catch on to what he is actually asking. When did I know I was an artist. As opposed to when did I know I *wanted* to be an artist, which is what the few people who know my dreams always ask me.

"Ninth grade," I say. "When Mr. Conway told me that he'd never seen talent like mine before and that I needed to do something with it. I guess I kind of took it to heart. But I fell in love with it when I was seven."

"Tell me about it."

My skin tingles. No one has ever asked how I started

with art. Even Mr. Conway was only concerned with where I wanted to take it. "I started by making coloring books," I say.

"Hold on. You made coloring books? Brandy, what the heck?"

"I had to. We didn't have a lot of money for random stuff when I was little because everything went to Mom's nursing school. Art was never long enough at school, and I loved coloring, I made my own books. And Ben, I had so much fun that I stopped actually coloring, only drawing. Then I started drawing pictures of the stories my grandmother read to me. Pictures of my mom and grandmother in their nurse's uniforms. I would draw a rock on the ground. I didn't care, I just needed to be drawing. Then, when I learned about watercolors and clay, art became everything to me. That's never changed."

For the hundredth time today, Ben smiles at me. There is so much tenderness in the way his lips are curving. So for the hundredth time today, I melt.

"I really do love your art," he says. "I can see you going far with it."

You need to be done. Mom's voice crashes into my head and I stop short.

"I won't be."

"What are you talking about?"

"Dinner tonight. Mom didn't take it well when I told her I wanted to go to art school. She's making me quit."

"How can she do that, though?"

"Her house, her rules."

"That doesn't seem fair."

Fair or not, there is reality and I need to face it. "My mom had me when she was seventeen. And she could've . . . not had me. You know? She gave up so much for me. Everything."

"I don't understand what that has to do with your art." He is staring at me, his forehead wrinkled in concern.

"I mean, you have a baby at seventeen and everything changes. I see it with Shai. She was training to be a ballerina. She had to give that up."

"But you're not a teen mom," Ben says. "Right?"

I shake my head. "No secret babies here. But my being able to take care of myself is super important to Mom."

"From what I can see, you're doing an okay job of it."

"Except the part where I apparently can't buy clothes on my own, feed myself, or regulate my emotions like a normal person. But the point is, she had her own dreams. And she sacrificed them for me."

"Brandy, you don't know that."

"You've never seen my grandmother's scrapbook collection. Grandma was so proud of her. But then she got pregnant." I look down in shame. "I ruined everything. Being a nurse would make it up to her. Won't it?"

"But you should never feel like you owe your mom. She made the choice to have you. It's not like you appeared one day like 'Hiii, it's meeeee!'"

"But then the scrapbooks changed and they were all about me. Mom never made it to college. Instead, she got her GED and then went straight to nursing school. And she loves her work, Ben. You don't know how much. I told her I wanted to be just like her. She's so *good*. When I told her, she must've figured I wanted to be a nurse, too, just like her. And for a while I absolutely believed that's what I wanted. She got my grandmother to make me a little set of scrubs, and I used to pretend to give shots to my teddy bear. And after all that make-believe, can you blame her for only expecting this from me? She shouldn't have her heart broken just because I changed my mind."

"Except you're totally allowed to change your mind. Plus, there's no way this is a whim. *You made your own coloring books.* That's not something someone randomly does."

Ben is seeing me. Really, really seeing me, and that's turning my emotions into a whirlwind.

"You don't think she'd still be proud of you no matter what you chose?"

My face warms. "I don't know."

"I get the whole wanting you to have a good life thing. If a parent doesn't want their kid to have a good life, I would seriously question why they had a child in the first place. But why is this *one* way so important to her?"

"It gave her security. She thinks it'll give me security, too."

He stops and snaps his fingers. "Your hair. That's what's different about you!"

"You're seriously *just now noticing?*"

"I've *been* noticing."

"Like hell!"

"No, for real! It just didn't register. But now it's blowing all around your face like flower petals. You should wear it down more often. It's really nice. Can't help but wonder if it's as soft as it looks."

There are only three walking people on this Earth I allow to touch my hair: Grandma, Mom, and Shai. I'm seriously considering allowing a fourth when that contender's pocket starts playing the theme to *The Incredibles.*

Which is freaking amazing. So much better than my own default theme.

Ben has frozen in place, his face as pale as the moon. "It's my agent."

22

Lights. Camera. ACTION!

9:10 p.m.

"BRUH."

"I know!" He pauses, then reaches his hand out to me. It happens so fast I don't have time to overthink it. I just do it. I take it and bring it to my lips. For luck. He squeezes lightly when he taps his screen. "Ben here."

I don't know what's happening on his agent's side, but on my side I only hear a bunch of "Okay. Okay. Okay. Okay. Okay. Okay." And Ben's expression is at baseline, except there are a few lines in the middle of his forehead. Which tells me *nothing*.

I want to explode! It takes forever for that call to end!

Then he has the nerve to slowly slip the phone into his pocket and turn to me. "Shall we?"

"Bruh!" I say again.

And then there's that grin everybody loves. "I got it."

"Are you serious?"

He nods. "I got it."

A million emotions rush at me at once, but the loudest is my resounding joy for Ben. I throw my arms around him. "Of course you did, you brilliant bastard you. All the congratulations in the world."

He squeezes me tight. "Brilliant bastard?"

"I'm so proud of you."

A weird expression comes over his face. "Yeah?"

"Yes! This is amazing. Would it be weird if I asked for your autograph now? Before I don't have you to myself anymore?" Oh my *God*. If there is a course about thinking before you speak, I need to sign up for it ASAP. "Pretend I didn't say that."

He squeezes me again. "You'll always have me, Freckles," he murmurs into my hair.

We stand there a bit, him resting his chin on my head. Me burying my cheek into his T-shirt. I'm trembling just slightly, and I don't want to be the first to step away.

He sighs, and I look up at him. He's so pale right now, and maybe even a little green. "Ben, are you okay?"

"Yes."

Liar. "Do you need to sit down?"

"No." He bites his lip. "Yes."

We settle onto the curb, not talking. Ben is hardly ever quiet. So this is weird.

But it's also kind of nice, just sitting here with him.

I give him a quick glance out of the corner of my eye. He's so still, which is so different from how I'm feeling. Adrenaline is spiking through my veins, but I try to control my breathing. For his sake.

His eyes are tracking the people walking by, probably on their way home or to Stella's Diner to stuff themselves with bacon and waffles.

"Do you people watch as part of your acting?" I ask him.

He nods. "I've always done it just for fun, but now it's useful for my work. Why?"

"Just curious." I wonder what he sees. Maybe he's capturing the way people move or gesture to use in the characters he brings to life on stage or screen. Maybe if I watched strangers like he's doing right now, drawing them—as real people and not cartoons—would be less intimidating.

I reach into my bag and pull out my iPad and Apple Pencil. I want to make a few quick sketches of the different ways people walk. "Maybe I can learn from that, too." Like how to create a decent swagger or a passable bounce, even if I have to start with rudimentary shapes and strokes.

My fingers buzz with anticipation as I wait for the

Procreate app to open. Then I get to work immediately, setting up the canvas with the tools and colors I know I need and tweaking the settings so they're just right. Because for me, even quick one-off sketches need to be perfect.

"Do you carry that thing everywhere?" Ben asks.

I nod. "Never know when the urge will strike."

"Huh."

I start making strokes, but they look terrible. I frown and undo. Start again, but these results are much worse. Ugh. People are hard to draw, and they rarely come out the way I see them in my head. Real people are always moving too much for me to really capture the essence of who they are. Their features never look quite right on paper, or on screen. The proportions are all off or the setting is all wrong. And hair? Forget it. Immediately.

But then I stop trying to force it. I don't really want to draw random people walking down the street. That's never been my style. Instead, I decide to make something familiar. And this time, when my pen touches the iPad, the image starts to flow out of me like water. The light initial circle and guidelines. The shape of eyes, a strong jaw, and upturned, Roman nose. Then the lips. A perfectly proportioned face. Then it hits me exactly who I am drawing.

Oh my God.

"Who's that?" Ben looks over my shoulder, and I slam the iPad cover shut.

"No one."

"Didn't look like nothing. In fact, I dare say it looked kind of like me."

"In your dreams, Eyebrows. If you must know, I'm trying to work on realistic drawings of people instead of sticking with my cartoon style."

He glances at the iPad in my lap. "Real people, huh?"

"Ben."

By some act of mercy, he drops it. Instead, he turns back to the street. He watches the occasional car drive by. I watch him. He is a statue. I can almost see his brain processing processing processing. I sneak open my iPad cover and try to add more detail to the drawing. But now I'm all discombobulated.

I'm having a hard time wrapping my head around a couple of things: the face manifesting in my drawing, and the person that face belongs to becoming a star. His life is about to change big time, and I don't think either of us can fathom how much. I close the cover again.

He's still sitting, his expression reflective.

"You're so subdued," I say. "Not like someone who's just gotten his dream role."

"I think I'm in shock."

I nod slowly. "I get that." I just hope his is a joyful shock, not the hopeless shock I felt this morning. I still feel hopeless, but the shock has worn off. There's only depression there now, when I allow myself to think about it. Which I won't because Ben is the lead in a major motion picture!

Holy shit. Ben's going to be a movie star.

"Holy shit. You're going to be a movie star!"

"Whoa, whoa, whoa. Not so fast. I mean, it's really, really unlikely."

"But—"

"So the thing about Hollywood is that things move really slow until they don't. Then it's a whirlwind until it's slow again. There's a lot of hurry up and wait, and a lot of 'is this even going to really happen?'"

It sounds more like he's talking himself out of it than anything. "I think you're past the 'is this going to really happen' thing. I mean, you got the part."

"Yeah, but anything can take it away, you know? Movies get delayed. Contracts get cancelled. The whole thing could come out and bomb. You just never know."

"Ugh. You sound like me, all storm clouds and rain. You're usually a sunshine."

He tilts his head. "Am I?"

I nod. "Totally. Being around you makes people happy. It's just a thing that happens."

He seems to be mulling it over. "That's really nice of you to say."

I shrug. "It's the truth."

He gives me a long look. "Does being around me make *you* happy?"

Here's the thing: Whatever weird things my feelings are doing around him now, at the end of the day, Ben is *fun*. He always has been. And he's easy to talk to. I spilled so much of my heart to him today without a second thought. Does this mean I trust him? It must. So maybe it does make me happy to be around him. Even though he gets on my nerves.

Can both things be true at the same time?

I poke his shoulder. "I guess you're all right."

He gives me the sweetest smile and my stomach swoops.

I need to finish that drawing. But not right now. It's enough being here with him for now.

"Can you tell me which movie?" I ask him.

He gives me a long look. "I'm really not supposed to say anything. But." He closes his eyes. Let's out a deep breath. Opens them again. "I want to tell you. You promise not to tell a soul?"

"Honest promise."

"It's *Shadows and Ice*."

I shove him. "Shut up."

"I know!"

"You're Trent?"

"I'm Trent."

"Holy shit." I can see it, too, even though Ben is nothing

like Trent, who is a deeply broody yet awkward wounded warrior who has to save the kingdom he's not sure he even likes. The book kind of pokes fun at the super serious fantasy bad boy trope, but it's also pretty entertaining. And an international bestseller. I'm not even that big of a reader and I've read it three times. "Ben. What the heck! That's, like, *everyone's* favorite book!"

He gives me a weak smile. "Yeah."

"There's no way you're not going to get famous with this movie. People all over the world are going to fall in love with you."

I didn't know it was possible for him get even whiter, but here he is. Pale as snow. "Hey, are you okay?"

"All over the world?"

"Oh God. I shouldn't have said that, should I?" I mean, my heart does somersaults when I think of more than my following seeing my art, but I can hide behind it if it ever takes off. If this movie goes as big as the book, there's no way Ben will ever be able to hide, not for a long time.

"I think it's kind of hitting me. No, it's really hitting me. Millions of people might know who I am. I can't even fathom it." He buries his head in his hands. "There's already all this pressure and I haven't even signed the contract yet. How is it going to feel when it's announced and my mentions get flooded with comments and people call me names and—"

"Okay, Benjamin? I need you to breathe."

"Ugh. Stop saying my full name."

"I need you to breathe," I say again.

"I am breathing."

How come in this moment he is arguing with me about semantics? "I mean the kind of breathing Shai would want you to do. Deep, soulful breathing."

"Soulful? What even is that?"

He is so *aggravating*. "You know what I mean!"

He nods. "I do know. It's just more fun to focus on making you mad instead of whatever the hell is happening with my career right now." He takes a few deep breaths, then nods again. But there's a vein jumping in his forehead, and he keeps tapping his foot on the ground.

Maybe he's feeling like me. Maybe emotions are crashing through his veins and neurons along with a strong desire to rip off his skin and let the feelings burst free. "I can help you get out of your head again. Do you want to?"

"Please."

Now I smile. "I know just the place."

23

I Wish You Would

10:00 p.m.

"YOU BROUGHT ME BACK TO THE CARNIVAL?"

"I did."

"Is this okay? What if we get caught?"

"Follow me."

The grounds are empty now. The lights are off, and the silence is eerie, especially compared to the chaos of just an hour earlier. They'll probably start breaking down the rides early in the morning, but for now, everything is still. I lead Ben to the Ferris wheel, and yes! The car I tagged this morning is right on the bottom. I hop over the guard rail and motion for him to follow.

"Brandy...what are you doing?"

"Shh."

The aluminum floor creaks as we make our way over to the car.

To my art.

White surfaces are always hard for me to resist. They never fail to awaken those tingles in my fingers—the all-encompassing urge to break up all that pure brightness. Maybe because there's always been something in me that wants to destroy all that purity. And a blank white surface is a never-ending temptation.

And do I feel guilty about that desire? Of course. But never enough to actually stop myself from giving in to it. It's been like this as long as I remember. Even the walls in my bedroom are covered with all kinds of art made by yours truly. I love expressing myself with colors. Swirls. Emotion.

My fingers tingle. My heart pounds.

I don't want to think. I just want to draw.

Once upon a time, I used spray paint. But spray paint is too messy even at the best of times. I can never get the effect I want. Plus, it wouldn't work very well on the shiny, smooth surface of the Ferris wheel car. The paint markers give me some sort of control. Control I need to feel while the rest of my life is spinning out around me.

I flip open my bag and select a purple marker.

Don't think. Just draw.

Ben is still as I carefully add shadow to the little carousel I drew this morning.

"Brandy. What the hell?"

I don't even dignify that with a response. But I do raise my eyebrows at him before turning back to my drawing.

"Oh my God," he says. "Your video from earlier. It was this!"

I give him a wry smile. "Wow. Nothing gets past you."

"I can't believe I didn't pick up on it. Wait. All those bruises."

I just keep smiling.

"Brandy, where was this car when you made this drawing?"

I look up through all the spokes at the top of the wheel. Then I look back at Ben.

"Brandy, no. Don't tell me you climbed this thing."

"Okay, I won't."

"Have you lost your mind?" Realization after realization dawns on his face. "The bridge? Was that you?"

I nod.

"And the statue at the park?"

Another nod.

He sucks in a breath. "Okay. Wow. I don't know whether to be impressed or to shake some sense into you. You know this is super illegal, right?"

"I know."

"And if you get caught—"

"I won't."

"But if you do—"

"I won't," I repeat. "Unless you say something."

"Which I'd never do."

"Exactly."

"Holy shit, Freckles. I knew there was something simmering under the surface for you, but I had no idea it was this. And what does that say about how clueless I was? It's so obvious now. Does anyone else know?"

"Not even Shai."

His expression softens. Then he looks at me. Back at the drawing. "How come you're showing it to me? And why now?"

"You shared a big secret with me." His profile is in silhouette against the orange streetlight. Straight nose. Lips that are slightly pursed. Hair lightly ruffling in the wind. It's really a gorgeous profile. But then he looks at me full on and my heartbeat speeds up.

"That's because I do trust you," he says.

"And I trust you." Admitting it out loud makes everything feel clearer. The rushing in my veins slows down. My focus becomes sharp. And this moment feels just right. "And that's why I'm sharing a big secret with you."

He doesn't say anything else, so I start by drawing a Ferris wheel behind the two friends. It rises behind them, magnificent and enormous. It might as well be the Eiffel Tower as far as the little people are concerned.

Then I start adding little butterflies to the drawing. There's no way these additions are going to be perfect. Not enough light for one thing. Too many emotions making my hand unsteady for another. And finally, being watched by the one making me feel all these feelings is keeping me from focusing like I usually would.

But the beauty of the butterflies is that they don't have to be exactly perfect. Because emotions are so messy, ruining a perfect line isn't a tragedy. At least I'm trying to make myself believe that in this moment. It's just how I feel.

And this Ferris wheel car will be gone soon anyway. The carnival won't be here forever. Whether or not the ride operators will eventually scrub off my drawing is a mystery. And I guess that's part of being an artist. Knowing how to let go, because at some point, it won't belong to me anymore. It'll belong to the viewers, the buyers, the collectors.

But I like that it's here now.

I turn back to Ben. He's watching me, the look in his eyes guarded. I give him a small smile because yeah, my feelings are a hot mess, but I'm also in my element here. Perfectly content. And safe.

Ben nods and turns back to the ride car. So I resume my drawing. This time, I pick a black marker.

"Why don't you use spray paint?" Ben asks.

"Doesn't do it for me. It's faster, but I can't ever get the effect I want. This way is cheaper and more portable."

"You've thought this through."

I shake my head. "I don't know. Maybe. I just needed something easy."

"Wouldn't just using paper be the easiest?"

"Are you mansplaining my rebellion to me?"

He throws up his hands. "Yes. And I am really sorry. Brandy, that's really cool. I love your little characters."

"Yeah? You're being honest?"

"Let's put it this way. If I ever get a tattoo, you're totally designing it for me."

My mouth drops. "Mr. Boy Next Door wants a tattoo?"

"I've been thinking about getting one since I was twelve."

"What? You never said!"

"A man's heart is an ocean of secrets."

"Did you just...quote *Titanic*?"

"It's a family tradition."

"Quoting *Titanic*?"

"And watching it."

I don't even know how to respond to that. "You would really let me design your tattoo?"

"For sure."

I can't help but feel warm and fuzzy inside. Tattoo design is a big deal. That's a *lot* of trust, and while I don't think I'd ever be able to actually ink anyone, the thought of someone wearing my art is thrilling. I know people can get them removed with lasers or whatever, but if someone got my art tattooed on their skin with the intention of it being permanent? That's really pretty awesome. And strangely touching.

"Ben...I don't know what to say." My throat is getting thick and my eyes are tingly. I don't cry. I don't. But if I did, I think I'd be safe to do so in front of Ben. "I didn't know you thought that highly of my work."

"Are you kidding? The set pieces you painted were always the best. You always added something extra to it. It's like—" He screws up his face. "Okay, you know how you watch certain movies and certain actors keep you coming back because they give something so special to every role they play? They really pull you in to the story they're telling."

I nod.

"And then there are the ones who you can tell are just phoning it in. Everything is technically correct. They're saying the lines and hitting all their marks, but things just fall flat because there is some sort of disconnect. I felt like a lot of the stage crew was like that. They were in it to pad their extracurriculars. But your sets, Brandy. I always, always felt a connection. You connected to the work, and you connected to me, as an actor."

I drop my marker. "I did?"

"And this." He gestures to the car. "At first glance, it's great, but you keep looking because you know there's more. So much more."

I'm staring at him and staring at him. How could he tell? I put everything into painting those set pieces. I wanted the audience to be fully immersed, no matter if the drama club was singing *Oklahoma!*, performing *I Remember Mama*, or doing *Our Town* for the fifty millionth time.

"You're going to make me cry," I say under my breath. Because this boy. He sees my art. Beyond my art, to the emotions and the messages and so much more. But more important, he sees *me*.

Except he seems kind of oblivious to the emotional turmoil that must be flashing across my face right now. He's still looking at the Ferris wheel car. "What if I get a tattoo, and then I accidentally let it slip in an interview that you were the one who designed it? And I tell them all about you and you get to be all famous?"

"Oh my God." I freeze.

He finally looks over at me. "Hey, are you okay? Does the thought of being famous freak you out?"

"I mean, I saw how you acted today."

"True."

"I guess I never gave it much thought because a lot of artists don't get famous like that. I just want to be able to make a comfortable living doing something I love."

"I get that," he says.

"I don't know if I'm like you, you know?" I turn back to the art. "Sometimes I want to be like Banksy, just throwing up stuff when no one's looking and making people wonder where it came from. Then I start imagining if I had pieces in

The Met or something like that. And sometimes I want to start a graphic novel franchise that explodes into movies or something batshit like *Creekvale*."

"I would've loved to be on that show," Ben says. "If it came out now, I would've definitely gone out for Rocky, but I was way too young and unskilled to audition back then. Maybe I can star in the viral graphic novel you'll make one day."

"Except I have no idea how to write a story, so maybe that idea is out the window." I pick up my marker, which, thanks to the corrugated metal flooring, hasn't rolled too far away. "Plus, the thought of being famous kind of scares me. Like, what happened to you tonight? I don't know if I could handle it with the grace you did. I like attention, but only when I'm in the mood for it."

Ben nods. "Nothing like that's ever happened to me before. Pretty sure my agent said something about me eventually getting media training or whatever, which probably has something about handling stuff like this, but I was in such shock I barely heard what she was saying."

"I can't even imagine what that's like," I say. "Basically you'll have to be *on* every single time you are out in public. What if paparazzi start chasing you when you're just trying to get gas or something?" Which honestly sounds exhausting. But Ben seems to get energized when he can perform for people. Different strokes for different folks, I guess.

"Yeah. I don't know. I guess I'll figure it out."

"Are you 'on' now?"

He stares at me. "You've known me for how long? And you can't tell if I'm faking it or not?"

"I mean, I don't know. You're the same as you always are. But I don't know if that's 'on' or if that's just you."

"I'm not 'on' right now, Brandy," he says. "Earlier today? When I was taking those selfies and signing those autographs, while super exciting but also scary, I was absolutely 'on'. My cheeks were hurting so much from smiling—maybe that's why celebrities smile with their mouths closed all the time. Huh." He stares straight ahead, a furrow in his forehead. "Yeah…that makes sense," he murmurs to himself.

"You're losing me, Benjamin."

"My point is: I just wanted to get back to you and Shai and finish my cotton candy, but I couldn't show that to them because again, it's really cool to have people look at me like that. But you'll always get the real me. Whether you want it or not."

I don't know whether to be alarmed, flattered, or relieved. I guess I'm a bit of all three. I lightly punch his forearm. "I'm glad. Even though you're a pain in the ass."

"Oh, you want to talk asses?"

I shove him. "Don't be vulgar."

Ben studies the new butterfly. "Okay, I have to say something weird. Don't take this the wrong way, but somehow that tiny butterfly you drew reminds me of me. But why?"

"I don't know. You're standing here?"

"Is that the real reason?"

"I needed to draw." I give him a smirk. "And you won't leave me alone."

He just keeps looking at me, his knowing expression irritating me. "Oh my God, just because you're about to be a big star, you think everybody's in love with you."

"Not everyone. Not the cute girl standing beside me doing something very illegal, for one."

"Ben."

He bites his lip, then looks down at his shoes. Then he peeks up at me through those ridiculous eyelashes. "What?"

This is so unfair. "Why are you looking at me like that?"

A devious smile. "If you haven't figured it out by now, Brandy Bailey..."

I stare at him, my mouth wide open. "You are unbelievable!"

"And you're so easy to get a rise out of!"

I shove him. "You cannot tease people about stuff like that."

He raises his eyebrow at me. "Who says I'm teasing?"

"You can't tell someone they're cute and not mean it."

"Again. Who says I don't mean it?"

I let out a long, long sigh. "Why do we always talk in circles to each other?"

"Because you start it."

"I do not!"

"You do too."

"Brandy Bailey."

"Benjamin David Nolan."

"What did I tell you about using my full name?"

"Benjamin David *Joseph* Nolan."

"My confirmation name? Brandy, how do you even know my confirmation name?"

I turn back to my little butterfly. I really want to make it look delicate, like a stained-glass window at midnight, which will be a challenge on many levels. First, I don't have a lot of time. Second, my markers tips are too broad. And third, it's harder to make whimsical art when my emotions are going up and down like a wooden horse on a merry-go-round, but I have to try. I'll feel a lot better once it's done. "It's a secret."

"You have a lot of those these days, don't you?"

I pause in the middle of attempting a thin, dark stroke. "Yeah."

We're quiet for a bit, and then ... "Me too."

"Maybe you need to let off some steam, too." I hold a dark blue marker out to him. "Want a turn?"

He stares at the marker. I hold it out again, and he takes it. "What would I even draw?"

"Whatever you feel like."

"Whatever I feel like," he says under his breath. "What even do I feel like?"

212

" 'Fraid I can't answer that one for you," I say.

He shakes his head slightly. "No. I—it's a lot. You know?"

I nod. "I know."

He stares at the car, a wrinkle in his forehead. No one should look that cute while thinking so hard, but I guess I should finally go ahead and admit to myself that Ben is not your typical person.

"It's messed up, really. I'm living my dream. And here I am, standing in the middle of an abandoned carnival, about to deface a large piece of mechanical equipment."

I bite my lower lip. "I think..." I shake my head. "Never mind."

"No. What were you going to say?"

"I was going to say that I think catching one's dream might even be scarier than chasing it. But, I mean, I don't know."

Now his expression is thoughtful. "Maybe that's why you're going to let your mom tell you that you can't go after your dream."

"You mean other than the fact that she'll kill me?"

"Be serious."

"Have you met my mom? I *am* being serious."

He points the marker at me. "One thing I noticed is that you shut down about things when they get hard. Or you joke about them."

"Why does that feel creepy? Were you stalking me?"

"See? You're doing it again. You seemed shocked when I asked you what you wanted earlier. Has anyone asked you that recently?"

I freeze. "My father did. Earlier."

"Hold on. You talked to your father? Actually talked to him?"

"I went back to NEO." Suddenly I feel so sad. "The funny thing is, I thought he'd be able to help me. Instead I'm more confused than ever."

"You talk about your dreams a lot, at least to me, but you never really *let* yourself dream."

"Because half the time they feel unobtainable. I've been kind of considering fine art, too. Do you know how hard it is to break in to freaking fine art?"

"I don't think that's it, though, Brandy. I think it's because you're scared they're going to come true, and that you'll betray your mom. I know you think you owe her everything, but by not living your truth, you're cheating both of you."

"Are you psychoanalyzing me?"

"You're joking again, and yes, I am. I'm learning a lot in therapy," he says.

"I never thought I'd say this, but I think I want to be like you when I grow up."

He snorts. "Please. I'm no role model."

"Well, I'm a mess." I gesture to the ride car. "Why do you

think I do this? Art is the only time I feel like I have some sort of center."

"*Center.* That has a slightly new age ring to it. Has Shai been making you do breathwork?"

"Every freaking day." I roll my marker between my fingers. "I could probably use some therapy myself."

Ben nods. "I mean, I told you that earlier."

"Yeah. You did."

He points to my bag. "What marker are you going to use next?"

"I think it's your turn."

Ben turns back to the car. "I have no idea where to start. How do you know where to start?"

"I—" I pause. "I guess I just start."

He turns back to me. "Really helpful, Brandy. I don't know what I would do without you."

I grin. "Do you need me to help you, Ben?"

"Yes, please."

I let out a slow, quiet breath. Then I put my hand over his. I try to ignore the bolt of tingles rushing up my arm to my shoulders, now down my side....

And then, out of nowhere, everything just feels so easy. This is Ben, and he's here, and it's okay. He sighs softly. I turn to him just as he turns to me. He reaches up and caresses my cheek. And I'm officially a puddle of goo.

"What are you doing?" I manage to get out.

"You're so pretty," he says.

"Ben—"

"Brandy."

And for one perfect moment, my brain empties of everything except the handsome boy in front of me. The handsome boy who I've been trying to deny my feelings for but well, apparently feelings have *no* interest in what I want.

Unless this is what I want?

Stop thinking.

I'm pretty sure he's looking at my lips, but I can't really tell because I'm so busy looking at his lips.

His lips.

His lips which suddenly shine super brightly.

Holy shit. "Hide!"

Ben is squinting into the light. "I think it's too late for that."

"Stop!" yells the holder of the flashlight.

We freeze. Hands up. Markers clattering to the ground. My teeth clattering with fear.

There is no way I'm getting out of this.

Uncle Myron moves toward us with the ease of a lanky cowboy. Frustratingly intentional, because he obviously wants to torture me. My favorite uncle—as long as we're hanging out at his house while he grills hot dogs and ribs. Or while he lets me and my cousins splash him from the pool. Not so much right now, tall and intimidating in his cop uniform. And even though I know I'm not really in any danger with him, my eyes fly to his holster.

"Both of you. Follow me. Now."

24

This Night of Reckoning

10:35 p.m.

UNCLE MYRON COULD YELL.

And he *would* yell.

Oh Lord, he would yell.

Once we're in his cop car, he lets loose.

"What the hell is wrong with you? I've told you time and time again to stop this! What if it hadn't been me who picked you up? You know I have three Karens and a Chad on my staff, and it's been a slow summer. They're itching to start some shit. I'd rather it not be with my niece!"

"Are you taking us to the station?" I ask in a small voice.

"I could book you for trespassing. Vandalism. Loitering. Any number of things."

"Sir," Ben says, timidly. "If you could maybe not do this."

My uncle makes eye contact with Ben through the mirror, and raises his eyebrows.

"Sir," Ben says again. "It's just that. I just got my dream role in my dream movie, and if it gets out that I've been picked up, I might get in big trouble."

Uncle Myron's eyes flip over to me. "Is he for real?"

I nod. "He's for real."

"He is a movie star."

"Going to be," I say.

"We don't know that," Ben says. "It's only my first major role."

"I saw a marker in your hand," my uncle says to Ben. "You're just as guilty as she is."

"Uncle Myron, no. This is all me. I promise."

Uncle Myron sighs. Long and deep.

Then he looks at Ben again. "I'll make sure you're clear. But you, young lady!" His eyes cut over to mine. "I told you last time. If I caught you out here again, I was going to call Alicia."

I wince. "Since when do you call me young lady?"

"Since I caught you doing the one thing I said I'd better never catch you doing again."

"She's going to kill me."

"You should've thought about that before I caught you. Again."

"The bright side is, if I'm dead I won't have to be a nurse."

"I am not getting in the middle of that," Uncle Myron says.

I've been to this police station before. We all have. The fire station, too. And the post office. Field trip after field trip when we were growing up. Shai and me giggling on the school buses, climbing into the firetruck, and sitting in the high seats. Watching the postal workers sort mail. Learning what the different sirens meant in the police car.

And sometimes, I'd just tagged along with my uncle. Watching him help people through incredible situations is super cool. I guess he's like my mother that way. They love community, and they love trying to make it better.

My uncle is good at his job. But he also loves me. I know it creates a conundrum for him. He's not only a cop—who are not everyone's favorite people these days—but he's a Black cop, which really puts him in quite a pickle (as Ben would say). He'd been doing me favors all summer, looking the other way with my street art. Only now it sinks in how much trouble he could've gotten in if one of the Karens had figured out what he was doing.

I have a lot to apologize for.

I feel sick.

And I want to cry.

Uncle Myron points to the two chairs by his desk before heading through the door marked EMPLOYEES ONLY. Ben and I plop down. I am still and silent. Ben jiggles his leg so hard the entire floor shakes.

"I'm sorry," I say to him.

"No you're not." He cut his eyes over to mine. "But you will be."

Oh hell no! "Was that one of your audition lines?"

"No." He crosses his arms. "I just always wanted to say it."

Is he teasing me? I can't tell. But then he makes eye contact with me, his lips slightly quivering.

This fool is laughing at me! "You know what."

He bumps my shoulder. "I *do* know what."

Uncle Myron thrusts mini bottles of water at me and Ben. "Alicia's on her way," he says to me. Then he stares. "What in the name of sanity did you do to your nose?"

I touch the piercing. Ow, still tender. "I got it pierced."

"I see that." He nods. "So that happened. Good luck to you when your mom sees that."

"She's already seen it." Remembering the dinner makes my hands shake so badly I can't get a good grip on the bottle.

Ben takes the water bottle from me and unscrews the cap. "You okay?" he asks me.

I shake my head. He opens his mouth as if to say something, but then his phone rings. He glances down and his eyebrows jump up. "I have to take this."

Ben goes over to the corner where we can still hear everything, so what's even the point of him moving? But whatever.

"Did you call his parents?" I ask Uncle Myron.

Uncle Myron glances at my hands, which are still trembling. "Not that it's any of your business, but yes. I did."

"I mean, it's my fault he's here, so..."

"That boy has a brain and two working legs. At any rate, it's not *completely* on you. But that's not to say what you did isn't completely cracked. My dear niece. My sister in Christ. I know you're going through a lot right now. But you need two things: perspective and a healthier way to cope with stuff."

So says everyone. Shai, with her "you just need to breathe more." Mom with her "you need to find something productive to do. But don't worry. Once nursing school starts, you'll be too busy to be so antsy all the time."

My eyes fill with tears. I upset Mom and ruined our fancy dinner. I got Ben in trouble. I'm a terrible person. That's all there is to it. Maybe I should tell Uncle Myron to put me in jail. It's the least I deserve. No one needs me tainting their lives. They can all be free, while I get what I deserve.

Oh God, I feel sick. I ate way too much at the carnival, and now my stomach is even more unhappy with me. If only I could disappear. Just hide away forever.

And now the tension, which had been at a manageable level up until now, is rope thick. It's getting harder to breathe, and all the lights are turning into little pinpricks. I close my eyes to straighten my vision, but when I open them, the room tilts. And my skin is on fire. Feels like spiders crawling under the surface, and I need to scratch them out *right now.*

"Brandy!" Uncle Myron's voice sounds like it's in a tunnel. "Brandy. Stay with me."

"I—"

"Feel your feet on the ground. Right now. Feel the water bottle in your hands." Uncle Myron keeps giving me instructions like that until the lights look normal again.

Now I really want to cry. "I'm sorry."

"You should get those checked out. The panic attacks."

"Is that what's happening to me?"

Uncle Myron nods. "I think so. I get them, too."

I stare at him. "You mean, this happens to other people?"

"Yeah."

"Why do they feel so bad?"

"I don't know."

"How can I make them stop?"

"Only your doctor can tell you that. Does Alicia know about them?"

I shake my head.

"I guess that's another thing you need to tell her, then," Uncle Myron says.

Ben sits back down. "Sorry about that." He looks at me. "Hey, Freckles. You okay?"

Myron and I exchange a quick look. Mine says *Please don't say anything to Ben*, and his says *Your secret is safe with me*.

"Was that your mom?" I ask. Because I need a distraction. Anything. "What did she say?"

"She said she was 'disappointed in me' but once I told her about getting the part, she freaked out."

"In a good way?"

He nods. "She says she's very proud."

"Good. She should be."

"This is still a ding in their books, but I think the movie thing will overshadow it soon enough. At least until Olive brings home a Surgeon of the Year award or something."

"Olive is...?"

"My older sister."

"But it's not every parent who can say their kid is starring in a major motion picture. Are you grounded?"

He shakes his head. "I don't know. It could go either way, honestly."

"They wouldn't make you give up your part, would they?"

"Not once they hear how much I'm getting paid."

"Ooh." I wiggle my eyebrows. "How much *are* you getting paid? Don't answer that. It's none of my business."

Ben just grins and he really needs to stop being so adorable, especially at a time like this. We're sitting in a *police station*, and my life is in *shambles*. He should have some respect.

224

This isn't funny. I know. But I am at a loss as to how to cope right now.

The door to the station opens.

Everyone freezes.

Especially me.

Because standing there, in her light pink scrubs and sensible white sneakers, is my mother.

The look on her face could make a grown man cower. Even Ben grips my shoulder in an undeserved gesture of solidarity.

I swallow, knowing that this is the last thing I might ever do.

God help me.

25

Crash of Wills

10:45 p.m.

THOUGH SHE BE BUT LITTLE, SHE IS FIERCE.

I don't even like Shakespeare all that much (something I know better than to ever admit to Ben, who spent years studying Shakespeare for acting purposes), but this quote is now running through my head on a constant loop as my mother locks eyes with me.

The anger coming from her direction is palpable. And yet, I swallow a pang as I take in how beautiful she is. Big brown eyes that flash with a myriad of emotions. Impatience. Exasperation. A hefty dose of fury. And disappointment.

The disappointment is the worst.

It's justifiable. I know that. But it still stings.

"Brandy Angelica Marie Bailey. What the fuck."

Mom is one of the most even-tempered people I know, and it takes a lot to get her mad. (Disappointment is another story. That comes way too easy.) She never swears, and she *never* drops f-bombs. So right now? I am terrified.

"Hi, Mom," I say in a tiny voice.

"Don't you dare 'Hi, Mom' me. What the hell is wrong with you? I've been looking all over for you ever since you ran out of that restaurant. You haven't answered my calls. I couldn't find you at the carnival, so did you duck out from that, too? I've been worried sick! And turns out that you're at the damn police station! For tagging? Have you lost your damn mind? You know good and well I raised you better than that!"

I know better than to correct her about anything, but it's so hard to keep quiet about the art. Technically, what I do is graffiti art, not tagging. But it's illegal either way and it was really stupid of me to get caught. I sit on my hands. "I'm sorry."

"No you're not. But you will be."

My mouth drops. Twice in one night?

There is a sudden lack of activity in the station. Everyone's stopped what they're doing and are watching the Brandy-Alicia showdown.

"And you!" Mom shoves her brother, who stumbles into the corner of his desk.

He throws his hands up. "What did I do?"

"You knew she was doing this! And you only just now are telling me? What the hell, Myron?"

"Keep your voice down. I'm not trying to have her get a record."

"Maybe she should have a record. Teach her ass a lesson." Mom turns back to me. "I ought to let you rot in jail overnight. Maybe you'll learn to act like you have some sense."

"She won't really be rotting," Uncle Myron says. "She'll just be in a holding cell. And she'll have it all to herself—"

"*Not helping!*" Mom yells.

Silence. You can hear a pin drop, it's so quiet. Then Mom points to me. "You. Car. Now. And hand over the bag."

"They took my markers," I mutter.

"Did I ask if they took the markers? No, I did not. Give me the bag."

I bite my tongue and hand over the bag. The container of my other two most prized possessions—my iPhone and iPad. And with a sinking feeling, I just know I'm not getting either of those back anytime soon.

"Do I need to pay anything?" Mom asks, still staring at me, a million emotions flashing across her face, none of them meaning anything good coming for me.

My uncle looks at my mother. She looks at him. Some

sort of unsaid communication passes between them. They do this weird brother-sister telekinesis all the time and it never ceases to fascinate me and also sort of freak me out. "Just get her home safe," Uncle Myron says.

"Bet," Mom says. She glares at me. "Let's go."

26

The Wrath of Alicia

11:00 p.m.

MOM HAS TWO TYPES OF RAGE. THE FIRST ONE I CAN HAN-
dle. The stern lectures, the mouth pulled into a thin line. But
this one now? The bristles of her anger reach across the car
and threaten to choke me.

She isn't saying a word.

The silent treatment kills me. Even though I deserve it.

I stare out the window, watching the storefronts go by.
The park. The carnival. That fucking Ferris wheel. Too
soon, we aren't far from our building, and the reckoning I'm
about to face makes me want to wet my pants.

What is wrong with me?

I wrap my arms around myself to keep from scratching my skin off. It just really sucks that disappointing people is the one thing I hate more than seeing blood, and here I am, disappointing every-damn-body. Why can't I just...act right? No wonder I don't feel like an adult. No wonder I don't feel like I have control over anything. How can I when I don't even know how to begin?

And why does it have to be so freaking hot? Where is all the air going?

When we get to the apartment, Mom's so mad she keeps dropping her keys. Finally, she thrusts them at me. I get the door open and am half tempted to stay in the hall after she stalks inside. But I know better than to argue after she snaps, "Get your ass in here."

I brace myself for the inevitable explosion but what happens is much worse. "Give me your laptop."

"Mom." My voice is hoarse. I clear my throat to clear it. "Please."

The look she gives me could melt ice. "I just know you're not arguing with me right now. I mean, is that what's happening? You're trying to argue with me? After I just picked your ass up from the *police station?*"

Now the explosion comes. "I cannot believe you embarrassed me like this. What is the matter with you, Brandy? Didn't I raise you better than this?"

I should've enjoyed that silence in the car because right

now? My ears are ringing. I clap my hands over them because all sense of self-preservation has apparently jumped out the window.

I know better than to try to reason with her when she's like this. Because when she gets to this volume, the entire meaning of the lecture is lost. It just sounds like one long scream. It would be fascinating and maybe even a little bit entertaining if it wasn't directed at me. But because it is, it's terrifying.

"Brandy, what on *earth* were you thinking? Not just with the tagging. All of it?"

"I'm thinking that I'm desperate!" I blurt.

She throws her hands up. "What could you possibly be desperate about? I'm breaking my neck to give you a good life. A good home. You've never gone without. What is making you so desperate that you're defacing buildings and running away?"

"Mom."

"And furthermore, do you know how embarrassing this is for me? I'm a well-respected nurse in this community, and you're just going to ruin that? What the hell, Brandy?"

"Mom! This is not about you!"

Silence. Ice cold silence.

"Bring me your laptop," she says again.

I really don't want to do this. But I'm scared of what will happen if I don't. So I go into my room and flip on the light.

The place is a mess of discarded outfits, random hair bows, and balled up pieces of paper.

Mom is sitting on the couch when I come back into the living room. She holds out her hand for the computer.

I don't hand it over.

"Give it here, Brandy."

I don't move. I'm frozen again, clutching my computer to my chest.

She stares at me, her expression unreadable. "Are you kidding me right now?"

"Nothing's changed," I say. "And nothing ever will change. I want to go to art school."

"I told you. You're done."

I shake my head. "No."

She doesn't seem to hear me. "You obviously don't get what an honor it is to get into Lucerne, especially with your grades. You sure as hell aren't taking your future seriously, and the only way you will is if you don't do art at all."

My eyes fill with tears. "But, Mom."

She jumps up and points at me. Accusingly. "You're ruining your life! Can you imagine how much better off we'd be if your father was a man and got a real job instead of standing around painting all the time?"

"Or if he'd just stuck around?" I ask quietly. She doesn't say anything, so I keep going. "I know about him, Mom. I've been in contact with him for a while now."

She freezes. "You've been in contact? You've been talking. To him."

"Nothing super deep, Mom. But yeah. He emails me sometimes." I shuffle. "I met him today."

Mom is speechless. She collapses on the couch and slaps her hand over her heart. "You might've mentioned that, Brandy. You might've mentioned *all* of this."

"But why? So you can have more reasons to be disappointed in me?"

She buries her head in her hands and doesn't say anything for a long time. When she looks up again, her eyes are red and wet. "I can't believe you'd go behind my back and talk to him. After all I've done for you."

"And that's why I didn't want to tell you. Anytime you talk about him, you get upset."

"Well, can you blame me? He abandoned us, Brandy, and it was three times as hard to survive after he left. Do you know what that was like? Every day I'm grateful to Mama for helping us out, but I had to do just about everything on my own. So yeah, I get upset when I even have to think about him, let alone talk about him. And you ran to him like...I don't even know what. *I'm the one who's been here!*"

"If he's that bad, then why did you keep me?"

Not a word out of either of us. The sounds of the apartment are extra loud now, and it's an all-around attack on my senses. The whirr of the air conditioning. Ice cubes clanking in the ice maker. My laptop fan randomly whooshing to life for some reason. Intermittent buzzing vibrating my bag, which is lying on the couch.

My skin feels like it wants to jump off and run down the street. The cold of the AC can't touch me because wave after wave of heat is washing over me. My breath is coming in shallow, short spurts, but I am here and everything around me is in sharp focus and I hate it.

"There was never any question I was going to keep you, Brandy," Mom says, her voice husky. "No other choice ever entered my mind, not even for a second. I want you to believe that. Okay?"

"But I have to be a reminder of him. Every single day. So why *would* you keep me?"

"How I feel about him has nothing to do with my relationship with you," she says slowly.

Except it seems like it really does.

I still don't know how *I* feel about my father. Sometimes I get angry, but I wasn't even here when he left. So am I angry for my sake, or because he hurt Mom? Or did I want to see him because I knew it would hurt her? Am I really that kind of girl?

I know his occasional emails and the few times he Venmoed me money will never compare to what Mom does for me. But for what it's worth, he doesn't pressure me to be someone I don't want to be. And for that reason, I don't hate him.

"I'm sorry," I say again. "But I don't believe you."

Her eyes narrow. "It's not about you. It's about what you want to do. Of all the things you could've chosen, it had to be what *he* chose. Do you know how that makes me feel?"

"And do you know how it makes me feel, thinking that I'll have to deal with blood and guts and—" I swallow to keep what's left of my funnel cake and cotton candy from coming up. "Art's the only thing I want."

"I thought you loved babies." Her face is a rain cloud, and I hate knowing I'm the one who made it like that. "I thought you were excited about following in my footsteps. That you were going to be like *me*. Not like him. And I was so excited to bring you along on my journey. That job, Brandy, I can't describe the feeling when you help deliver a new baby. It's magical, and I want you to experience that magic every day, like I do."

There are a lot of words I'd use to describe childbirth, but magical is not on top of the list. The miracle of life is absolutely amazing, but there was a lot of screaming and fluids and wires and tubes and beeping machines in Shai's delivery room, and I don't know if I'll ever get over it. And I didn't even have to actually go through it like Shai did!

I swallow. "Which is why this is so hard. I'm sorry, but

I don't want to be a nurse. I don't want anything to do with medicine at all."

With jerky movements, Mom picks up her bag. And mine, too. "I can't be here right now."

I hold my computer tighter and look down at my shoes. Converse with colorful doodles all over the white parts.

"We aren't done discussing this. In the meantime, you are grounded. No phone, no electronics, no TV. As long as you're living here, I can still do that."

One of these days I'm going to move out on my own and no one will ever be able to ground me again. But for now, I'm stuck. And pissed. Takes everything in me to not roll my eyes to the top of my skull. "How long?"

"Until I say you're not grounded."

My jaw is stiff, and my eyes are burning. "Yes, ma'am."

At the door, she turns to look at me. "I'm furious at you, but that doesn't mean I don't love you. And even though I want to wring your neck right now, I never regretted you."

Then why are you walking out right now, I think. But my throat closes again.

And the door closes behind her.

She forgot to take the computer, but I can't bring myself to care. Because I'm standing here alone with no iPad and a million emotions storming throughout my body. Electric, lightning zinging through every nerve. I don't like it, and I have to do something about it *right freaking now.*

I.

    Need.

        To.

           Draw.

Printer. Printers always have paper. Desk, with pens. All kinds. I grab what I need and get to work.

27

The Art of Rebirth

11:20 p.m.

SOMETIMES, WHEN I'M LUCKY, I KNOW EXACTLY WHAT I WANT to draw, and when I sit down with my iPad and Procreate, the illustration flows out of me like honey. It's never perfect the first time, but I'm usually happy enough with it that tweaking it is a thing of joy.

Most of the time I'm not that lucky. I know what I want, but it doesn't come so easily. A hot mess vomits onto my iPad, and it's all undo undo undo until I figure it out.

I don't get the undo luxury with paper. It's either erase erase erase, or it's crumble and toss. Crumble and toss.

Crumble and toss.

My sketchbook is spiral-bound, so I don't really toss whatever I put in there. It's my playground, a safe space for me to experiment with no judgement. But using this fancy laser printer paper right now feels like I shouldn't be messing up like this. I grumble and stab the pencil on the paper, breaking the tip. And of course the pencil sharpener is nowhere to be found. I don't like drawing with stubby instruments, but I'm desperate. I have no idea what I want to draw. I just need to do something. So I close my eyes, take a deep breath, and *do something.*

The first few pages are chaos. Heavy strokes. Sharp lines. Ragged edges. So very unsatisfying when I want my Procreate and Apple Pencil. Or markers and a smooth, white wall.

But it would be worse to not be drawing at all, so I push through.

I toss aside those pages of hot mess and close my eyes again. Try one of those breathing techniques Shai taught me from her birthing class or yoga or something. I don't know. It seems to work for her. Maybe it'll work for me.

Inhale . . . two . . . three . . . four . . .

Exhale . . . two . . . three . . . four . . .

My eyes pop open.

I've got it.

I start with a circle. Then the guidelines: a cross that intersects in the middle of the circle. Next: a square that sits in the circle, its four corners touching the perimeter.

I'm making a portrait.

My characters are easy. My lettering is easy. They're abstract manifestations of whatever I'm feeling at the time. But this portrait? I want to do it right. But there's not much paper left.

I close my eyes and let out a breath. It's time to let go of perfection and just freaking draw. I mean, who even cares? It's not like this is going into my portfolio or a gallery. But I need to do this. If Mom has her way, this will be the last thing I ever draw. And soon, I'll have bigger things to focus on. Like not killing people.

So I just do it. Lines and shades and circles and triangles and on and on and on. My hands are covered with pencil dust because I'm not the most disciplined when it comes to sketching. Some of it smears on the paper, but I can't be bothered to care because this portrait. *This portrait!*

The nose is perky and upturned, and the mouth is wide, lower lip catching in a slight bite. The eyes are sideways teardrops, slightly tilted up at the outside corners. They shimmer with a million feelings.

There are little lines in the forehead, almost like this person is afraid of all those feelings. Scared they're going to take over and push her to a place she is terrified of going. But maybe it's time she goes there. Maybe she already has.

I sprinkle freckles across her nose, which is peeling from a slight sunburn. For the first time in hours, I manage a smile.

Her ears are small, and adorned with multiple piercings. Her nose is adorned with the piercing she just got today.

I don't know how much time passes before I can sit back without my skin crawling. Without my brain running a million miles an hour. Without my mouth clenched so tightly my jaws ache.

The portrait is almost done, but not quite. I want to add just a little bit of color. I go into my room, and as usual, the walls assault me when I flip the light switch, but in the very best way. No plain white walls for me. Just random drawings everywhere. Tiny little aliens from when I was small, whimsical kawaii stuff from when I was younger, even Jesus art because I was once really into that. I go to my desk and pull out my colored pencils. Faber-Castell. I stand there, staring at the box for a long time.

Sometimes things register so briefly you don't have time to dwell on it. Then it gets pushed to the dark recesses of the subconscious, only to resurface at the weirdest times. This is one of those times. These pencils aren't cheap, and Mom gave them to me for Christmas. Why would she give me expensive pencils if she was so against my art? Even if she only wanted it to be a hobby—wouldn't she have gotten me cheaper ones?

Maybe I'm thinking too hard about things. Alicia Bailey is nothing if not proud, so even if she doesn't agree with my art, she's not about to let me use shabby stuff if she can help it. So that's what this is. Right?

It's been so hard to relate to her these days, and that makes me really sad.

There's a knock on my ceiling. Shai, banging the "Can I come down?" code.

This has already been a night of self-revelations, and apparently it's not done.

All those times I felt I was alone—I never was.

And my best friend is pretty damn awesome.

I knock back. "Of course, you dork!"

28

Friend Connection

11:40 p.m.

SHAI COMES INSIDE, LUGGING A LITTLE SLEEPER FOR ELSA, who is deep into dreams. She briefly rests her hand on my cheek before setting up the little sleeper and gently laying Elsa on it. Elsa sniffles a bit, then falls right back to sleep. "You okay? I heard some yelling."

"Did we wake you?"

Shai kisses Elsa's little head. "I was already up. Now if you'd woken Elsa, we would be having words right now. But as it stands, I'm here to offer a distraction." Shai comes over and wraps her arms around me. "Thought you might need one."

I lean into her embrace. "I do. Thank you. But you didn't need to come down, especially if you were having a hard time getting her to sleep."

She shakes her head. "Thankfully, Elsa's a heavy sleeper. Once she's out, she's out. It's *getting* her to sleep that's the problem. But that's the joy of motherhood. And teething. Here. I know this is the last thing you want to see, but it was in my mailbox by mistake." She hands me a thick eight-by-ten envelope. The Lucerne logo is enough to make me toss it aside. Instead I stare at it so hard the words start swimming.

Shai plops on to the couch and pats the space beside her. "Sit with me."

"I'm grounded for the unforeseeable future," I report.

She looks around. "Where is your mom anyway?"

"Apparently, she can't be around me right now."

Shai screws up her face. "Ew. I'm sorry."

I shrug. "Whatever."

"That's one thing I do not miss about living at home. Julia's too cool to even think about grounding me. Hold on. Is it okay that I'm here?"

"She said I couldn't go out. Not that I couldn't have people come in."

"You're playing with fire and I'm here for it," Shai says. "Why are you grounded?"

I toss the packet on to the coffee table. "Long story."

"I have time."

I sigh.

"Okay, you don't want to talk? Fine. Then I'll talk." She sits up straight and looks me in the eye. "I think it's time for you to have a come-to-Jesus moment," she adds.

"You don't even believe in Jesus."

"That's patently untrue. I'm no longer a Christian. That doesn't mean I don't believe in Jesus."

"But—"

"We're talking about you right now. So."

"I can think of a million things that would be more fun than talking about me."

"I'm sure you can. But it's high time you face your demons!"

"What if we play *Dream Life* instead?"

Shai's face lights up. "You know I love *Dream Life*." Her expression turns back to solemn. "But that's fun, and, Brandy, my dear, we have to be serious for now."

My shoulders slump. "I know."

"How are you *really* doing?" Now her expression is concerned. "You've had a hell of a day—your emotions have to be in turmoil. You've barely talked about your father, and I heard the yelling, so you were obviously fighting with your mom." She tilts her head and squints. "Do you need to do some breathwork?"

"I really have no idea."

Shai wraps a blanket around her shoulders and opens it

so I can cuddle in with her. Mom keeps the temperature at Arctic Circle, so this is very understandable and acceptable even if it is ninety-two degrees outside. "I'm going to be honest, and you probably won't like it."

I brace myself. Because even though Shai has this way of doling out truths in the gentlest way and she is never harsh for the sake of being harsh, it still hurts to hear those truths.

"I'm just going to say it." She lets out a deep breath. "You have chances that I'll probably never have again, and you're kind of throwing them all away. You need to cut all the bull-shit and just fucking choose. Your mom and dad can't do it for you. Ben can't do it for you. I can't do it and Elsa sure as hell can't."

"But my mom said—"

"I know what she said. So what? It's your future, and I hate seeing this eating you up when all you have to do is put your foot down. Really put your foot down, and fight for it. Like I know you're going to do with that stud in your nose. But that's not your real battle, and I think you know it."

I swallow. She's absolutely right. The reason I feel all unbalanced is because all this time, I've been all talk and distraction. Fumbling and bumbling around with a fistful of markers and a dream. Everyone around me is making bold choices. Ones that actually matter. It's time I stop talking about it, and make mine.

For real this time.

"How come it feels like everyone is brave except me?" I ask.

"Brave? I had a whole-ass baby when I was seventeen years old. If that's not terrifying, I don't know what is." She gestures toward Elsa, who is still slumbering away. "And I love her with everything in me, but, Brandy, I'm scared. All the time."

Wow. She always seemed to have it all together. Even during those first few delirious weeks, when I'd get up super early to help her before leaving for school. Even when she was struggling to get Elsa to latch on so she could eat, Shai kept at it. She still puts on this strong, happy (albeit tired) face, making mommy-hood look like a joy.

"I know you do what you can to help," she continues, "but you'll never truly get it. And that's okay! But it's hard. It's fucking hard, knowing that every decision I make will affect Elsa. And people are judging me, no matter what I do or accomplish, someone's going to have shit to say."

"Like your parents."

"I mean, I knew they'd flip out. Still. I didn't think they'd kick me out. I wish I didn't still crave their fucking approval and forgiveness, especially because I haven't done shit wrong." Her face flushes, and her eyes fill with tears. "But they make me feel like I have!"

"I hate that they did. I hate that they still do."

"I thought—we all thought—that once they saw Elsa, they'd have a change of heart."

"Your parents suck."

She snorts. "Understatement of the year."

"I should've seen that it's still bothering you."

She gives me a strange look. "There's really no time for breakdowns when you have to keep an infant alive. Why are you acting like my life is your responsibility?"

"You're my friend. You're my sister."

"And Elsa's my daughter. *Mine.* I know I'm dealing with stuff, but we all are. It's not your job to fix it for me. You... you realize that, don't you?"

"I should be doing more, though."

Shai gently shoves me. "You didn't leave." Then she tilts her head, regarding me. "Brandy Bailey. Bran. My wonderful BFF. The world doesn't revolve around you, and it's not going to end because you won't always be able to drop everything for me. And you have to know the world's not going to end if your mother's upset that you're choosing your future."

"So why does it feel like the world *is* going to end?"

"Because—and I really do mean it in the nicest way possible—you have no perspective."

"Ugh. I have to be exhausting."

"My point is that my whole world had to change when I got pregnant. But you still have the freedom to get the life you want. So go get it."

I turn to her. "Do you ever miss dance?"

Her expression turns thoughtful. "Sometimes. But I

don't miss all the pressure and the hours and hours and hours in the studio. I really don't love it enough for all the hustle I have to put into it. It's not like Ben with acting. He is passionate about it with his whole being. And it's not like you with your art. That picture above Elsa's crib? It's stunning, and I'm so proud of you all the time. I've seen you when you're in your zone. It's like you go to a whole other planet. I never felt like that with dance. But I was good at it regardless, and I would've stuck with it if Elsa hadn't come along."

I nod, but I don't really understand. Art's the only thing I've ever been good at. I've always been terrible at science, and as for anything else? Mediocre at best.

"Did you ever consider...?" I let my question trail off.

She shakes her head. "No, but I worry, all the time, if I'll be able pull off being a single mom and going to school. I know your mom did it, but she had her mom to help. And sometimes when it's really hard, I'm scared I'll end up resenting my daughter and everything that happened. I really hope not. I love her so much."

"Make sure you remind her you love her. All the time, okay? Because I know what it's like to worry about being resented. It's not fun."

She gives me a watery smile. "And explains so much about you."

My tears are falling freely now. "I guess it does."

"For what it's worth, I don't believe, for a second, that your mom resents you. Okay?"

"It's like my head knows this, but my heart doesn't get the message."

"It's not impossible to recalibrate your view, though." She lays her head on my shoulder. "Except your piercings should remain part of that view."

"I'm absolutely keeping the piercings." I stare at the Lucerne packet on the table. "Have you ever considered psychotherapy? Lucerne probably has a nice program."

She shoves me again. I fall over and burst out laughing.

29

Right-Hand Man

12:15 a.m.

SHAI'S PHONE BUZZES. SHE GRABS IT AND READS THE NOTIFI-cation. Her thumbs start swiping all over the screen. I swallow and look away. The way she texts makes me dizzy.

But the curiosity. It burns! "Who are you talking to?"

She doesn't answer. She jumps up and grabs my hand. "Come with me."

"Where?"

"The bathroom, silly. You look a hot mess."

I don't move. "Who cares?"

"You can't take charge of your future looking like that."

"I don't think my future is watching me right now."

"The future is *always* watching."

"That makes absolutely no sense."

Her phone buzzes again. "Hold that thought." She reads the notification, smiles, and starts swiping again.

I try to look at her screen. "Shai? Are you texting a *man?*"

She snatches her phone away and gives me a shit-eating grin. "Don't be so nosy."

"I mean, you're the one standing here grinning like a hyena."

"Cheshire Cat."

"Whatever! *Do you have a man?*"

She ignores me, her thumbs flying over her phone screen. "All will be answered soon. You just relax."

As if I can!

Her phone vibrates again. I try to sneak another peek, but she's having none of that. "Mind your business."

"Why do I feel like this *is* my business?"

She shakes her head. "Always so suspicious. Anyway, come on. I have to fix your face. As I said, it's important to look the part. Dress like the life you want. And right now, you look like you walked into a door."

I feel like it, too. "Your brutal honesty is really something, you know that? "

"Yeah, it's great." She grins and drags me into the bathroom. The white walls in this room tease me every single day, but up until a few weeks ago, I was good about keeping my art confined to my own private space. So the bathroom remains safe. For now.

"Do you have cucumbers?" Shai asks. "Your eyes are all puffy."

"Since when do you care when I'm looking ugly?" I ask her. "And my eyes aren't puffy! That's some white people stuff right there."

"You are half white and your eyes are puffy and in case you didn't know, your cheeks turn red when you blush, and they are so red right now. So do you have cucumbers?"

I glance at the mirror and yeah, I can see what Shai means. Not that I go walking into doors often, but I've had better looks for sure. I splash some cold water on my face and let it cool my warm cheeks.

Why am I blushing?

"Cucumbers?" Shai reminds me.

"Oh right. Of course we have cucumbers," I say. "Mom loves to make fancy pitchers of water with the stuff."

"I thought so. I'll be back."

Shai takes her phone with her, so no peeking. Not that I'd do that anyway. Even though I'm pretty sure whatever private thing she is texting about has everything to do with me.

What did Shai just tell you? I ask my reflection. *Not everything in the entire world is about you. Get over yourself.*

My hair is a mess. This is a multiple-times-a-day occurrence. The super fine and slippery strands constantly unravel.

I style it into its usual two braids. Not the neatest, but it'll do for now. Tangles contained for a while, and another benefit: playing with my hair is a huge source of comfort for me, and braids are easy to grab.

"You look much better," Shai says when she comes back into the bathroom. "Although I do wish you'd wear your hair down more often. It was so freaking pretty tonight."

I glance over at her. "Who are you texting?"

"Your mom."

My heart jumps. "Really?"

She shoves my shoulder gently. "No. Clown. Come on. Let's get these cucumbers over your eyes. You'll feel much better."

"And is that *really* the only reason you're making me do this?"

She puts her hands on her hips and glares at me in the mirror. "Just do it."

"All right, all right."

I lie on the couch and let Shai cover my eyes with the cucumbers. To be fair, they do feel really good. All the crying (I still can't believe I cried, and it felt...okay?) and the air conditioner means my eyes are like a desert. The cukes are refreshing and cool.

"Now we can play *Dream Life*," Shai says. "I'll start. In my dream life, I'm making loads of money as a celebrity doctor. Or a doula. I have my own practice where people can choose any sort of birth that they feel most comfortable with."

"Can you do that and live in your dream cottage, too?"

"I think I've outgrown my fantasies of being a cottagecore kitchen witch, but we'll see. I don't have any immediate plans right now other than taking care of Elsa and studying all the biology. Eventually I'll go to college, because like I said, I have to go to medical school. Then I can deliver your celebrity babies!"

Um. "What do you mean, *my* celebrity babies?"

"We all know Ben's going to be famous. And when you two get married and have kids—"

I take the cucumbers off so I can stare at her like she's lost her mind. "Shai, what in the green hell—"

She gives me an expression like *bless your heart.* "Please. I see how you look at him. You *like* him."

I cover my face, which is heating up despite the air conditioner unleashing its most on me.

Shai's mouth drops open with glee. "You didn't deny it!"

"Please stop."

She jumps up and starts dancing around. "You didn't deny it! You didn't deny it!"

"Remember not even *five minutes ago* when we were talking about you?"

"Hahahahaha," she laughs. Maniacally. "I knew it! I *knew* it!"

"Shai, you're going to wake the baby!"

"You love him. You're going to marry him," she sing-songs.

"*You* need to calm down."

She stops dancing and grabs my hand. "Can I help plan the wedding?"

"Shai, what the hell. We're eighteen."

She rolls her eyes. "I mean in the future."

I just blink at her.

"Oh, look at you! You're speechless. Undoubtedly dreaming of living in a fancy Hollywood Hills house with Ben."

She grins. One of her knowing grins where her eyes are sparkling extra sparkly and her dimples are dimpling full force. "I remember when we were still in school. Any time he wasn't around, you were looking for him. And any time you weren't around, he was looking for you. And don't think I didn't see the hug he gave you on graduation day. He was holding on to you for dear life."

"No way." My denial is feeble because I remember the hug, too. But I'd assumed Ben hugged everyone like that. Except…he hugged me the same way tonight. I never even considered what it looked like to other people. I jump up and pace back and forth, thinking. Remembering.

We'd just done the recessional, and people were out in the lobby taking a million pictures. Some people were filming videos for social or whatever. But a bunch of us were giving each other hugs. It was the end of an era, but in that moment, we were frozen in time. I'd just stuffed my phone into my little clutch when I looked up and saw Ben making a beeline for me. "You're not going to sneak out of here without hugging your best boy, are you?"

"Bring it in, Ben," I'd answered. He wrapped his arms around me and squeezed. But not too tight. Just the right amount. I buried my head in his chest and inhaled his soap and clean laundry and sunscreen scent, thinking it would probably be the last time I'd ever see him unless it was on a TV or movie screen. I'd ignored the bittersweet emotion that had swept through me, but yeah. It had been there. I realize that now.

She raises her eyebrow at me. "Brandy. The boy did not want to let go of you. My heart broke when you walked away from each other because I knew better."

I sway on my feet. "I don't know how to deal with all of these feelings."

"I know it's a lot," she says, "But you're stronger than you think."

"Am I?"

She squeezes me tight. "You are, Brandy. You just have to believe it."

This time I really do relax, because she's not the first to let go. "Okay. I'll try."

30

Too Much to Lose

12:20 a.m.

"BE RIGHT BACK!" SHAI SINGS. BUT I FOLLOW HER ANYWAY, and I have to do a double take when she opens the door. A triple take. Because Ben freaking Nolan is standing in the doorway. Then he's in my living room.

What. The. Hell.

He waves. "Hi."

"You're in my apartment," I say. "Why are you in my apartment?"

"I invited him," Shai says.

"But...why?"

"Because." She smiles one of her beatific smiles, and I bite the inside of my cheek to keep from screaming.

Ben is standing next to me now. He's too close. The tingles traveling down to my feet and back up are loud and clear. I sit down and hope he doesn't notice how much I'm trembling.

"I texted her to ask how you were doing," he said. "Because I hadn't heard from you. It was kind of intense back there."

Shai is turning from me to Ben and back again. "What was intense?"

"Long story," I say.

Hang on.

"You were texting Ben this whole time?"

"Yes, ma'am," she says in a Southern belle accent, so it sounds like "yay-es, may-am."

"Since when are you two on a texting basis?"

"It wasn't hard to find Shai's number," Ben says. "Or yours. I've been texting you since your mom picked you up."

Ben has my number?

"The old student directory still works." He sits next to me. "How are things? They looked pretty rough when you left the police station."

"Police station?" Shai whips around to stare at me. "You got arrested? What for?"

He grins the most grinniest grin. "You don't know?"

"We did *not* get arrested. My uncle just escorted us in."

Shai eyes get really big. "*Us?* What the hell happened tonight? Brandy?"

Ben pokes my shoulder. "Go on. Tell her why your uncle escorted us to the police station."

I growl. "I will eat you, Benjamin Nolan."

He waggles his eyebrows again. "Is that a promise?"

I clench my fists. "Ooh! I cannot—"

"—stand you," Ben finishes. "I get it. You hate me." He moves slightly closer to me and locks his eyes on mine. Which makes my heart forget to beat. "For the record," he murmurs, "I don't believe for one second that you hate me."

I make a fist and punch my palm. "What if I show you? Will you believe me then?"

"Nope."

"You know what, Benjamin Nolan?"

Shai gently clears her throat. I jump about a mile.

"My uncle picked me up for making street art," I blurt.

Her face lights up. "You mean like graffiti?"

"I prefer the term 'street art,' but pretty much, yeah. That."

"She tagged one of the cars on the Ferris wheel," Ben says.

"I did not tag. I... decorated."

"That is so freaking badass." And Shai does look super impressed. To be fair, it isn't that hard to impress her. Not in a bad way. In a very open-minded and welcoming way.

"And that's part of why I'm grounded," I say to her.

"Damn, Brandy. You really are that bitch."

"I don't know about all that. I mean, I'm *grounded*." I pause and turn to Ben. "Hang on. Did you say you've been texting me this whole time?"

He nods. "I wanted to make sure you're okay."

"My mom has my phone."

The color drains from his cheeks. "Does she read your notifications?"

"Why? What have you been sending me?"

"I might've texted you some pictures of the stuff you showed me today," Ben says. "I'm sorry. I didn't know she had your phone."

I sigh, then shrug. "I'm already grounded."

Shai reaches for Ben's phone. "I want to see what you texted her."

While she's scrolling through his picture roll, he turns to me. "How are you, though? Like, really?"

"To be honest, I've definitely been better. But it helps that I'm not by myself right now."

He gives me his sweet smile, and something in me melts.

Shai holds Ben's phone out to me. "Is this what you got in trouble for?"

My little carnival is front and center on Ben's screen. "It is."

"Was it your first, um…installment?" Shai asks.

"Installation. And no." I shake my head. "I started making them right after the senior award ceremony."

"The one where you *won an art award*," Ben says. I stare at him. He remembers that?

"I wish you'd told me," Shai says. "What, you think I can't keep a secret?"

"Plausible deniability," I say. "If you don't know, then you can't get in trouble."

"Speaking of," Ben says, "you won't get in trouble for me being here? Since you're grounded and all?"

This is so embarrassing. "It's fine. But you don't have to stick around if you have better things to do. And why aren't *you* grounded?"

"I'm not grounded because I haven't even been home yet."

"Dude, what?"

"Maybe *you* are that bitch," Shai says to him. "What have you been doing all this time?"

"Freaking out."

"With good reason," I add.

"About what? Being arrested?"

"We weren't arrested," I say.

"Okay, then spill it before I explode." Shai squeals, then she covers her mouth. Elsa sniffles but doesn't wake up.

Ben looks at me. I look at Ben. Then we both look at Shai. "I got a role," he says.

She holds her hand up for a high five. "Right on."

"Tell her which role, you doofus," I say.

"I'm really not supposed to tell anyone," Ben says. "But I trust Brandy. And if Brandy trusts you, I trust you."

"That's really sweet and all, but hurry up and get to the juicy stuff," Shai says with a wink.

Ben takes a deep, fortifying breath. "I'm going to be playing Trent."

Shai doesn't need to ask what movie this Trent character is from because duh, everybody knows. Her mouth drops wide open and her face lights up with so much delight. "You're kidding. Wait, of course you're not kidding. Ben! That's incredible! Oh my God!"

He smiles. "Thanks."

Shai holds up a hand. "Is that why those girls ambushed you at the carnival?"

Ben shakes his head. "There's no way anything leaked that fast. I hadn't even gotten the call yet."

"But they *are* your groupies," I say.

He crinkles his nose. "They're *twelve*."

"You'd be surprised at how resourceful middle-schoolers are."

"How do *you* know?"

"I have cousins."

"Maybe they're your fans from *Triple Threat Mix Party*," Shai pipes in.

Once again, Benjamin David Nolan is speechless. His cheeks darken. "You did not watch that show. Tell me you did not watch that show."

"Oh, we watched it, all right," Shai says. "And I have *all* the episodes recorded."

"Mortified," Ben says. "Absolutely mortified. And about two seconds from walking out that door."

"Don't you dare," Shai says.

"Don't worry," he says. "I'm not really leaving. I don't think I can go home right now. I can't be alone with my thoughts. Like, I keep waiting for my agent to call me and tell me it was a prank. Or for those kids to bust through the door and demand more autographs. I know that's irrational, but...how can I explain it?" He taps his bottom lip, thinking. "So. I love acting, right? I really, really love it. It's what I want to do, it's all I've ever wanted to be. You know this."

I nod. "Mm-hmm. It's like me and my art. I can't think of anything else I'd rather be doing. Ever."

"So the getting famous part is...ohhhh." He covers his mouth. "Oh my God."

"Ben? You okay?" He doesn't look okay. All the color has drained from his face again, and his hands shake slightly.

"Breathe, Ben," Shai says in her calming voice. "In, out. In, out."

"I think I just had a breakthrough," he says. He jumps

up and starts pacing. Shai and I look at each other, eyebrows raised.

Shai leans over to me. "Trust his process."

"I'm not scared of the acting," he says. "It's all the *Hollywood* stuff I'm scared about! Acting I know. Hollywood? Not so much." He keeps walking, but now he looks excited instead of like he's just been dipped in a bucket of chalk.

"I completely understand," Shai says. "Okay, I really don't, but I am proud of you for figuring this out!"

"Yeah, I'm going to tell my therapist—hey, what's this?" Ben's pacing stops as suddenly as it started. And once I figure out why, it's my turn to be mortified.

He is *holding my self-portrait.*

No one was ever supposed to see that! "Give that back!" I reach for it, but Ben holds it higher. I stand up on the couch, but *I still can't reach.* Damn these short-person genes! "Benjamin!"

While he's looking at me with the most infuriating smirk, Shai, who is at least four inches taller than my five foot one, snatches the paper from Ben's hand. "Ha! Hahaha!"

I reach out my hand for it, but she doesn't give it over either. *Wow.* What kind of friends have I got?

"It's gorgeous, Brandy," Ben says.

"It's not. It's me."

"Yes, exactly," he says. Then he looks at me, all amusement gone. He's serious.

The arctic blast of the AC can't touch me now. Every inch of me is burning. "Give it back, please."

"You should put this on your social." Shai hands the drawing over and I clutch it close.

"Not even a chance," I say.

"Talent like that deserves to be shared everywhere," Ben says. "And Brandy, I truly mean that. I'm not teasing you."

He's not. I can definitely see that. But no. "Thank you, but I can't show this. Not yet."

"I hope you reconsider, because—"

A big thump and a loud screech makes us all jump. Elsa's lying there, screaming like her life depends on it. And based on the amount of blood running down her face, it just might.

Holy shit, holy shit, holy shit.

Those are the last words running through my mind before everything goes black.

31

Come to Jesus

12:45 a.m.

WHEN I COME TO, SHAI IS CRADLING ELSA, WHO IS *SCREAMING* eardrum-piercing shrills of distress. The poor baby's face is red, and the tears are nonstop.

Meanwhile, Big Baby Brandy over here has a flipping flopping stomach and can barely breathe. This is so embarrassing, and it's taking everything in me not to start screaming myself.

"It's okay, sweetie," Shai murmurs.

Elsa is inconsolable.

Someone else is yelling at me, but it sounds like a white-noise machine, for all I can understand. "What?"

"...first aid kit?" Ben's asking.

"Huh?"

"Where is your first aid kit?"

"Um..." I stand up, half-heartedly point toward the bathroom, then freeze. Helpless, I look over at Elsa. Shai is singing to her softly and rocking her, and her cries are lowering to sweet little whimpers.

I sway on my feet and sit down quickly before I take another tumble. Ben appears (through a haze) with a first aid kit and wet paper towels, which he hands to Shai. She sings a different song while she makes quick work of cleaning Elsa's face. I can't look without feeling woozy, so I close my eyes and try not to rock back and forth myself.

"Et voilà," Shai says, and I finally pry my eyes open just in time to see her putting a Minnie Mouse bandage on Elsa's temple, near the hairline. "That wasn't bad at all, now was it?"

"She's okay?" I ask shakily.

"Oh yeah, she's fine. Just the teeniest tiniest cut. Looks like she banged her head against the corner of the coffee table."

"Oh no, I'm so sorry." I glance at Mom's fancy glass coffee table. I don't think it's broken, but I'm having a hard time seeing clearly. But I know from experience that the corners are pretty sharp. Some of my own bruises are a testament to that.

"It's fine," Shai says. "I should've put her down in a better spot, but seeing as she's only six months old, I didn't expect her to roll over that far!" Her voice changes to her sing-songy voice. "You're a genius, aren't you? Yes, you are!" Then her eyes focus on me. "Hey, are you okay?"

My face is hot and I'm embarrassed. I turn away.

"Hey, hey. Brandy. Look at me."

I can't look at her. I can't look at anyone.

"Brandy." Ben appears in front of me. He puts his hands on my face. "Look at me."

I try to focus on his eyes, but they just keep blurring away.

"I need you to breathe."

"I can't."

He puts my hands on his heart, then grasps his over mine. "Yes, you can. In. Out. In. Out."

With my eyes fixed on his, I follow the rhythm of Ben's heartbeat. His breath. *In. Out. In. Out.* I'm here and I'm safe. *In. Out. In. Out.* Elsa is okay. *In. Out. In. Out.* It's okay. I'm okay. I'm fine.

After what feels like forever, but also not long enough, I feel like I can adequately take in air again. "I'm so sorry," I choke out.

"Brandy." Ben's face finally comes into clear focus. And his expression is so tender I want to cry.

"I'm useless," I say. I'm being pathetic and I don't even

care because I couldn't even help little Elsa, who I love more than anything.

"You're not useless," Ben says. "Stop being so hard on yourself. That was a scary thing you just saw. And what just happened to you? This isn't the first time I've seen it. Remember earlier? Do you know what that is?"

"I do now. My uncle told me," I say quietly. "It was a panic attack."

"Oh my God, Brandy," Shai says. "Does this happen a lot?"

Ashamed. I look at my lap. Then I nod. "Only recently. I've been having more and more lately. My uncle says I need to get help but, like...I get upset over silly stuff. It's embarrassing."

"It's not embarrassing, Bran," Shai says. "It's a disorder."

"It sucks."

Shai nods. "I think you need to fill out that application. Right now."

"Right now? While I feel like I want to scratch my skin off? While Elsa is hurt?"

"I told you. Elsa is fine. And would you do it otherwise? I bet not," she says. "It's time."

I'm not sure I'm convinced, but Shai's eyes are shooting firebolts at me. I'm not interested in crossing her while she's looking at me like that. So, with shaky hands, I pick up my laptop. The application is already bookmarked, my password saved in the browser so at least I don't have to use too much brainpower for that. I look at Shai again, but she pointedly gestures toward the screen.

So I begin.

My fingers tremble and I keep making typos of the easiest things, like my name and address, so I'm really not sure I'm in the right mind for this. But Shai's firebolt eyes press me to keep going. By the time I'm done, the shaking has stopped, and I feel a zing of something in my stomach. Excitement.

"Do you think you'll be ready to submit it tonight?" Ben asks.

"She'd better be," Shai mutters.

I chew on my lip. "I feel like my portfolio is almost there, but not quite. I think it needs one more *wow*."

"Any contenders?"

I wrack my brain trying to decide. The portrait of Ben *might* be a good possibility, if I had time to clean it some more. Except, Mom has my iPad. And I probably have to ask his permission anyway, which would be super awkward. If he ever finds out I drew him...

I shudder just thinking about it.

Shai and Ben are both looking over my shoulder and I'm going to be honest, it's super unnerving. "Oh my God, really?"

"I'm not letting you weasel your way out of this," Shai says.

"Do you have the cash for the application fee?" Ben asks.

"Yes. I'm good on that."

"Excellent."

"Did you finish the art on the Ferris wheel?" Shai asks. "Your tag? I'm sorry, I mean 'installation'?"

I kind of dig how even Shai calls it an installation now. It feels more real somehow, and not just some silly thing I keep in my head.

"I don't know," I say thoughtfully. "I kind of got interrupted the last time I was there."

"I'm thinking," Ben says, "that we should go so you *can* finish it."

I stare at him. "You're not serious."

"I'm very serious. Remember, I saw it, and it's super cool. And also, the fact that you put a Ferris wheel on the Ferris wheel itself is seriously impressive. I think that's your *wow* piece, Brandy."

"There's one big complication, though. I can't exactly dismantle a Ferris wheel and submit it online."

"Duh. You'd take a picture and send that," Ben said.

"And you shouldn't get caught if you frame it just right," Shai adds.

I'm such a clown. "Of course! I did it just this morning for my social." I wonder how many views it has? I automatically reach for my phone and then I remember. Crap. "I'm grounded. How am I supposed to take a picture if I don't have a phone?"

Ben and Shai look at each other and then look back at me.

"I'm sitting here like, you're eighteen," Ben says. "So how on earth can she ground you?"

"I live under her roof. Her rules."

"Ugh." Shai shudders. "I hate that sort of reasoning. Like, really hate it."

"I do, too. But it's not like I can afford to move out on my own." Or that I'd even know how to get started with such a thing. Shai did it in a way and she'd probably be willing to help me figure it out, but I can't ask that of her. Not when she's already so busy. And not when she's already here taking care of me while she has a whole-ass child of her own to care for.

"Anyway," Shai says, "so there is this thing called the internet. And imagine: One of us takes the picture and emails it to you."

"Come on, Freckles. Where is your fire? Your *spunk*?" Ben asks.

I shove him.

"Why is it always *me* who has to get shoved?" Ben asks.

"One of the perks of sitting the closest to me."

Shai stares at us with a soppy look on her face. "You're adorable together."

"Stop it!" I say. "We're teasing each other, like we always do."

That ship has sailed for me, but for the sake of not

embarrassing myself in front of Ben, I have to keep playing along with my old game. It's silly, but it feels safe.

"Okay," Shai says in a way that I know she doesn't believe me. I don't blame her. I don't believe me either.

One of these days I'm going to find a balance. If I'm not blurting the first thing that pops into my head, I'm over-thinking everything. And people are looking at me like "you okay, sis?"

I just don't know if today is that day.

"Whoa, look at the time!" I point to my wrist, on which there actually is a watch. Too bad an Apple Watch is pretty much useless without a phone connected to it. "I should really get—"

"It's either the Ferris wheel thing or this!" Shai holds up my self-portrait from earlier.

I point to the self-portrait. "Yeah, that's going to be an extra pile of hell no from me." It's honestly pretty decent, but still. I'm not there yet.

"All right. So go back to the carnival," Shai says.

"You realize that if I get caught, I'm dead. My mother will kill me. I will become a ghost."

Shai's eyes light up. "Who will you haunt first?"

"You've said it a million times. If you go to nursing school, you're already dead," Ben says. "So you might as well go out doing what you love."

I look at Shai, but she's absolutely no help. "He's right, Bran."

I know he's right. "Okay." I reach for my bag, then remember it's with Mom.

"Um, slight hiccup. I need my markers."

"Not really," Shai says. "I know you have a stash somewhere."

"Oh right!" It had been so long since I'd used them that I'd practically forgotten about them. I go to my room and dig out my second-best paint markers. "Found them!"

"Elsa and I will hang out here," Shai says. "I trust you two can behave yourselves?"

I smile sweetly at her. "Since when do I not behave?"

Ben's standing in the hallway. "Come on, we need to go!"

"Shh!" The last thing I want is to disturb Ms. Jane across the hall, who will yell "Stop that damn noise!" for hours if she thinks anyone is being too loud. I stuff the markers into my backup messenger bag and grin at Shai and Ben. "Let's do this."

32

War Paint

1:10 a.m.

THE GROUNDS IN THE DEAD OF NIGHT ARE EVEN CREEPIER than they are in the morning. At least there was some semblance of daylight then. But now, the structures are illuminated in shadow against the orange glow of the streetlights, and they rise like a haunted house on Halloween.

"I don't like this," Ben says.

On the entire walk over, I kept looking over my shoulder, nervous that Uncle Myron or my mom would pop up out of nowhere. But now that I'm here, the adrenaline is pumping and I want nothing more than to get to work. "We have to hurry."

He and I climb over the barrier to the car. "I *really* don't like this," Ben says.

"We won't be long. I promise."

"I'm setting a timer in my phone. If it goes off while we're still here, we need to bounce."

"Okay." I kneel down. "Hello there, friend."

I tilt my head and study the lines. The colors. I have to be more mindful of how these markers will behave, since they're not my usual choice. Then everything clicks. "I know just what it needs."

"Is that us?" Ben asks after I sit back on my knees, satisfied.

I start stuffing markers back into my bag. "In a way." This morning, there were only two little people. Now there are four: me, Ben, and Shai, who is holding Elsa. The Ferris wheel rises behind us. But we're not all that recognizable, I hope. Except to those of us who are in the picture.

"This is incredible," he says. "And I'm honored that you added me."

"You should've been there all along," I say.

He squeezes my shoulder, which makes me feel warm and fuzzy all over. It's nice. I watch as he pulls out his phone and starts snapping photos. Apparently his has some sort of lowlight setting on it, so there's no flash needed. Which is great because we don't need to draw any sort of attention.

He points the camera at me. "Smile!"

I pose with my artwork because I really do love it, and I am proud of what I pulled off. Then Ben wraps his arm around me and holds out the phone. "Let's take a selfie. To commemorate this night."

"Really? This night? Shouldn't we be leaving?"

"We have time for one picture."

One selfie turns into seventy million. We smile, we make goofy faces, he sneaks rabbit ears behind my head. "You know what? We look good together," Ben says.

I look closer. "Yeah, I guess we do." There's a twinkle in my eyes that I haven't seen in a long time. It matches the twinkle in his. Might this boy who drives me bananas also bring out something good in me?

He gives me another one of those leading-man heart-breaking smiles. Wow.

Ben's phone buzzes. He finally looks away from me, and glances at the screen. "Let's get out of here."

He holds his hand out. I grab it, and we scramble over the barrier.

33

Left in the Dark

1:35 a.m.

I AM DELIRIOUS WITH EXHAUSTION, HAVING BEEN UP FOR hours and hours. And yet my heart is racing so much that I might as well be gallivanting around Paris. Adrenaline is a heck of a drug.

The apartment feels nice and cool after being out in the humid air. Or maybe that's just my relief at having made it back without getting caught.

Shai's on the couch, scrolling through her phone.

Ben and I are sucking down some slushies we grabbed on the way home. He had the genius idea to sneak a bit of vanilla ice cream into the bottom of the cup before putting the slushie on top, and it tastes amazing. He and I both have blue tongues, which he also had to commemorate with his phone.

I plop down next to her and hand her a slushie. "Enjoy."

"Thanks! Oh, this looks yummy!"

I lean my head on her shoulder. "Where's Elsa?"

"In bed. Julia's home now, so I can be down here."

"But why? You should go to bed, too. I know you're tired."

"I'm here to make sure you send that application."

"Not a good reason for self-induced sleep deprivation, but okay."

She scrolls some more. "It looks even better than earlier! Brandy, you *have* to submit this with your application! Don't you agree, Ben?"

But Ben isn't listening. He's staring at his phone (which has just started buzzing like a million angry wasps) with his mouth open. And I watch, in real time, as the color drains from his face. Then he thrusts the phone toward me and Shai.

SPOTTED: HEARTTHROB NEWCOMER CANOODLES WITH MYSTERY HOMETOWN GIRL

By K. Elle | Friday, June 21, 2024 | 1:30 a.m.

Could your new celebrity crush already be off the market?

Photographers captured rising star **Ben Nolan**, who is rumored to be in talks to play Trent in the much-anticipated **Shadows and Ice** (based on the blockbuster YA series of the same name), Thursday evening at a quaint carnival with an unidentified girl. The couple shared sweet treats and sweet looks as they made their way from ride to ride.

Nolan, best known for **Triple Threat Mix Party**, a show that has already churned out superstars **Leanna Brooks** and **Jordan Reed**, consistently dodges questions about his romantic life...

Please sign in or subscribe to continue reading

"Are they talking about me?" I ask.

"They sure as shit aren't talking about me," Shai says. "You don't think they would be all over the baby thing if they were?"

"I need to log in," Ben says.

I let out a soft snort. "You actually subscribe to that thing?"

"It's my publicist's log in. She has to, it's her job."

"Are you sure you want to do this?" Shai asks him. "Maybe it's better not to know."

"My morbid curiosity craves all the knowledge. I have to satisfy it." He scrolls, and then thrusts his phone at us again.

It's not just words. There's a photo. The sky is inky, but streetlights shine from above. In shadow are a boy and a girl standing, holding hands, the Ferris wheel rising behind them. It's a beautifully composed shot. Except for one thing.

"I'm pretty sure that is me," I say. The tight feeling is inkling back, and I try to squash it down. I cannot have another attack.

"Those are definitely your braids," Shai says.

"And those are definitely your sneakers," Ben adds.

"What the fuck?"

"That's us. Together. Me and you," Ben says.

"I got that. How? We literally took those pictures like ten minutes ago! Ew, were you papped?"

"But *why*?" Ben asks. "I'm so confused."

"Dude, you just landed the role of the year, and not everyone's as scrupulous as we are," I tell him. "Somebody must have blabbed."

Ben drops his phone on the table and plops down on the couch. "This is freaking weird. Like, I knew my life would change but I didn't expect it to happen this fast. And...I kind of like it? I think? But also...no? Like, who sneaks pictures like this? And who cares who I'm hanging out with? I'm a nobody!"

I watch Ben's phone travel across the table, fueled by all the vibrating. "Far from it," I say. "Plus, you admitted earlier you've been practicing your autograph. You must love it."

"But there's you."

"Oh yeah. There's me. Hold on, there's me! I don't want people to see me! Oh my God. What do we do?"

"I mean...at least they can't see your face." Shai says. "That's a relief. Right?"

"How is any of this a relief?" I can hardly breathe. "Can you please stop that thing from buzzing?"

Ben grabs his phone. "I'm calling my publicist."

"Brandy. Brandy!" Shai grabs my shoulders. "Look at me."

"I can't breathe."

"Yes. You can. Remember what I taught you!"

For the millionth time today, my skin is crawling. "Why is this happening?"

"Brandy, are you really that oblivious?" Shai asks. She grabs my laptop and clicks a few times, then thrusts it at me. A different gossip blog, one without a paywall, is up, and there's the photo of Ben and me. "Look at your body language in this picture! His fandom is going to go wild."

I gulp. A bunch of local preteens is one thing. This? A whole other level. "Fandom? There's no way Ben has a real, live fandom."

"I can hear you," Ben says.

Shai pats my hand. "Oh, sweet summer child."

"I'm standing *right* here," Ben says. "And unless you count the kids at the carnival, I do not have a fandom. Layla. Ben here. Did you see—?"

"Have you really not been paying attention?" Shai asks me.

I lower my voice. "I'm so embarrassed."

"Why? The picture is gorgeous and looks like the cover of a freaking YA novel."

"Because I like him."

The world tilts, splinters, cracks, then rights itself.

Saying it out loud makes it very, very much real. It's not an abstract in my brain anymore, or a thought (or a lot of thoughts, if I'm being honest), or fodder for Shai to tease me with. I can't explain it away anymore because it's there. The seeds have been there for a while now but today? It's blossoming. Boy is it blossoming.

"I like Ben Nolan."

Admitting it out loud makes the punch hurt that much more. I've been grappling with this roller coaster of feelings all day, but now it's really out there. Solid. Almost palpable.

This crush is real.

Which . . . *of course* it is! Now that he's going to be all rich and famous and won't need little old hometown me. Not when he's in Hollywood surrounded by rich and famous people who are also super gorgeous, and I can't even imagine coming close to in terms of awesomeness.

"This is so freaking cliché," I groan. This guy has been in my life for ages and only now do I realize I like him. There's no way he's not going to think I'm after him because he's got this big role and he's going to be famous.

I'm so frustrated. What if I could've been with him all along? I shake my head. Ben's a flirt, but *I'm* the nobody. And it's not like he's ever admitted out loud that *he likes me*, so there's really nothing for me to be panicking about! Shai has already planned our wedding, but I think I need to hear the words from the boy himself.

If such words are meant to materialize between us.

Then the question becomes: Do I even *want* that? And what would I even do if I got it?

Grrr. This is so unnecessary. I should be focusing on all the other shit that happened today. Like seeing my father in person for the first time in my life. Shouldn't I be freaking out about that more than freaking out about crushing on a soon-to-be movie star? And what about Lucerne? I mean, priorities, Brandy, my God.

Ben pops up behind us. "The good news is...hey!" He turns to me. "You're wearing the dress!"

I look down. "Of course I'm wearing the dress. I told you I would."

"You've been wearing it all night. It's in the picture." His expression softens. "I knew it would look good on you."

"Thanks." His compliment makes me feel warm all over. "So what's the good news?"

"The bright side is that no one's being nasty," Ben says. "If they ever are, I'll make them fix it."

"Since when can you dictate what a gossip blog does?" I ask.

"I need to know," Shai cuts in. "Is there bad news?"

"Why would you ask him that?" I say.

"Because when someone says 'the good news is,' there is usually something bad that follows," Shai explains. "So spill, Ben."

"Yeah, there's bad news. They've identified you, Freckles."

"What? How?"

"I don't know." He shakes his head.

"How are you so calm, Ben?" I ask.

"I'm not, actually. This entire night has been one thing after another. But. I signed up for this. You didn't. They can say all the shit they want about me. They don't get to fuck with my friends."

Record scratch. We both stare at Ben, open-mouthed. He stares back. "What?"

"This is the first time you've ever dropped an f-bomb," Shai says. "Well done."

"This is not the first time I've ever said *fuck*."

"When *was* the first time?" Shai asks, her eyes shining.

"What are you—? I don't know—that's not what we need to be worrying about now. Brandy, turn off your phone notifications. All of them."

"For the last time, I am grounded. I do not have my phone."

"Can you call your mother and ask her to silence it?" he asks.

"No. Phone."

"Don't you have a landline?" Shai asks.

"Oh. Yeah!" I pick up the receiver and pause. "No. We're in a fight. Remember?"

"Of course you are," Ben groans.

Shai giggles. "Good lord. Y'all are a mess."

"A boiling one," Ben agrees.

"What even is happening?" I ask.

"Is your phone on vibrate?" Ben asks.

"It is, but what does that have to do with anything?"

"That's good news. Your battery will eventually die from all the buzzing," Ben says.

"Who is Layla?" I blurt.

"My publicist. She strongly advised me to turn off my notifications and close my DMs for the love of God, and to also turn my AirDrop to contacts only. Actually all of you should do that with the AirDrop. Some of the stuff I've gotten…"

"Oh, believe me, I know," Shai says. "Randoms have sent me some of the most messed up stuff."

"I just have one question," I asked. "Who could've done this?"

"Sent me nudes?"

Gross! "*No*. Who would've put our picture up like this?"

"It's all over social," Ben reports. He's scrolling wildly. "This is madness. I'm not even famous! Why do people care?"

"How many times do I have to say it?" Shai asks. "You're the next big thing and you're going to be huge." Then she stares harder at her phone. "Oh wow."

"Oh wow what?"

"My prediction didn't take long. You are blowing up," Shai says. "This is going to be great publicity for you, Ben! And for the movie!"

We stare at her. "Did *you* call the paparazzi?" I ask.

"Why would I have done that, my dear Brandy?"

"I don't know. I don't know anything anymore. Do you really think my phone is blowing up right now?"

"I'm sorry, but yes," Ben says, nodding. "This is the second time tonight my work is getting mixed up in your life. I thought this was the one place I could escape to." He sucks in his bottom lip and oh. I melt. Because for the first time since I've ever known him, Ben looks terrified. Like, now that his dreams are coming true, maybe he wished on the wrong star.

I don't think I'll feel that if/when I do the art thing. I just need to actually send my application. But first, I need to get the picture that...

Wait.

"Ben?"

"Yeah?"

"Did you text the pictures from tonight to me?"

"Yeah. Why?"

"Um. I am grounded, remember?"

"I know. You've told me approximately seventy times."

"My *mom* has my *phone.*"

The color drains from Ben's face. Again. "Oh shit. I forgot."

"She's going to see everything. Everything! Oh God." I start pacing. "I'm dead, I'm dead, I am so dead."

"Would that be a bad thing, though?" Shai asks.

"That my mother really *is* going to commit capital murder right here? Yes, that would indeed be a bad thing!"

"I mean, you sure as hell aren't going to show her, so maybe the universe took things into her own hands," she explains.

"Not. Helping."

"Don't you have Face ID?" Ben askes.

"Yeah, but she has my passcode."

He pushes his hair back. "Man, you weren't kidding when you said she pays too much attention to you."

"I know."

"I sent stuff, too," Shai says. "I'll take full responsibility if it comes down to it."

"No, you won't," I say. "You didn't force me to go out, and you didn't make me draw on that Ferris wheel car."

"I mean, we kind of did," Shai says.

"I could've said no. But I didn't. So there we go."

"Being grounded sucks," Ben says.

"Tell me about it."

The lock turns. We all freeze.

The door creaks open.

Oh no. Oh no, oh no, oh no.

This night. This *freaking* night.

34

The Wrath of Alicia II

2:00 a.m.

MOM DOESN'T SAY A WORD. SHE STALKS INTO THE APARTment and holds up my phone, which is buzzing like a thousand angry bees. Her lips are pursed. Normally, seeing her standing there with that expression would scare the bejesus out of me. But I'm so emotionally drained that I can't even muster up a smidgen of fear. Or anything.

So I wait.

"What in the world is happening with this thing?" she asks. "And why are all these people here? You are grounded. Or did you forget?"

"You told me I couldn't leave the apartment. You never said anything about people coming to me."

"You really want to argue semantics right now? You know I'm not afraid of lecturing you in front of your little friends."

"Should we go?" Ben asks.

"Yes," Mom says.

"No," I say. She glares at me. "You said you're not afraid of lecturing me in front of them. So do it."

"Brandy Angelica Marie Bailey."

"Mother."

"Since when do you call me *Mother*?"

"Since when do you use all four of my names?"

We're staring at each other. My fists clenched by my sides. My phone still vibrating in her hand.

Then her face crumples. She drops the phone and gathers me in her arms.

I feel my face crumpling, too. I've been emotionally raked over the coals tonight, and forgive me, but it feels so good to just...let go.

I let Mom hold me for as long as she wants.

Because I need it, too.

She pulls away and finally gets a good look around the living room. "What the...what *is* all this?"

Crumbled pieces of paper. Colored pencils rolling all over. Paper towels, now crusty and brown. The first aid kit, its contents scattered everywhere. Dried blood dotted all over the laminate floor. "Brandy, what happened?"

I can't answer, because I'm right back to earlier tonight, when I couldn't even help the very best baby in existence. That, with the incessant buzzing, is doing my head in. I want my skin gone *now* but I can't move. I can't breathe. I can't.

I can't.

"You can't what?" Mom puts her hands on my shoulders. "Look at me, baby. What can't you do? Brandy!"

I can't think.

"Brandy! What is wrong with you?"

"I can't do it, Mom. You can ground me forever. I don't care, I cannot be a nurse. I cannot do it. I can't. I can't. I can't."

"It's been a crazy day," Mom says. "You're just emotional."

"No! Please listen! Elsa hurt her head, and she bled. A lot. And I couldn't help her. I love her so much"—the tears start flowing—"and I couldn't help her."

"Brandy. I told you, it's okay," Shai says.

"But it's not. It's really not."

Her phone beeps. "It's Julia. I'm going to go check on Elsa." She turns to me. "I'm sorry."

"For what?" I ask her.

She shrugs. "I don't know. The blood. The panic attack. All of that."

I shake my head. "None of that. You're amazing."

We hug, and then Shai heads toward the door.

"What do you mean, *panic attack*?" Mom asks.

"You have to tell her," Shai says. "Be brave, Brandy. I know you can." And then she's gone.

"Tell me what? Does it have to do with why your phone's been buzzing non-stop for thirty-five minutes?" Mom asks.

"No, that's something different," Ben says. "And that's all my fault."

Mom looks up at Ben. Then back at my phone. Then back to Ben. Then she gets a knowing look on her face. "You were with my daughter earlier today."

"Yes, ma'am."

"At the police station."

And I swear I can audibly hear Ben gulp.

"Did you sneak out again?" Mom asks me.

I don't answer. She turns back to Ben. "Are you influencing her to do all this stuff?"

"I, um, I...what?"

"Just seems awful suspect that the one day she's hanging with you, she...I don't even know what you're doing, Brandy. What are you even doing?"

How am I even supposed to answer that?

"Did you sneak out again?" she repeats.

So here is where I almost get caught. "What do you mean, *again*? Or ever?"

"Brandy." She holds up my phone, which just about *has* to be out of juice by now. "I saw the texts. All of that art and pictures with him." She points to Ben. "But now your phone's covered in all these notifications. What the heck is going on?"

"Can I have my phone back? At least to silence it?"

Mom closes her eyes, then opens them. Then she tosses me the phone. "It's all gotten away from me anyway."

I silence my phone and finally, I feel a little bit of my panic abating. I swipe and swipe and swipe, but the notifications keep coming. So I go into settings and turn off *all* notifications. Then I slip the phone into my pocket. Maybe Mom won't remember that I'm grounded.

Mom is studying Ben, her expression thoughtful. Then she pulls out my iPad. She swipes a bit (I don't even want to know what she's looking for) then hands the iPad to Ben. And that's when I realize.

I freaking realize.

"Mom!"

Ben is staring at the iPad, transfixed. Then, mouth open, he thrusts it at me. "You drew me," he says. "I knew you were drawing me!"

I'm so embarrassed I might wet my pants. But who even cares at this point? I'm at my threshold, so that would barely register on the humiliation scale.

"Freckles..."

"Yeah. I drew you. Okay? I had to get you out of my system."

Ben is speechless. His mouth opens and closes. Opens and closes. I'm not sure what expression my face is showing, but once he sees it, his own expression softens. "Brandy."

Maybe it's time to finally admit it, out loud, to him, what's been brewing all day and all night. Maybe even all four years I've known him. "I—"

"Now is not the time," Mom says. She opens the door and turns to Ben. "It's getting late. I'm sure your parents are worried."

His expression falls, but he doesn't argue. "You're right. Thanks for having me over."

He gives me a look asking if I'll be okay. I give a barely perceptible nod in return. He clocks it, gives me his own nod, and then walks out the door, closing it gently behind him.

35

Such Is Your Destiny

2:15 a.m.

MOM SITS AND PATS THE SPACE BESIDE HER ON THE COUCH. "Come sit with me."

"Are you going to yell at me?"

She hands me my bag. "No. I think it's time for a heart-to-heart."

"Okay." But I don't move.

"First things first," she says. "The nose piercing."

"Oh. Yeah." This time I refrain from touching the thing.

"I'm not a fan. I never will be a fan. It's unnatural, putting holes in your body like that."

Says the nurse who gives injections on a regular basis. "I'm not taking it out."

Her forehead scrunches up. "Did you think I'd make you take it out?"

I nod. "And I probably would have. To keep you from being disappointed."

A million expressions cross her face at once. "Brandy, why did you apply to nursing school?"

"I had to. You gave up your life for me. You could've made it so I never existed."

She stares and stares and stares. "But what does that have to do with nursing school?"

"The scrapbooks. I ruined all your plans."

"What are you talking about? What plans?"

"Your PhD and all that fancy science stuff."

"Peanut, my plans weren't ruined. They were redirected." Her eyes fill with tears. "I was the one making the choices. I love my job and my life now. And I love you."

"You don't regret having me? You don't look at me and see... *him*? My father?"

"How long have you been thinking like this?"

I shrug. "Ever since you told me you were glad I wanted to be like you."

Her shoulders slump. "Brandy. You are my beautiful daughter with her own dreams, and—" She grasps my hand. "I want you to listen to me, and listen good. I have never and will never regret having you. Not in a million years. If I had to do it all over, I would make the same choice again and again."

I hate seeing Mom look so sad. Every instinct in me wants to erase her sadness, even if it means giving up everything I want.

"You do not owe me your life. Okay? Even if... even if that means I have to accept that you don't want to work beside me."

"But what about all the stuff you said earlier about security and having a good life?"

She twists a loc around her fingers. She twists and twists and twists. "I had this vision of you in my head, wearing cute little scrubs and your hair in braids and taking care of babies in the nursery. Being like *me*. Not... being like *him*." But then her expression turns serious again. "You let art consume you, just like he did. He made it, but like I said before, that's a one-in-a-million thing. And not everyone gets successful that way. I'm so scared chasing it is going to sweep you up like a tornado and destroy everything. Destroy you. How are you going to find your way if that's the only way you can see?"

We're quiet for a bit, and then it dawns on me. It's so freaking obvious I want to smack myself upside the head for not seeing it sooner. There are other ways. There are always other ways. The signs have been there all along. I just didn't really *see* them until now. Literally. A memory flashes: a NOW HIRING sign in a window. "I think the real question is—why does security *only* have to come this one way?"

She taps her chin. "I'm listening."

"I'll start with getting a job."

She frowns. "I don't really want you working while you're in school."

I let out a deep breath. "I have to say something, and you're probably not going to like it. But how can I find another way when you shoot down every idea I have?"

"I haven't been—"

"Mom. You have. Ever since I brought home that D in science and that F in English."

"I simply want you focused."

"But I'm done with high school. Why couldn't I work? At least part-time? I already have, in a way."

"What are you talking about?"

I sit down and pick up my laptop. The screen lights up with that gossip blog. I try to click away, but I'm not fast enough. "What's that?" Mom asks.

"Celebrity news."

"Since when do you read that stuff?"

"I don't." I navigate to my webpage. "My shop. Please. Just look."

Mom takes the computer and clicks through the website,

stopping at the "laptop stickers" section. "How are you managing the inventory?"

"That's the best part," I say. "I don't have to do anything. I upload my designs, people buy them, and I get paid."

"And what are you doing with the money?"

"I started a bank account the day after I turned eighteen."

She looks sad again. "You've been keeping so many secrets from me."

"I'm eighteen, Mom. I'm allowed to open my own bank account. And—" I swallow. "I'm allowed to get a nose piercing. And choose which school I go to."

"That may be so, but if I'm paying for your education, then I'm not okay with you just studying art. You're hell-bent on doing this thing. But I *need* to know you have something you can fall back on. At least pick a more practical minor."

Oh my goodness. She's right. It doesn't have to be all or nothing!

I google. A bunch of websites pop up to answer my query. "It says here that a good minor for someone majoring in art is business administration. Or marketing." Of course! That makes perfect sense. "Those minors can help me with my art business, but they can also help me find other paths if art doesn't work out right away." And marketing is interesting in a way. We studied it in social studies and that was one of the lessons I did okay with.

Mom nods slowly. "That could work."

For the first time in a long time, the knots in my stomach start unraveling. Things are starting to fit together. I'll need to know how to do invoices and things like that. How to sell my work beyond my online shop. "I think it could be a good thing. And in the meantime...the art supplies store at the Shoppes is hiring. I can really prove I'm responsible, and I'll be making even more money." Not to mention possible discounts. And access to all those materials. It's perfect! "Maybe that can even make up for tonight?"

Mom picks up the iPad. "Maybe." She gives me a sideways glance. "I have a confession to make. I looked through your portfolio."

My stomach flips. "And what do you think?"

"It's really good. Like this picture right here. The details. Looks like his hair is curling as we sit here." She gives me a thoughtful look. "You really like this boy, don't you?"

"Yeah," I say with a breath. "I think so. Except I don't know if I've ever actually had a crush, so I don't know if this is normal."

She smiles over at me. "In some ways, you are so innocent."

My face grows warm. "Mom."

"I like it. Never change."

"Mom!"

She swipes on my iPad. This feels kind of violating, but also, I want her to see my work. I *need* her to see it. So I don't stop her. "You really are talented. And very serious about your art."

"I did almost go to jail for it."

"Please. Myron would've never put you in jail for real."

"I also won an art contest. It came with a cash prize and a workshop. And I'm going to take the workshop. I can learn so much from those instructors."

"Well." She looks at her lap and plays with her hands, something I've never seen her do. "I guess you're on your way, then. Have you applied to that art school?"

"Not yet. I mean, I started filling everything out, but..." I trail off, leaving so much unsaid.

She seems to pick up on it, though. "If I didn't do all this"—she gestures around—"to make it so you can live the life you dream of, then what was the point? So..." She bites her lip, and I can tell it's hard for her still. "As long as you prove yourself responsible, and you really work hard on things besides just art..." Another sigh. "I'll support you."

I jump up. "Really? You really mean that?"

"I do. It's hard to let go, but..." She squeezes her eyes shut. "I do mean it."

My hands are shaking. "Oh my God. Okay."

When she opens her eyes again, they're shining and wet. "So I think it's about time you pull up that application."

I turn back to my computer. I click to the tab with the

application. I've been timed out, so I have to sign in again. "I really have your blessing?" I ask her.

"As long as you keep up your end of the bargain."

"I will."

"Okay then. You have my blessing. Now you need to give it to yourself." She points to my nose. "Just like you did for that."

"You're never going to let me live this down, are you?"

"Maybe in twenty years."

I shake my head. Then I go back into my application.

"Do you want me to look it over?" she asks.

I consider it. She knew how to get me accepted into nursing school. The email still sitting in my inbox is evidence of that. But I really need to start doing the things that matter to me on my own, without thinking about who's going to approve, or what people will say. Is that part of feeling grown-up? Doing what will work for me, instead of doing what everyone else wants? And not thinking the world's going to fall apart if I'm not giving up everything I want for what they need?

I think it might be. "Nah, I got it."

I open my portfolio. And then I remember. I need to add one more thing.

I pull out my phone, which has two percent battery left. Just enough juice to email myself the pictures that Ben texted over and the pictures that Shai texted earlier. A whoosh sound, then the phone goes dead.

My email dings right away, and without fail, I get a little bit excited even though I know I just sent myself the message. The pictures download, and I upload the picture from the Ferris wheel to my portfolio.

"Is this the tag that Myron caught you doing?"

"I will only answer on the grounds that you will not incriminate me in any way."

She holds up her hand. "Amnesty here. Brandy, that's stunning. Where is it?"

"I'm *not* going to answer that because you'll freak out." The upload confirmation pops up on the screen. I flip through all the images there. There are so many, all my favorite pieces. The message from Breaking Free flashes in my head. It's possible those are my favorites because they are also my safe pieces.

"Brandy?" Mom asks.

"It still feels unfinished."

She holds up the self-portrait, then raises her eyebrows at me.

"I don't know...."

"At least let me email it to you."

"Okay."

Mom takes a picture of my picture with her phone, and about thirty seconds later, my inbox dings again. "I just think that they should see who their artist is," she says.

I download the picture and open it in my photo editing

software. It's simple, and I use it to brighten and adjust the shape of the picture. The more I look at the self-portrait, the more I like it. Definitely outside of my comfort zone, and absolutely not perfect, but that feels like it's okay.

I flip back to the application and repeat the process. Drag and drop. Then upload. Colorful spinning wheel, then the confirmation.

It's part of the portfolio now. No going back.

"I think...I know it's ready now." But what I mean is that I know *I'm* ready now.

Mom squeezes my shoulder. "Let me type in my credit card information for the application fee."

"I can pay for it."

"I've got it." She takes my laptop and types in her number. That seems like another grown-up thing I should do: memorize my debit card number.

I bite my lip. "Promise you're not upset about me not choosing Lucerne?"

She sits back. Her mouth is turned down slightly at the corners and her eyes are still shining. "I'm not going to lie. I'm literally grieving this vision I've had of you for almost all your life, and I'm sad you won't be joining me in the maternity ward someday. It's going to take me a minute to get over it. But as much as I wish you'd follow in my footsteps, I think I would rather you be happy. Just don't..." She trails off, but I think I know what she's saying.

"I'm not going to let art take me away from you. Okay?"

She squeezes my hand. Her voice is all muffled because of her stuffy nose. "I know. And I'm so sorry for ever, ever making you think you owed me. And I'm sorry that my feelings about your father got mixed up with my feelings about your art."

My eyes sting for the millionth time today. I swallow. "Thank you."

She tilts her head toward the screen. The payment information form is all green. "Submit it already!"

I smile. "Okay. Here goes. For real this time."

36

This Night Is Ours

3:15 a.m.

I SHOULD BE DEAD ON MY FEET. YESTERDAY MORNING'S SUM-
mery haze feels so far away. And yet, my body is still completely
wired. Somehow this night managed to turn itself around! I
sent off the application, yes! My nose piercing gets to stay in,
yes! And Mom and I are good again. For real. Triple yes!

When Mom is in the bathroom doing her nighttime rou-
tine, I sneak and put the remaining two hundred and fifty
dollars she gave me earlier on her nightstand. Maybe I'll need
to get a new dress someday. I don't know. Will an acceptance
to the Preston Academy of Art get me dinner at the President's Club? I hope I get to find out.

I head back to my room, my phone still in my possession. I stick it on its charger and after a few minutes, the screen lights up. I open social media, and oh my God, my follower count is exploding! The internet works fast. Social media even more so. I hope this will get more people to see my art and hopefully appreciate it. And maybe even buy it.

Then it hits me.

The tag in Ben's post. That must be how they identified me. Oh God.

There is another Venmo notification from my father. Two-hundred dollars and a note to "use it wisely," followed by a winky face emoji and an artist's palette emoji.

I open my text messages.

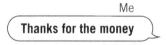

Me

Thanks for the money

It's so late, I don't expect a response. But a reply pops up almost immediately.

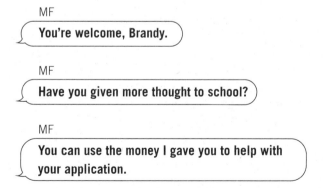

MF

You're welcome, Brandy.

MF

Have you given more thought to school?

MF

You can use the money I gave you to help with your application.

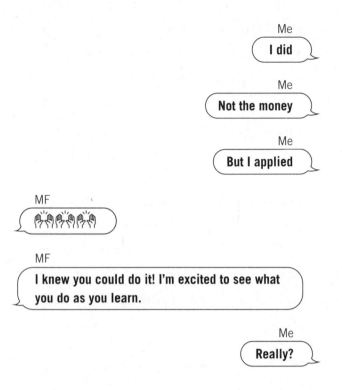

Me
I did

Me
Not the money

Me
But I applied

MF

MF
I knew you could do it! I'm excited to see what
you do as you learn.

Me
Really?

Three dots appear and disappear. Appear and disappear
again.

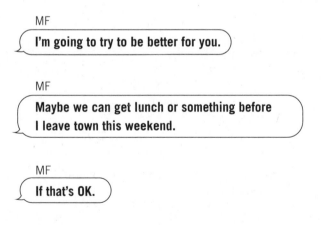

MF
I'm going to try to be better for you.

MF
Maybe we can get lunch or something before
I leave town this weekend.

MF
If that's OK.

We just met in person today — Me

It's all still new, you know? — Me

So IDK... — Me

MF
I get it.

MF
Just let me know.

MF
I can't promise I'll be perfect. But I want to try.

MF
And for what it's worth.

MF
I'm sorry.

I sit there, staring at that last message. I don't know how to answer it yet. So I save it for when I do.

✧ ✧ ✧

I open my laptop so I can organize my files. My room might be a mess, but my computer is pristine. I click on the icon for

Ben's portrait and drag it to my Portrait folder. Inside that folder are more folders: Shai. Elsa. Mom. I make one for Ben, and drag the icon there.

Then I pick up my phone again. I've never texted him before, but there is a message with an unfamiliar number, and that message is full of familiar pictures.

I tap it.

My phone lights up two seconds later.

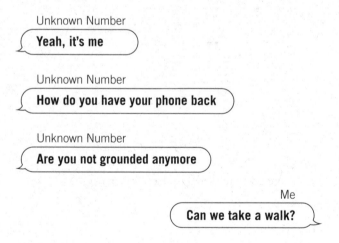

Three dots.

Three dots.

Threeeee dots.

> **I'll come get you**

I honestly don't know if I'm still grounded or not, so I'm quiet as I brush my teeth, splash cold water on my face, and rebraid my hair. Then I sneak out of the apartment again. Not for the first time, I send blessings to the sky that our property manager keeps the door hinges nicely oiled. Because grounded or not, being out at three in the morning is never my mom's idea of a good time.

Ben's waiting for me in the lobby. I walk up to him just as he holds out his hand.

"Let's take that walk," he says.

I let my fingers wrap around his. "Okay."

The heat and humidity from earlier have calmed way down. The air feels clean and fresh, and the petrichor scent hangs all around us. Rain is coming again. It'll make tomorrow super humid, but it'll be nice tonight. I close my eyes and inhale deeply. Being outside hits different when you're grounded for the foreseeable future.

"You're so quiet," he says. Then he gives me a smirk. "For once."

"Okay. You know what? I was trying to behave and of course you had to act up."

He bumps against my side. "You know you deserve it."

I bump back, slightly harder than necessary. "So?"

"There you go again with the shoving."

"You know *you* deserve it," I mock. Then I turn more serious. "So earlier. I'm sorry you had to see all that, with my mom and all. And I'm sorry that she kicked you out."

"No worries, Freckles. I needed to stop by home anyway."

"Everything okay?"

"Parents are on board, and I'm not grounded. Is everything better with you?"

"Yeah. We had a long talk and worked things out. So it's good. For now."

"And how are you feeling?"

I take a deep breath, and it feels like a true, cleansing breath. My chest feels lighter than it has in ages. No opinions and thoughts pressing into me or weighing me down, at least not tonight. I finally fit in my skin. "Better than I have in a long time. I'm actually really excited about my future."

"Did you send the application?"

"I did."

"Awesome." He squeezes my hand again. "I'm really proud of you. You're going to tell me as soon as you get the acceptance letter, right?"

"I love your confidence in me." Because now that the anxiety of finally choosing art school is starting to wear off, another kind is sneaking in. "What if I went through all this and they don't even want me?"

"You apply to another art school. And if they don't want

you, pick another one. It's just like auditioning, in a way. You'll find the right fit. I believe that with my whole heart." He stops and takes my other hand. His are just the right amount of warm, and that warmth radiates all through me. "But for what it's worth, I can't imagine any school turning you away."

He's smiling that sweet gentle smile, and my knees go weak. "Th-thank you."

He lets go of one hand and flicks my braid, then we start walking again. The Ferris wheel looms in the distance, still and silent. "I mean it. You text me as soon as you hear from them. Okay?"

The thought of legitimately texting Ben, one on one, thrills me. I make a note to save his name in my contacts. "I will. I promise."

"And you don't have to wait until then to text me," he says quietly. I look at him again, and he's biting his lip, but not in the flirty way that makes me lose my mind. In a vulnerable way that makes me want to pull him close.

"And the same goes for you," I say. "I want you blowing up my phone."

"I'm glad to hear that, because..." He screws up his face. "I fly out tomorrow evening."

I stumble over a crack in the sidewalk. "Already?"

Ben steadies me. "You okay?"

"You're leaving so soon."

He nods again. "Yeah. I know. I'm torn. I feel like I'm

starting to get closer to you and I *definitely* want to keep doing that, but..."

And now I understand how Mom felt when Aaron left. Not on the same scale. Nowhere near that. But having to let go of someone so they can chase their dream. The difference here is that I hope Ben never feels like I'd hold him back. Not like how my dad felt. Maybe still feels in a way. "I get it. You have to do this."

"I do. I really do. And I'm...nervous. Really, really nervous. But it feels right. You know? I'm scared shitless, but I know it's what I'm supposed to do."

"It's weird. Like, once we opened ourselves up to the possibilities, they started raining down on us."

He smirks. "You sound like Shai."

"I'm starting to think Shai knows her shit."

"I think you know *your* shit. Brandy, you never, for a second, believed I wouldn't get that part."

"They'd have been losing out big time if they didn't pick you. I've seen you onstage. I've seen you on TV. I am in awe of your talent. No other outcome made sense."

"And I never believed, for a second, that you wouldn't apply to that school. You just needed a push."

"I think I got more than just *a* push today. Hey, I don't know if I ever thanked you."

"For what?"

"Everything. This day. This night. All of it."

"Brandy."

"No, I mean it. You came through for me in a way I never even imagined. And I'm really glad you're in my life."

His hand trembles in mine. "Today was one of the best days ever. And that's because you were in it. Hollywood's going to be strange. I'm going to wish you were there with me every day."

I flush all over. "Me too."

"Knowing you're here is going to help me, though." He squeezes my hand again. "I'm still kind of freaking out. I just don't want to let anyone down."

I nod slowly. "I kind of know the feeling. For what it's worth, I one-hundred-percent believe that you're going to blow them away, in the best way."

It's quiet except for the sounds of crickets chirping.

He eventually says, "I know you mean well when you tell me I'll be great, but that doesn't take away how scared I am."

I nod. "You know what? That's fair. It doesn't help to hear 'you got this' when you don't even think you have the tools to get it." A beat. "Hey, Ben? You know you don't have to worry about letting me down. Right?"

He gives a wry laugh. "You're actually the person I worry about the most."

"Me?"

"Yeah. You. Brandy Angelica Marie Bailey."

He puts his finger on my lips. It takes everything in me not to kiss it.

We walk quietly for a while more. Then, "So things really are good with your mom?"

"If not, she's almost as good of an actor as you are," I say. "I can't wait to see you on the red carpet."

He lets out a soft laugh. "And I can't wait to see you kick ass at that school."

The way he says it makes me truly believe I have a shot at getting accepted.

His expression turns thoughtful. "Do you remember the day we met?"

"How could I forget?"

"You walked up to me with the most peculiar expression. I couldn't tell if you liked me or hated me."

"To be fair, I didn't know myself. But I did know this: you were in my seat."

I still remember it so clearly:

Lunchtime. Second day of freshman year, so our seats were already established. And let me tell you, securing that table was hard work. The seniors got first pick, then the jocks. Us art kids were usually shunted to the side, and being the babies of the school didn't help. So, when I saw him sitting there, sitting in *my* seat, I stopped in my tracks and made everyone pile up behind me.

"What the heck, Brandy?" Shai had been right behind me. She shoved me gently, then noticed the kid in my seat. "Oh hell no. Not today."

Shai wasn't as much of a sunshine back then. Being part of a cutthroat ballet team made her super fierce, and she didn't take anything from anyone on anyone's behalf. Plus, she was strong and flexible. People knew to stay out of her way.

But I wasn't that keyed up. Probably helped that the interloper was kind of cute. I stepped over to him while everyone else sailed to their seats around me. Up close, golden green eyes fixed on mine and brought to mind delicate, rolling fields like from the farm my school visited during fourth grade. I knew from that moment I would never forget eyes like that. Even if it would take me more than four years to appreciate them. "Hi. Um, this is me."

"I kind of gathered," he said. "Sorry. I didn't realize."

"No. I... how would you have known?"

I set my tray down next to his. And that's when he stole his first Tater Tot from me. And I knew. I *knew* from that moment that my life would not be the same.

And it really hasn't been ever since.

Right now, Ben gives me a smile that almost makes me forget my name. The smile disarms me every time, because it reminds me of that first day. The day he made me question everything I thought I knew about myself.

The day I decided that maybe I didn't mind sharing my Tater Tots, but naturally, I wasn't going to make it easy for him. He got an earful from me every single Thursday until we graduated.

But I never stopped him from taking the Tots.

"What was that expression about anyway?" he asks.

"Let's just say I needed to figure some things out."

"Have you? Figured them out?"

I laugh. "No. But maybe I don't have to have *everything* figured out right now."

"Mood," he says.

And then I feel it. The full unblocking of that throat chakra. "Ben?" I ask again.

"Yeah?"

"I like you. I think I liked you since you stole that first Tater Tot from me."

Oh my God, that smile. "I like you, too, Freckles. Why do you think I stole the Tater Tot?"

"Well, Eyebrows. Will you still like me when you're tempted by your new rich and famous friends?"

"First of all, I'm not cool enough to make rich and famous friends. Second of all, I like you now, as difficult as you are. So yeah. I think we'll be okay."

I yank his arm. "You know what I'm about to say."

He steps closer to me. Brushes a spiral from my forehead. "Brandy Angelica Marie Bailey."

"Benjamin David Joseph Nolan."

He presses his lips against my forehead. "I think being with you is going to be a wild ride."

Tingles are traveling clear down to my toes and back up again. "So we're really doing this?"

A shadow comes over his face. "Unless...earlier, you said you don't want to be famous. But if this movie is a success, my life will change. Big time. And if you're with me...I'll do what I can to protect you, but being with me might make fame happen to you anyway. Will you be okay with that?"

"I can't say for sure," I say. "Not until I'm in it, you know? For now, I like when you're around. Even if it means dealing with all that other stuff."

"I can't promise people won't be mean. Just remember to keep your phone notifications off. Limit your comments. Maybe have a private account that only a few of us know about. Maybe even consider getting a whole separate phone. You never know when the gossip blogs are going to pop off."

"A whole new phone?"

He shrugs. "Just an idea." Then he grins, lighting up his whole being. He's still such a sunshine, even on this dark street, on this dark night. "I can't wait until you design my tattoo. And when I can hang your paintings in my big Hollywood Hills mansion someday. And when I can go to the Met Gala knowing your paintings are on some of the walls."

I bump against him again. "Again with the confidence. Do you want to share?"

"You did a bunch of brave things today." He strokes my

thumb with his. "The confidence is there. You just have to believe it."

I let out a sigh. "I'll try."

He looks at me, his expression gentle. "Okay." Then he yawns the most enormous yawn I've ever seen.

"Ben. What was that?"

"I'm tired! I flew across the entire country this morning, if you recall."

"No! That yawn! See, I knew you had a big mouth."

"Excuse you. It is a leading man's mouth. Have some respect."

"Oh my God. It literally is! How do I keep forgetting?" A thought pops into my head. Because I've read the books that Ben's movie is based on. "Ugh, you're going to be kissing other people and you haven't even kissed me yet." And apparently the thought decided to pop right out of my mouth.

He raises his eyebrow and steps closer to me. I can smell his spring scent and the air on his skin. "Do you want me to kiss you?"

Do I? I can't take this! I grab his collar. Pull him down to me. And then.

I kiss him.

I gently touch my lips to his, just enough to feel how soft his are. I linger just a little bit, feeling myself getting lost before I jerk myself to reality.

"I'm sorry, I—"

"Mm-mm." He shakes his head. "Get back over here."

Then he's kissing me. And it's the most amazing, spectacular kiss. The fireworks have nothing on this and I don't want it to end.

Oh my God.

I'm kissing Ben Nolan.

I'm really kissing Ben Nolan.

Oh my God.

We're kissing. And I'm loving it and hating it because it's so so so so good, but he's leaving soon and...

Stop thinking.

He's so tall I have to stand on my tiptoes. But I am not wobbly because he is solid and holding me tight. He's always been solid. How did I never notice before now?

I pull him closer, closer, closer, taking care to avoid my newest piercing. I tangle my fingers in his curls. Absolutely inhale him. He smells and tastes like Coke. His hair is silky and smooth. And we just keep kissing and kissing and kissing.

"Wow," he says after ten hours or ten minutes. I don't know. What is time?

"Yeah. Wow."

He bites his lip and smiles at me. Then the smile turns into a shit-eating grin. "I knew you liked me." Then he takes off down the street. "Ha ha ha! You like me! Woooo!"

Ooh! I chase after him. "I cannot stand you, Benjamin Nolan!"

Acknowledgments

Whew! When people tell you that second book syndrome is a Thing, believe them! This book was such a challenge on so many levels. It wasn't all just me, though. So many people helped me bring this book to life, and I'm very grateful to have them in my corner.

Thank you, Nikki Garcia and Milena Blue Spruce, for your amazing and thoughtful notes as we worked through the drafts and edits of this book. You knew the story I was trying to tell and got me to break through my walls and make it happen. I am in awe of the skills and instincts you both bring to the table when it comes to stories. I'm so lucky to get to work with you.

Production is such a big part of making a book, but it's all behind the scenes. I don't think this team gets enough recognition. Therefore, Jake Regier, Lota Erinne, and Jenn So, thank you for all your help in making everything clean and shiny. Patricia Alvarado, I'm not sure what a production and manufacturing coordinator does, but thank you for doing it!

I love, love, love the art on the cover and throughout this

book, and I deeply, *deeply* admire the artists and designers who made it look so good. Gabrielle Chang, Karina Granda, Andi Porretta—holy cow, you blew it out of the park!

Dear Emilie Polster, Alice Gelber, Savannah Kennelly, Hannah Klein, and Christie Michel, thank you for using your marketing and publicity expertise to spread the word about Ben and Brandy's story.

Thank you, Caitie Flum, for helping me with this project for literal years! It's finally a real thing, and it's so exciting!

A heartfelt thanks to Nia Davenport, who listened to me read aloud my (very different) first drafts and fell hard for Ben and Brandy. Your enthusiasm for their love story helped me through some of the hardest writing days.

I could not have done this without dear J. Elle, who, in between superlong Marco Polos, FaceTime calls, and life in general, helped me really work out the story I wanted and needed to tell. J. Elle, you are one of the kindest, most giving people I know, and you deserve everything good coming to you.

Adib Khorram, thank you for just being a really good friend and supercool person. And also for letting me borrow *Kiss & Tell*. I think this means all our characters have to officially be friends now.

I am so grateful for the lovely people I've met on this journey. This is by no means an exhaustive list. I know a lot of great and talented people…but I have only four pages this time! Forever ChiYA: Anna Waggoner, Gloria Chao, Kat Cho,

Lizzie Cooke, Samira Ahmed—where would we be without our quarterly brunches and Chicagoland book events? Lost, that's where. Reese Eschmann, Mia P. Manansala, Miranda Sun, Cat Novara: I adore all of you, and we really should go get pizza at that one yummy place again soon. Traci-Anne Canada—for driving completely across town to shop with me on a random spring night and for being one of my biggest hype people. Becky Albertalli—thank you for the *Animal Crossing* visits and being so sweet and supportive. Claribel Ortega for *The Sims* and the writing sprints; Karuna Riazi for being such a considerate, kind, and intentional person; and Swati Avashti for our long phone calls and "nope!" Ha! Julian Winters—I stole your name for two of the celebrities in this book. I hope you don't mind.

I want to thank the authors who inspire me all the time: Sarah Dessen, Nicola Yoon, Judy Blume, Zoraida Córdova, Angie Thomas, Stephanie Perkins. I'm in awe of the work you create, and I can only hope to be half as good as you all someday.

My most favorite Twitch content creators, TotallyKayt, celeste_starr, and sheilur, for getting me through my long days with entertaining gameplay, coworking sessions, and general cozy chaos. You've all helped enable my *Stardew Valley* obsession, and I am forever grateful that I got raided into your streams.

The young ones in my life: Luca, Ashton, Ansley, Braylon, Juju. I love all of you like my own, and I hope my stories resonate with you someday.

Wanda Lotus, my dear friend with the musical voice,

you're welcome for the *Sims* obsession. But seriously, thank you so much for being my center. You've gotten me through a lot. I don't know if you know that, but I am so grateful.

Jennifer Niven, my forever sister, thank you, thank you, thank you for your unconditional love and support and just being you. Here's to so many more late-night giggles, shopping sprees, boat rides, and international travels together. And maybe even some writing! (And Justin—yes, I did borrow Mr. Conway's name from you.)

Rena Barron, I don't even have the right words to express how much you mean to me. No matter how busy life gets, you are always there to encourage me, laugh with me (or at me), listen to me vent, and eat sushi. You're the very best bestie ever.

Aidan Davis, my son, my favorite person ever, and the best person I know. Brandy's love of art is inspired by you and your talent. You're going to go far, and I can't wait to see you do it.

Adam Selzer, my partner in crime and in life. Just kidding, we don't do crime. Thanks for indulging in my hyperfixations, my McDonald's obsession, and my love of all things pink. Sorry not sorry about all the Mickey Mouses in the house.

Readers…thank you! I hope that you love this book, and that you adore Ben and Brandy even more than I do.

And last but absolutely not least, the most special thank-you to my mommy, Lenora Kita, who never pressured me to be something I didn't want. You're the very, very best, and I love you so much.

RONNI DAVIS

lives in Chicago, where she copyedits everything from TV commercials to billboards by day and writes contemporary teen novels about brown girls falling in love by night. She is the author of *When the Stars Lead to You*. Ronni invites you to visit her online at ronnidavis.com and follow her on Twitter and Instagram at @lilrongal.